I

Matthew J. Olson

Copyright © 2021 Matthew J. Olson
All rights reserved.

First Edition

Edited by Cynthia Shepp, Editing Services

To the fans of *Flaming Curse* who wanted a little more!

Contents

CHAPTER 1—CHURCH	1
CHAPTER 2—WHO IS RATHBONE?	5
CHAPTER 3—ARGUMENT	10
CHAPTER 4—NIGHT	14
CHAPTER 5—FARM	18
CHAPTER 6—CAMP	22
CHAPTER 7—TRACKER	25
CHAPTER 8—WIND ROCK	30
CHAPTER 9—MISSION	36
CHAPTER 10—DEATH CURSE BLOCK	42
CHAPTER 11—HOME AGAIN	45
CHAPTER 12—HEALING	49
CHAPTER 13—BREAKING	51
CHAPTER 14—MORE HELP	54
CHAPTER 15—DREAM REALM	57
CHAPTER 16—TRAPPED	60
CHAPTER 17—SLAVE LABOR	65
CHAPTER 18—ON THE ROAD	69
CHAPTER 19—ABILENE	73
CHAPTER 20—DREAMING	76
CHAPTER 21—TRAIL JUNCTION	79
CHAPTER 22—PHANTOM	83
CHAPTER 23—RATHBONE	87
CHAPTER 24—QUESTIONS	90
CHAPTER 25—DINNER WITH MCKINLEY	94
CHAPTER 26—MEETING IN THE DREAM REALM	98
CHAPTER 27—TRAVELING WITH A PHANTOM	102
CHAPTER 28—SOLOMON RIVER	107
CHAPTER 29—TIME	111
CHAPTER 30—ANOTHER DINNER	115
CHAPTER 31—OUTLAWS	120
CHAPTER 32—TRADING POST	127
CHAPTER 33—FIRE	131
CHAPTER 34—WHY BE A SHERIFF?	136
CHAPTER 35—REVENGE	141
CHAPTER 36—TAKING THE LEAD	146
CHAPTER 37—LINCOLN	152
CHAPTER 38—SCOUTING	157
CHAPTER 39—LAST SUPPER	161
CHAPTER 40—DREAM COUNCIL	164
CHAPTER 41—TORTURE	169
CHAPTER 42—FAMILIAR VOICES	173

CHAPTER 43—MCKINLEY 178
CHAPTER 44—CURSE 185
CHAPTER 45—HOME 194

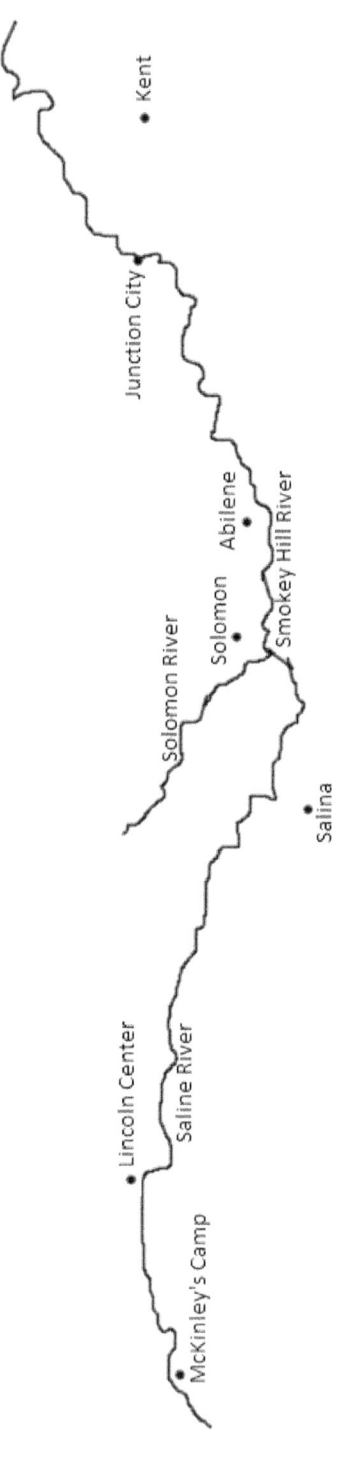

CHAPTER 1—CHURCH

There was a certain peace in attending this morning's service at St. Joseph's Church. The building was about a year old now. The spring sun shone through the stained-glass windows, giving the flock in attendance a rainbow glow. Marta took it all in, not minding the pew in front of her being empty or most everyone avoiding her, Beth, and Greta. It was an uneasy peace, but a peace all the same.

Sheriff Jethro Bourne sat next to Marta, holding her hand. They'd been courting for about nine wonderful months now. She was happier than she ever thought possible.

Marta shook herself from her reverie. She was on a mission today—and every Sunday—to watch Pastor Goodman's replacement, Pastor Sheppard, like a hawk.

He was droning on about not worrying. "And lest not forget the teachings of Matthew chapter six, verses thirty-one through thirty-four. 'So do not worry, saying, "What shall we eat?" or "What shall we drink?" or "What shall we wear?" For the pagans run after all these things, and your heavenly Father knows that you need them. But seek first his kingdom and his righteousness, and all these things will be given to you as well. Therefore, do not worry about tomorrow, for tomorrow will worry about itself. Each day has enough trouble of its own.'"

Yes, so what if Marta were worried? She was worried this pastor was another warlock bent on killing witches like her, Beth, and Greta for no good reason. Just because he hadn't proven himself to be a magical being in the eight months that he had been assigned to this church didn't mean a thing. Goodman had been there about ten years before it came out that he was a warlock.

Since his demise at her death curse, there hadn't been any other threats to the peace of Kent and the surrounding area. Sure, there was still petty crime, but Sheriff Bourne's watch kept that to a minimum. It didn't hurt that his reputation had expanded when he took down McLeod.

Sheppard continued, "Remember, my brethren, if you worry, you end up facing your ordeal twice. I'd like to end the day by..." His eyes fixed on the church door at the back of the room.

Marta turned to see what had stopped the pastor in mid-sentence. A man stood just inside the door, dusty from his travels. He looked unarmed, but he had a cross hanging from his neck. Marta recognized the cross. It was one of Goodman's talismans.

Marta tried to reach for the power. Well, it was a reach in her mind's eye for the magical orb that constantly followed her and from which all magic in the world flowed. The reach stopped short since the orb was farther away than usual. The talisman must be dampening her reach. She tried not to panic but felt her pulse race and sweat spring forth.

"Sheppard," the stranger said with a nod.

"Rathbone," Sheppard called back. "What are you doing here?"

Bourne let go of her as he slowly worked his right hand toward his revolver. Beth and Greta were already working with Marta to get the magic. In her mind's eye, Beth was pushing Greta and Greta was pushing Marta. They had previously planned this in case they ever encountered a talisman again.

"I am here to rob you of a few of your flock." Rathbone looked at the empty pew in front of the witches and Bourne. "Given the wide berth y'all are being given, you must be Marta, Greta, and Beth." He indicated the women.

Marta wondered why he was being so cocky. Just because he had a talisman didn't mean he could come in here like he was the second coming of Jesus and accost them. She felt her brow furrow as she still hadn't been able to reach the orb. "What do you mean by robbing Sheppard of a few of his flock anyway?"

Rathbone smiled. "You can either come with me quietly or I can force you." He outstretched his hands before him, and arcs of lightning played between his fingers. There was no doubt that this man was a warlock in addition to having a talisman.

The closest people were quickly moving out of their pews and against the walls. With the main entrance blocked, some were trying to make their way to the only other exit behind Sheppard. Parents made sure to pull their young ones with them. A few cried out in alarm, but most tried to be quiet to not draw the attention of Rathbone.

Bourne jumped to his feet with his gun rising as he rose. "You aren't kidnapping anyone today."

Then the gun flew from his hand toward one of the pretty stained-glass windows. Her power made possible by Greta and Beth, Marta gave her strongest effort to reach the rest of the way for her magic. She succeeded, then cast an air spell to keep the gun from hitting the window. It was a basic spell and easy to do no matter how strenuous her hold on the orb was.

Marta putting a shield up around Rathbone so he couldn't strike out at anyone with the power was harder. This involved a lot of air with a little bit of the other threads of earth, water, fire, and spirit. More complicated, but still relatively easy. She returned the gun to Bourne's hand so she could quit using that spell and focus on the shield.

All this was done in a split second. Her breathing came in labored huffs at the exertion of breaking through the talisman.

"How?" Rathbone questioned.

"Three against one aren't very good odds." Marta then worked another spell to grab the warlock and force him outside. If this man wanted a fight, she would rather do it where the least amount of damage could be done. This spell, though, failed to grab Rathbone.

"I knew you were powerful, but I didn't know you could break through the block of a talisman. No wonder my master wants you." Rathbone laughed as he flung a fireball.

The laugh died as soon as the fireball hit Marta's shield. She didn't have to look at her body to know that her defense mechanism had kicked in. The gasps from the churchgoers who hadn't exited were enough to let her know she was a skeleton. It was good to know this worked outside of practice and in a real fight.

Rathbone's shock turned to anger. He started hitting the shield with lightning, fire, and other things to try to break it. Nothing was doing much to the shield. At least not anything Marta couldn't handle. She let him fight for a minute.

Suddenly, he stopped his current mode of attack. Marta remained wary as Rathbone cocked his head, staring at her with beady eyes. "You're a little more than what I am prepared to handle today."

Before Marta could react to that statement, Rathbone took a step back. "I think we are at a stalemate."

Marta felt her grasp of the shield weaken as Rathbone approached it. She had to move the shield or risk it collapsing. She said, "Stalemate? I haven't tried anything yet."

She knew the warlock had his shield, so she didn't bother with fireballs or anything like that. Instead, she issued the death curse. Like the air spell, the curse died before reaching its target. She hadn't realized anything could stop that spell before now. She gulped. Now what?

Rathbone smirked. "I know you've tried the death curse at least once. I wish I could perform my own, but my master wants you alive."

Marta felt the small pendant grow cold against her breastbone under her Sunday finest. This and the skeletal state were the two biggest accomplishments that the three witches had worked out this past winter. But all the preparation hadn't been enough to stop this warlock here and now. There had to be something else she could do.

Rathbone continued to back toward the door. Marta asked, "Who is your master?" in part to stall him, but mostly because she wanted to know who was after her.

Rathbone smiled, but he did not answer. Marta stamped down her anger so she could remain cool in this fight. He was almost to the threshold since they were so close to the door to begin with.

Marta picked up a bible that was sat on a vacated pew with her magic. She flung it at Rathbone. Unlike her other spells, the speeding book reached the warlock and hit him square in the face.

Rathbone shook his head, then grabbed it with one hand. That was going to leave a mark. There was no time for excitement as there was still a warlock to vanquish.

Knowing that something was making it through, she grabbed other items with the power to throw at the man. Firewood, other bibles, and even parasols left next to the door sprang into the air. Not all of it was Marta—Greta and Beth also added things and threw them. Bourne even fired his pistol a few times.

Rathbone caught on, making a shield to block the onslaught of items. The witches and Bourne quit throwing things at him and shooting him.

Rathbone turned and crashed into the door, flinging it wide open. He bolted. Marta was surprised the man didn't turn into a skeleton. Did he not know about that?

Marta grabbed her skirt to run after the fleeing man. Her shield was dropped as he was moving too fast for her to follow him with it and have it hold up.

She didn't make it two steps before an explosion detonated on the church steps. Marta was blown back by the blast with the door wide open, but she was uninjured in her skeletal state. She bounced right back up.

As she ran through the flames, she made a hole through them with an air spell so her dress wasn't scorched. She would fight the flames in a moment. First, though, she had to give chase to the warlock.

Rathbone was already driving away in a covered wagon, heading up the trail to the west. Marta turned to the hitching posts for her horse, only to find they had all been set free. Most were grazing in the cemetery while others had been spooked by the explosion and ran toward McDowell's Creek. They had to have been set free before Rathbone went into the church.

Marta could feel Greta and Beth behind her, working on putting out the fire. Rathbone was now at the top of the hill, almost out of sight. He was going faster than she thought those horses could go naturally, so he must have been doing something with magic to aid his escape. By the time she could get her horse, he'd be long gone, and she didn't know how to track him.

How in the world had this happened? She had been on the lookout for a warlock, and one had gotten right into her area. Yet, he hadn't succumbed to the death curse. How was she going to defeat someone impervious to the only thing that worked against her previous foe?

CHAPTER 2—WHO IS RATHBONE?

Marta was able to catch her horse with ease. It hadn't gone far, and it didn't run away when she approached it. Once she had hers, she was able to get Beth's horse. Their harnesses were still on as Rathbone had just undone the pole straps to let them loose from the wagon. The horses needed to be hitched before they could leave.

When Marta returned with the horses, Beth and Greta had the fire out and had even worked to fix the door that had fallen off its hinges in the explosion. Most of the womenfolk and children stood well away from the witches. The menfolk were all out gathering their horses.

Bourne had ridden with Marta, Beth, and Greta in the wagon, so he didn't need to catch a horse. He stood with Pastor Sheppard. When he saw Marta coming, he headed her way. Sheppard came with him.

Marta shuddered at the thought of having to converse with Sheppard. There was so much she didn't know about him, and he just had to be a warlock. She couldn't prove it, but his interaction with Rathbone had certainly been damning. She guessed she could put up with Sheppard long enough to see what he had to say about Rathbone.

Bourne wordlessly took Beth's horse to hitch to the wagon. This left Marta with just one horse to work on.

"I'd like to thank you for protecting us." Sheppard glanced at the church. "And also for minimizing the damage to the church."

Greta and Beth were also coming over, so they heard this last part. Marta glanced at the women and children still standing apart from everything else. "Are your parishioners also thankful?" she asked.

Sheppard glanced at the women. He said, "They think they wouldn't have been in danger if you hadn't been here in the first place."

Marta didn't disagree with this assessment. She noticed Sheppard didn't include himself in that statement. "And you think otherwise?"

Sheppard nodded. "I think Rathbone was looking for me to find you. He lucked out in you all being in the church as well."

Marta finished her snaps. She glanced up the hill that Rathbone went over. She didn't think he was coming back, but kept an eye out all the same. "It didn't sound like he was looking for you."

"Of course he was," Sheppard started. "I mean, his ultimate goal was to find you."

"Do you know him?" Bourne asked.

"Yes," Sheppard said. He seemed hesitant to continue.

Marta stepped a bit closer with her hands on her hips. She wasn't going to accept any nonsense from him.

"He was at St. Mary's seminary school at about the same time as I was," Sheppard continued. "He was one of the students who worked under Bishop McKinley. You know, the warlock who taught magic."

"We know. He taught Goodman," Bourne said.

Sheppard nodded.

"Did he teach you?" There was some venom to Marta's question, but she couldn't help it. Why mask what she was feeling anyway?

Sheppard's eyes grew wide. "Heavens no," he called as he raised his bible. "I was at St. Mary's to follow my calling and nothing else. I have no magical abilities like McKinley, Rathbone, Goodman, and yourself."

He cocked his head, squinting at her with a furrowed brow. "Is that why you always come to church? To keep tabs on me and see if I'm a warlock?"

Marta ignored the questioning. She was certain Sheppard was a warlock, and she wouldn't take the man's word that he wasn't.

"We aren't accusing you of being a warlock, Pastor," Bourne said. "We enjoy your sermons. Especially the one today on not worrying." He shot Marta a look.

He was always getting on her about not stressing so much. So what if she looked through all the newspapers that she could get her hands on for anything that seemed remotely magical to point to warlock or witch activity. She wanted to find warlocks before they found and killed her. If she found a witch, then that would be another resource to learn from.

Sheppard smiled. "Thank you, Sheriff. I'm glad you are enjoying my sermons. Are you also benefiting from them?"

"I'd like to think so," Bourne said. "I'm just not sure the rest of the congregation is letting your teachings sink in."

Marta knew this was another dig at her. She decided to flip things around on her beau. "Like you never worry. I remember you stressing over your job not so long ago. You were sure you would get recalled."

Bourne shot her a scowl, which made Marta's mood a little better.

Sheppard arched an eyebrow. "I can't believe that. What did you do to warrant recalling, Sheriff?"

Bourne kicked a stone on the ground. Maybe Marta shouldn't have gone this far since she knew he didn't like talking about it. She was sure everyone knew about it, so how the heck did Sheppard not know?

"I fell in love with a woman, and I decided to help her even though it put my job in jeopardy," Bourne muttered.

Sheppard smiled. "Ah yes, the classic story. Ever since Eve, men have been tempted by women."

Sheppard eyed Marta. "Despite her untrusting nature, this one does seem worth it, though."

"That she is," Bourne replied.

Marta rolled her eyes. She noticed that Beth and Greta were now seated in the wagon, watching in silence. They, at least, weren't sucking up to her.

Marta glanced up the hill again. *Rathbone isn't coming back*, she thought. Aloud, she said, "Let's focus on the here and now. Just how well do you know this Rathbone?"

"Not well at all," Sheppard said. "He was in the seminary with me for just a short time. I haven't seen him in probably twelve years."

"Besides McKinley, do you know any other warlocks?" Marta asked.

Sheppard shook his head. "They tended to not expose themselves. I knew Goodman was one and others left with McKinley, but I don't know their names. Heavens, that was years ago. I'm lucky I remember that much. If I hadn't seen Goodman make a talisman with magic and Rathbone make fireballs, I wouldn't have known they were warlocks."

Marta found it suspicious the pastor knew what a talisman was. "And you can't make a talisman?"

"No," Sheppard said. "I already said I'm not magical. I don't even know what they do."

Marta decided not to fill him in on that. Besides, she was able to get around the one today with Beth and Greta's help, so to explain they blocked powers was just going to add confusion.

Sheppard straightened, his brow rising. He pointed over his shoulder at the church. "Today was the first time I've seen a talisman since I caught Goodman making one at St. Mary's."

The man didn't ever seem to trip up. Everything he said was worded as if he were innocent—like "caught" when referring to someone performing magic and reiterating that he wasn't a warlock.

Marta just came out and asked it. "Are there any non-magical clergy out there?"

Sheppard sighed. "Yes, Marta, there are. In fact, there aren't many I know about who went with McKinley and Rathbone. Surely, just a handful. I've met hundreds of other bishops and pastors who weren't warlocks." Sheppard stopped, emphasizing, "And I am not one, either!"

Even though it wasn't a good try in tripping him up, it hadn't worked. She still didn't believe him, but it was time to drop that subject.

From the wagon, Greta asked, "How much longer are we going to be?"

Marta shot her a look, not bothering to mask her annoyance. She was trying hard to get some damning evidence here. Beth was also sitting there, watching on with a glassy stare. They didn't think Sheppard was a threat. Marta had reminded them over and over that she didn't think Goodman was a threat until he attempted to burn her at the stake.

She turned back to Sheppard, reminded of something else, and asked, "What about talismans? Do you know where any are?"

Sheppard shook his head. "I've only seen one."

"You said you saw Goodman making one, and now you've seen Rathbone wearing one." Marta had caught him in a lie!

Grabbing the power, she did an air spell to lift the warlock a foot into the air and bound his arms. She stuffed his mouth with a gag of air as well.

Sheppard arched a brow, but he didn't react otherwise.

"Marta," Bourne called. "Let him explain. Don't jump to conclusions."

Marta returned Sheppard to the ground, then removed his gag. So what if she rushed her discovery? She was victorious here. She should just issue the death curse here and now and rid the world of one more warlock. Instead, the stern look from Bourne made her release Sheppard entirely. She didn't let go of the magic. Instead, she put up a shield.

Sheppard slowly said, "I am near certain the talisman I saw Goodman make was the same one Rathbone was wearing today. So, yes, I've seen the talisman twice, but I've only ever seen one. How many more are out there?"

Marta didn't know the answer to that question. She was also disappointed Sheppard had yet another comeback. She released her shield and let go of the magic.

Instead of apologizing, she just dropped the issue. His lack of reaction during this when anyone else would have run screaming made her think of another question. Marta indicated the other parishioners. "Why are you talking to us when nobody else is?"

Sheppard shrugged. "Just because someone is different from someone else doesn't mean they don't deserve to be treated the same. From what I've heard, you three have only ever used your magic to protect yourself and others. That makes you good people, just like them." He indicated the parishioners. "I just wish they saw it, too."

"Fear is a powerful motivator," Bourne said. "You just keep preaching the good word. Eventually, they'll come around."

Marta doubted they ever would. But Sheppard seemed different. Could he be a good guy? It could be dangerous to assume him to be good. Then again, if she did start killing people for no good reason, that would make her the evil one. Killing Goodman was in self-defense. Her attempt to kill Rathbone was also defensive.

Then again, she was tired of being on the defensive. It was time to go on the offensive. It was time to hunt warlocks, especially now that one was so keen on her. She knew Greta and Beth wouldn't see it her way. Nor would Bourne. How could she convince them it needed to happen?

CHAPTER 3—ARGUMENT

Bourne took the reins after they all were in the wagon, which was fine with Marta despite it being her wagon and one of her two horses pulling it.

Bourne glanced over his shoulder after being on the trail for a few minutes. Marta didn't have to look to know the churchgoers were out of earshot. Her senses were that attuned. He asked, "So, how long have you known how to turn into a skeleton?"

Marta felt a twinge of guilt. She hadn't been entirely forthcoming with the details of the training sessions that were going on at her house.

"We had a breakthrough about three months ago," Greta said.

"Yes," Beth said. "Marta failed to block…"

"Shush," Marta interrupted before the damage was worsened. She glanced at Bourne out of the corner of her eye. He had one of the best poker faces she had ever seen.

"Three months, huh?" Bourne asked, tight-lipped and glowering. He wouldn't meet her eyes.

"Yes," Marta replied, a little relieved he wasn't asking about what she'd failed to block.

"You didn't think that was newsworthy?"

Marta shrugged nervously. She hated when he was like this. "You don't like hearing about the things we do."

Bourne huffed. "Because you tend to do things a little dangerously."

Marta patted his arm. "I've been doing this a long time, dear. Long before I met you."

Sighing, he shook free of her pat. "So, what was it that you failed to block?"

Just when Marta hoped he wouldn't broach that subject, he had to bring it up. Bourne turned to Greta and Beth. "Marta doesn't have to be the one to answer that question."

Marta's silence wasn't unnoticed. She was sure Greta or Beth would squeal, so she beat them to it. "I failed to block a fireball one day. Purely by accident. I didn't get a shield up fast enough, and it slipped through. I wasn't harmed, but I did lose a dress in the fire."

"You weren't harmed because you became a skeleton," Bourne said.

"Yes," Marta said. "Though, I would have been faster to put out the flames had I not been celebrating the fact I had finally been able to turn. Also, any injury I might have sustained would have healed quickly."

Bourne shook his head, but he didn't say anything.

"I'll remind you that we are careful when we practice," Marta said.

"Careful…" he muttered. He seemed to be considering that word.

Marta thought they were being careful despite his misgivings. Just because an accident happened occasionally, and a dress went up in flames, it didn't mean they weren't trying to stay safe.

"We also have pendants that protect us from spells now," Beth said. "They work. I think Rathbone issued some curse against us, or at least me, as mine went cold against my skin."

Marta nodded. There were many victories today despite not getting Rathbone. "Mine went cold against my bones. It's good to see they work instead of just going off those instructions we found in my spell book for making them."

Bourne cut into their good mood. "What I want to know is who is Rathbone's master and what does he want with you guys?"

Marta didn't know the answer, so she stayed silent.

"Maybe Rathbone's master wants us dead," Greta said.

"Why?" Bourne asked.

"He heard about Goodman's death and wants revenge," Greta replied.

It made sense to Marta. This brought up another thought, and she knew how the others were going to react. "I still think we need to go on a warlock hunt. Two have found us, and we need to get the drop on them before they get the drop on us."

They rode in silence for a bit. Marta thought this was a good sign that they were mulling it over.

"It's too dangerous," Beth said. "We don't know enough about our abilities to find one before they find us. We also don't know enough about this new threat or threats. We are better able to defend ourselves on our turf as we planned."

"We aren't safe with them out there," Marta shot back. "Sure, we have things planned for when they show up, but we won't know when that will be. Taking the fight to them would make it so we are fighting on our terms."

"I have to agree with Beth," Bourne said. "You now know two warlocks are looking for you, so now you are better prepared."

"But we aren't prepared enough," Marta said. "Rathbone's abilities exceed Goodman's. What if his master is even more powerful?"

"I think you are making my argument for me," Bourne said. "If you go looking for trouble, especially trouble that is more powerful than anything you are ready for, you are going to end up dead."

Marta clenched her jaw. She didn't end up dead after encountering

Rathbone. She wasn't going to die fighting his master. She just didn't want to sit on her thumbs, waiting for the fight to come to her.

The town of Kent was coming into view. She watched it as another thought came to her. "Greta, you've been quiet during this. What do you think?"

Greta hesitated, which meant she was going to disagree with Marta. "We have practiced fights at our house just in case something like this happens. I don't think we should abandon that practice now."

Marta huffed. "Fine. I've been outvoted, so I'll respect the quorum."

It was the only way they were able to keep the peace. Anytime Greta, Beth, and Marta disagreed on an issue, the majority ruled.

"So, I take it you won't be staying for our weekly courting night?" Bourne asked.

For months now, Sunday after church had been Marta and Bourne's night. He was off policing the county the rest of the week, which meant he was only around on Sundays. They made the best of it.

"I mean, I'd hate to miss a chance to court, but there are some extenuating circumstances here," Bourne added.

Marta thought she could hear disappointment in his voice. "I don't see why we have to break with tradition."

"But we need to go over spells tonight," Beth said.

"We know there is a threat, and we need to prepare for it," Greta added.

"We are prepared. Rathbone will need time to regroup before he makes another attack," Marta said. "He'll probably just alert his master to where we are. Who knows how long that will take?"

"You'll all be safer together," Bourne said.

Marta was surprised to hear this from him. "I let you go off to fight bandits on your own. We are prepared to fight on our own as well. If anything, we'll run away if the fight is too much. Our pendants will protect us."

Marta's friends fidgeted with sour expressions. Now was not a good time for them to lose their nerve. "We've practiced this, ladies. We're ready."

They nodded. Since they agreed, there wouldn't need to be a vote. Besides, they were romantics at heart and wouldn't get in the way of Marta's only night with Bourne.

"So, you guys take the wagon down to our house as usual. I'll be back in the morning on Greta's horse," Marta said.

Greta had ridden the horse to Bourne's house that morning for just this reason. They always planned for this.

They were now on the outskirts of town, which meant they were just a few hundred yards from Bourne's house.

"You know as much as I do. We shocked Rathbone today," Marta said. "He won't come looking for a fight so soon. He'll lick his wounds at the very least first. If Sheppard is right, he's a scout anyway. He will report our location back to his master."

Greta and Beth nodded. They pulled up in front of Bourne's house. He passed the reins to Beth before exiting. Marta also climbed down as Greta and Beth took their spots on the front seat.

Marta watched them go. They were letting fear dictate their actions. Where was the confidence they had after prevailing over Goodman? Surely one encounter wasn't enough to ruin that.

She still itched to go on the warlock hunt, especially after having one right in her grasp. How had she ever let that one go?

CHAPTER 4—NIGHT

Marta awoke sweating and finding it hard to breathe. A nightmare was to blame for yet another restless night. Bourne was lying next to her, their naked bodies spooning through the cool night. She reached to pull him close as she felt a chill.

It was then she realized she couldn't move. Her heart skipped a beat as she tried to vocalize her surprise, but she was gagged with an air spell.

A hoarse whisper said, "Hurry and collar her. She's awake."

Marta's eyes fought to adjust to the darkness. She realized she was in the air above Bourne and being slowly moved. The quilt she and Bourne shared moved with her, exposing him. The person whispering was Rathbone. Two other men were in the room.

Marta grabbed for the power, only to find it was elusive. As Marta took in more of her surroundings, she saw Rathbone had five talismans hanging from his neck. That was more than enough to prevent her from accessing the magic. Without Beth and Greta, she had little hope to reach the magical orb.

"I brought all five of Goodman's talismans with me this time," Rathbone whispered. "There is no use fighting, and you can't escape me now with them in my possession. I was so fortunate to find them all buried under a tree after his failed attempt to do you in."

Bourne stirred under her. Could he do anything? She was doomed if something wasn't done fast. Was he in danger, too?

Marta clawed for the power. She now realized she hadn't woken up from a nightmare—she had awoke to one.

"You should have just slept through this, Sheriff," Rathbone said, no longer whispering.

Bourne was no longer moving, except for his eyes. He was taking in everything he could in the darkness.

"What do we do with the naked guy?" one of the warlocks asked.

"Cover him up, meathead," the other one said.

The first said, "That isn't what I meant. I meant..."

Rathbone cut him off. "We bring him with us. McKinley can use him as leverage against his prize witch. She'll do whatever McKinley wants."

"She'll do whatever he wants because of the collar," the second warlock said.

Rathbone grunted. "Call it extra motivation. Hurry and collar her already."

"She has a talisman of her own that is fighting me," the first said. "I'm trying to defeat it. Until I do, she can't be collared."

Marta closed her eyes, forcing herself to quit listening. These people wanted her, and they were willing to use Bourne to get her. She needed to save them both, and she needed to focus to do it.

Her pendant hung from her neck. It was cold against her skin. That was the talisman the warlock was talking about. At the church, it didn't let any of Rathbone's spells touch her. How were they doing this much?

In her current state, it was a little tough to breathe. She was being held by an air spell inside the quilt. She did her best to take a deep breath to calm her. In her mind, she saw the orb of power. It was miles away, but she could see it. From all the practicing Greta, Beth, and Marta did, they could simulate this with a spell. It was like they put a wedge between the witch and their power.

Marta reminded herself to keep calm even though she could feel her pulse racing. She needed to be near meditative as she performed her next trick. It was something that neither Beth nor Greta could do, but she could.

Normally, it was like a hand in her mind reaching for the power. For this, she imagined a fist punching through the wedge to the power. She did this now.

The punch bounced back. It shocked her. Ever since she figured this trick out, it had never retaliated. It either connected with the power or it slid away. It never bounced.

Her calm threatened to turn to panic. She couldn't have that. She took another breath before trying again. This time when the punch bounced back, she just sent it right back against the wedge. Each time, she got closer and closer to the orb, or at least it felt that way.

Her pendant flew off. The first warlock said, "There. I've gotten through the talisman."

She ignored him as she had a task to focus on. Finally, a punch made it through, and she had the power. She opened her eyes to see a half-inch-wide gold collar held open on a single hinge by the second warlock. He was about to snap it around her neck as she was now clear of the bed, and he could reach her. She used the air spell to send the collar flying. She didn't know what it was, but she knew she didn't want it around her neck.

Her next move was to cut the spell holding her. She turned her air spell into a shield around her. She braced for impact with the floor. Instead, she realized she hovered in place.

"Quit struggling, or Bourne dies," Rathbone said.

Bourne was still in bed behind her. He was frozen in place, eying her. She tried to move her shield more to surround him, but she failed to make it bigger than a foot around her.

She needed to move to get to him, but couldn't while airborne. She had to get her feet on the ground to free him.

"Don't move," Rathbone said. "I'll kill him if you do. Drop your shield and allow us to collar you."

The second warlock had already retrieved the collar. He brought it back. Marta figured they couldn't put that thing on someone they couldn't see. She used Greta's invisibility spell, and the quilt fell right through her to the ground. Really, the spell made her immaterial, but, to other onlookers, she was invisible.

Like a shot, Bourne was whisked out of bed and stood up next to Rathbone. He had a dagger out and at Bourne's throat. Marta's breath caught.

"Last chance," Rathbone called.

Something must have changed with Bourne's bonds because he called out, "Save yourself, Marta."

Marta lightly set her feet on the quilt so she wouldn't fall through it, then on the floorboards. Being invisible meant that only ground would hold her up unless she also used the Earth spell on her feet to keep from falling through, which was what she was doing.

She couldn't get her magic to work beyond her shield, so she had to sneak up on Rathbone and his knife. She would pry him apart from Bourne. He was near the entrance of the room, so just a few steps away. The second warlock stood between her and Rathbone with that damn collar still held open.

Rathbone flexed his hand, pressing the blade a bit more against Bourne's neck. "Do you hear me, Marta? If you give yourself up, the sheriff lives."

Marta circled to stay away from the second warlock. She tiptoed to keep quiet. She would free Bourne in just another couple of steps.

Suddenly, the second warlock lunged forward. The collar closed on air, but it went through her shield and struck her in the head, knocking her to the ground. With the invisibility spell, she fell right through the floorboards.

She landed on the floor of the cellar. Pain emanated from her head. Not the back of the head where the collar hit her, but the front. She also felt dizzy.

From up above, she heard Rathbone ask, "What was that?"

"I saw the quilt move under her weight, so I guessed where her head was," the second warlock said. "Apparently, I missed."

"Well, where is she now?" Rathbone asked.

There was no answer, and Marta's eyelids became heavy. As she lost consciousness, she heard Rathbone yelling, "Find her!"

***

Marta awoke to sunlight streaming through the gap between the cellar doors. Even with the dim illumination, she could see almost everything with her enhanced vision.

When she sat up, she realized her head still hurt. Reaching up, she felt bare skull. A glance at her body confirmed she was a skeleton.

Marta flipped back to human before rising. She had a dizzy spell, so she put an arm to the wall to steady herself. She continued to feel her head with her free hand but found no injury. Ignoring the pain, she headed up the cellar stairs, afraid that Bourne was dead with a knife wound to the throat.

It took the air spell to open the doors since it was latched from the outside. Stars swam in her vision that she hadn't noticed before because of the dark. She ignored it and rushed inside, conscious of the fact she was naked and outside. She just pushed down her embarrassment since she needed to find out what had happened to Bourne. Once inside, she rushed to the bedroom.

No one was there. The quilt lay on the floor where it had fallen when she turned invisible. Bourne was gone.

Marta grabbed the quilt, wrapping it around herself. She ran back out the front door, which still stood wide open. A few people milled about, but none paid her any attention. There was no sign of Bourne or the warlocks.

They had to have taken him. If he were dead, his body would have been left behind. Rathbone mentioned Bourne could be used as leverage against her. Even separated, he could still be used against her.

Marta groaned as she realized this was her fault. If only she had figured out some way to detect when someone came near. Then these warlocks wouldn't have been able to sneak up on her and Bourne. She didn't know how, but she was going to get him back. To do that, she would need Greta and Beth. Three witches against three warlocks were much better odds.

CHAPTER 5—FARM

Marta could see a single plume of smoke during her entire ride south of Kent. She had a bad feeling about what it would be. The closer she got to her place, the more confident she was on what she would find. She rode the horse as hard as she could, occasionally healing it. She was using her strength to keep up the horse's, but, damn, she had a feeling she needed to get to the house soon.

Cresting the final hill, Marta stopped Greta's horse. She had resolved her nerve, but had ended up clenching her fists on the reins and grinding her teeth after seeing what was left of her house smoldering. A tear ran down her cheek.

Marta yelled, "Greta. Beth. Where are you?"

She listened for an answer. A few chirping birds were the only sounds she heard. Her breath caught as she wondered if Greta and Beth had been killed.

Marta eased the horse forward, looking for any sign of another being. Was this the work of Rathbone… or had McKinley been here? She guessed McKinley could have sent other warlocks here, but she needed to find her friends.

Her teeth ground as she visualized finding a warlock and issuing the death curse on him. He'd be dead before he even knew what hit him. Never mind that she didn't know what a warlock looked like. She would recognize Rathbone and the other two who attacked her at Bourne's. So, she visualized the death curse taking them out in an instant.

The outhouse and tack shed still stood. She passed them, getting even closer to the house. The wagon and two horses were in the corral. This didn't bode well for the chances of Greta and Beth being alive. If they were taken, an extra couple of horses would have helped. Then again, neither of Bourne's or Greta's horses were taken from Bourne's house. Also, Rathbone had gotten away from the church in a wagon that could easily hold captives. Marta shuddered at the thought of them being captured.

Upon reaching the house, she dismounted and began searching through the rubble. She was looking for human remains more than anything at this point. Where the beds would have been, she found nothing but ash. There was nothing to suggest a person had been on either one when the fire started. Marta even searched where her room was, but she found no sign of death.

The acrid smoke was starting to get to her. She choked a bit, her eyes watering. At least she blamed the ash. She performed a quick air spell to snuff out the smoldering pieces of house and knock the smoke out of the air.

She made her way to where her hiding place for the spell book was. The floorboards had also burned. She used the air spell to move the debris covering the spell book. A few flames burst up in the sudden exposure to air. She easily snuffed that out. The book was there, but charred up badly. She had the air spell lift and open it.

The first page was charred so badly that it was unreadable. She flipped to the middle. One corner was burned away, but most of the page was charred black. Only one corner was readable. Sweat beaded on her forehead as she flipped to near the end. This was more like the beginning. The book was useless.

Marta dropped the air spell, letting the book slam to the ground. She was now without a resource. Even though she had gone through it many times before, she hadn't tapped into the full potential of some spells as many times she didn't have the context to know what to do with it.

In the middle of the charred mess, Marta flopped on the ground. Emotions she had been suppressing flooded in. She closed her eyes and wept. Bourne's terrified expression showed in her mind. She hadn't been able to protect him. Hell, she hadn't been able to protect Greta and Beth.

Marta felt a chill come over her. She shivered. It was plenty warm out, but thoughts fluttered through her mind in an instant. She had no idea if Bourne, Greta, and Beth were still alive. They could have been captured and killed elsewhere, though Marta didn't see what the point of that would be. If they weren't dead, then maybe there was hope. The warlocks had wanted her alive, for some reason.

Marta jumped up. Of course there was hope. She just needed to track them down, kill the captors, and get her beau and friends back.

Having a purpose now, she ran to the horse. She nearly jumped on in her rush to mount.

Now that she was on, she pulled on the reins to turn the horse. It was then she realized she had no idea what direction to go. She stopped it again. "Holy crap," she said. "What am I going to do?"

She scanned the ground around the house as she thought about what to do. When she spotted something in the garden, she had her horse rush to the new object. Plants were just sprouting in the garden, so it made everything visible, unlike if it were in the tall grass everywhere else. It was a slipper. It had been deliberately set there since it was far enough away from the house to have been taken there. Either Greta or Beth had left it.

Here was proof of her suspicion that they were alive. Now she tried to figure out where to go from there. The toe of the slipper was pointed south, but did that mean that was the direction they went? Marta wasn't a tracker. She had no idea which direction to go. New tears flowed down her cheeks, and she clenched the reins.

With them being alive, it also meant they weren't in immediate danger, or at least Bourne wasn't. She was trying to comfort herself, sure, but there was some logic to this. Bourne was bait to get her. Maybe Greta and Beth would also be pressed about her whereabouts. They were alive, which meant she could rescue them.

Before she could go after Bourne, Greta, and Beth, she needed to find a tracker to help her, that much was clear. Where could she find a good one?

***

Bourne woke with a start. The wagon jostled over rough terrain, which jarred his teeth. He fought to remember what had happened and why he was in a covered wagon. He clammed up, realizing he had been abducted by warlocks.

He raised a hand to the bump on the head, which had caused him to pass out. His other hand came up when he raised the first, and he stopped his movement. He'd been restrained. Bourne continued to raise his hand to scratch the bump on his head, inspecting the shackles. There wasn't a keyhole to unlock them.

The reason there was no keyhole made Bourne's blood boil. Having a girlfriend who worked magic made it easy to see that magic was the only way to get these shackles off. He found a similar set on his feet since he was propped up against the side of the covered wagon. He had been dressed before being shackled.

He lowered his hands, balling his fists. Jerking his palms out, he tested the restraints. He ignored the pain in his wrists as he realized the shackles were well forged. He ground his teeth.

He looked around for a means to escape. Greta and Beth also shared his wagon. They were closer to the back, so they must have been loaded up after him. Their hands and feet were shackled, they wore riding dresses, and they were sleeping. Both had gold collars tight around their necks.

Bourne felt his throat, but he didn't find the same jewelry there. He wondered why such an expensive piece was around their throats. They had to weigh quite a bit even as narrow as they were, but it was thick.

Bourne searched the rest of the wagon. Two people sat in the front seat. Out the rear, he spotted a couple of riders tailing them. There wasn't a way to escape, especially shackled the way he was. He had to force himself to slow his breathing back to normal

He kicked Greta since she was closer to him. "Hey," he whispered.

Her eyes fluttered open, and she took a look around. "Oh, you're finally up."

Bourne was surprised to hear the 'finally'. "Have I been out long?"

Greta nudged Beth. "Bourne's up."

Greta then replied to Bourne's question. "Yes, for quite a while."

Beth came to with a yawn. "Nice to see you're alive. We wondered for a bit."

"Yes, why do they even want you alive?" Greta asked.

Bourne sighed. "They said something about using me as leverage against Marta."

Beth cocked her head. "She's alive?"

Bourne cringed at the thought of Marta dead. She had to be all right. "She turned invisible, and I think she got to safety."

Beth and Greta brightened at the news.

"I take it they have you blocked, which is how you were captured," Bourne said.

Greta sighed. "We can't reach the power, but it feels different than when we are blocked by a talisman. It's like the power is right there within reach, but our hands are chopped off. Usually, the magical orb is a mile away when a talisman has us blocked."

"We think these collars are a different kind of talisman," Beth added. "They put them on us in our sleep before we had a chance to react."

"Marta was the only one who could figure out how to break through a block," Greta said. "Even though we didn't have a talisman to try against, we thought we had a good simulation of one."

"She seemed able to perform magic even though Rathbone had five talismans on," Bourne said.

Greta whistled, and Beth's jaw dropped. Both their eyes widened. Bourne hadn't realized just how impressive that feat was until now.

His compatriots were quite calm as they rode in the back of this wagon. They seemed calmer than he felt, though he tried to keep his poker face on. "Any idea where we are heading?"

Greta and Beth both shook their heads.

"Any idea on why they captured us?" Bourne asked.

Again, the ladies just shook their heads.

Bourne felt his hopes deflate. They were in a hopeless situation, and he couldn't help them out of it. Even worse, Greta and Beth couldn't help them. Even if Marta managed to find them, could she rescue them?

CHAPTER 6—CAMP

For the first time since Bourne had regained consciousness, the wagon stopped. He still had not found a way to free himself from his shackles in the six or so hours he had to work with. Chafe marks now ruled his wrists.

Suddenly, the shackles at his feet sprang open. How had he done that?

Greta's and Beth's feet shackles had also opened. Something was up. Bourne heard a noise, seeing Rathbone at the back of the wagon.

"Come along," he said as the boot board dropped.

Bourne shuddered at the thought of all the magic being performed by this sinister man. Why was Bourne even being kept alive anyway? Why was he here? Where was here?

Greta and Beth stood, then walked stiffly down the ladder on the boot board. Bourne followed suit, taking in the surroundings. It was nearly noon, which meant they had traveled all night to get there.

They were in a wide valley. Red rock outcroppings marked the rim of much of the canyon they were in. Dozens of tents stood near a small river or large creek that snaked through the valley. One huge house stood halfway up the hillside. It could be called a mansion.

About a dozen men were at various places throughout the tents with two or three women around each one. The women all had collars and were doing some chore or another. Laundry, food preparation, and washing dishes looked to all being done with magic.

Beth and Greta stood at attention awkwardly. Something was up, and Bourne couldn't figure it out. "Are you okay?" he asked.

Neither answered.

Bourne became aware of Rathbone at his elbow. It made Bourne nervous that the man had been able to sneak up on him.

"They are in my control." Rathbone held up a pair of golden tokens. "They'll get used to the collars, and be able to better heed my commands."

Bourne glanced at the women, feeling pity for what they were going through. Since Rathbone was being talkative, now was the time to get information. "I take it you removed my shackles?"

"Indirectly. I controlled one of them to do it."

Bourne shuddered at someone's magic being in control of someone else. Especially someone of Rathbone's ilk. He pushed his qualms down as he needed to know more about their situation. "Where are we?"

"Near Lincoln," Rathbone responded.

Bourne thought about the amount of time they had traveled nonstop. It hadn't felt like they had gone north, but his sense of direction might have been messed up. They had taken more than a few turns, but he thought they were going west.

"Nebraska?" Bourne asked.

Rathbone shook his head. "No. Lincoln, Kansas."

Bourne's mind flipped as he tried to readjust the image in his head. "I've never heard of Lincoln, Kansas."

"How about Salina? Have you heard of it?"

"Of course," Bourne said, exasperated.

"We are about forty miles west, northwest of Salina."

Bourne had never been farther west than Abilene. He was now truly on the frontier. If he weren't in danger, he'd be excited at visiting such a lovely valley.

With Rathbone being so chummy, Bourne wondered if he could get a jump on the man. Maybe if he kept Rathbone talking, Bourne could land a good punch and get out of here. There wasn't anyone else close enough to be a threat. He looked over the camp again.

A tall man with long black hair and a beard stood out as he walked through the encampment. He wore no hat in the blazing sunshine that made Bourne long for his. He wore jeans and a blue button-down shirt. The oddest thing was that he didn't wear any shoes.

As he walked by, women curtsied, and men bowed. At the last of the tents, he kept coming toward them. Bourne's thought of escape was replaced with intrigue. Who was this guy?

Rathbone seemed to cower back from the leader when he reached them. This person was spooky.

"Greetings, brothers and sisters," the man said.

"Greetings, Bishop McKinley," Rathbone replied with a bow.

Rathbone nudged Bourne, then held up two tokens. Bourne found himself saying, "Greetings."

Greta and Beth both called, "Greetings, Bishop McKinley." They awkwardly curtsied. They had to have been forced into action.

"I haven't had time to work with the new pets," Rathbone nervously said.

McKinley nodded before cocking his head at Bourne. He felt like he was being inspected. Bourne didn't think much of this McKinley fellow that Goodman had spoken of before his death.

"Where's Marta?" McKinley asked.

Rathbone shook his head. "Don't know. She disappeared on me. We couldn't find her. I've tasked Monterey, O'Rourke, and Rhodes with finding and capturing her."

"That isn't good enough. She is the key to all of this," McKinley spat.

Bourne wondered what Marta was the key to.

McKinley pointed at Rathbone, and a fireball shot forth. Rathbone turned into a skeleton as the fire hit him. He issued no block.

"Find her!" McKinley roared.

The flames quickly died, and Rathbone turned back to a human. With a nod, he said, "As you command, my bishop."

Rathbone then handed over the two tokens to McKinley before returning to his wagon. Bourne watched as the wagon headed off.

McKinley grabbed Bourne's shoulder. With wild eyes, he said, "The witches are easy to deal with. What am I to do with you?"

Bourne stiffened to hide his fear. He was being kept alive for a reason he couldn't fathom while in the clutches of a madman. How was he going to get out of this one?

CHAPTER 7—TRACKER

Marta slowed her horse at the outskirts of Council Grove. It was past dark, not that her heightened sense of sight didn't see her through. Instead, she was giving her horse a break since it probably didn't like the sudden brightness of the streetlamps.

The decision to come to Council Grove wasn't an easy one. She could have found trackers in Junction City or Manhattan, but Council Grove was closer. Also, she was pretty sure her house was hit after Bourne's, though she wasn't positive on that. Rathbone was likely heading south since he started at the church, was at Bourne's in Kent, and then hit her place. It made sense that he would keep heading south, so Council Grove was on the way. The slipper also indicated south. She had decided on this direction while saddling her horse, grabbing her bedroll from the shed, and packing some coin and currency that was hidden in a cache for the trip. A neighbor curious about the fire came, and Marta got him to feed Beth and Greta's horses before setting out on her mission.

Now to go to the best place in Council Grove to find a tracker. On approach to the saloon, Marta heard loud, rapid piano music and a general loud crowd. It wasn't anything like the peaceful Kent saloon that would play some soft, slow music and the loudest it got was when there was some cursing at the poker table.

Marta stopped her horse at the trough, then tied him to the hitching post. She then steeled herself before going inside. She opened the door to find about forty people playing cards, milling about, or watching the show. On a dais at the other end, a girl with a low-cut dress and short skirt danced next to the piano. She made sure people got eyefuls of her bouncing bosom, flicking her skirt up from time to time to show off her legs. Marta couldn't believe the girl would expose herself like that.

This wasn't what Marta was here for. She needed a tracker, and this sorry lot was her best chance. But how was she going to get their attention? She couldn't compete with a dancing whore. Well, except for the fact she was a witch and in a bad mood.

Normally, she would think twice about using her powers in public. Despite most people knowing about her and her compatriots, they were still afraid of her abilities. It helped that she only used her power with the best of intentions, so her Kent neighbors at least put up with her presence. How would the Council Grove people react?

If she didn't get a tracker, what would happen? She thought the worst for a moment before deciding her friends couldn't wait on her being subtle.

She spotted an empty chair near the door. It had an obstructed view of the dancing girl. It wasn't at the table with the poker game going on, which was why it sat empty. She pulled the chair out from the table, then stood on it.

She called the air spell to create a cone that magnified her voice. "May I have your attention?"

The piano died, the dancer stopped, and every single head in the place turned to her. That was it. They didn't move. She expected a dozen or more to run from the room in fear, but that wasn't happening. The only different thing was the general mirth in the atmosphere turned to ice. It was like being in church and how the parishioners treated her.

Taking this in stride, she decided not to question why they didn't run. She dialed back her cone to increase her volume of speech only slightly. "I require a tracker," she simply said.

A few chuckles answered her, but most everyone stared at her blankly.

"Have I said something funny?" she asked with a bit more venom than she intended.

One man at a table nearby said, "If a witch needs a tracker, then the job is going to be dangerous. There isn't a tracker in this room worth his salt willing to accept the risk."

Marta's heart sank. He was right. The mission was dangerous, though she supposed the tracker could leave before she fought Rathbone and McKinley to get her friends back.

She kept her emotions in check, eyeing him. "I have a twenty-dollar gold piece for the person to take the job, and I am willing to pay another twenty dollars a day until my friends are found. I'll pay first thing in the morning each day, and the tracker can leave if they feel they are in danger." She thought that was reasonable, but it sounded too much like danger was guaranteed. She added, "Assuming, that is, there is any danger."

The man stared hard at Marta through squinted eyes. He wasn't laughing now. Was he considering the pay? He finally asked, "Where did you get that much coin?"

It wasn't all coin, but she didn't bother to correct the man. She also didn't see why it mattered where the money came from. Her family had done well, making arms during the Revolution and War of 1812. "I've been able to save my money, so far. The important thing is that I have it."

An outlaw type seemed to perk up. Marta added, "And since you all know I am a witch, you should realize I can protect it."

The outlaw shrank back. The rest of the folk didn't seem to care. Nobody volunteered, either.

The man, who was the only one to speak so far, asked, "Why can't you use your magic to track?"

Marta cocked her head. The truth was that she didn't know if it was even possible. If it were, she never learned. "If I could, I wouldn't be here."

Marta decided to add an emotional plea to her request. "Please, my friends have been abducted and I need to find them."

"Sounds dangerous to me," a man nearby said. "No way in hell am I risking my neck."

Marta rolled her eyes. Why had she added the info about abduction? It made her position worse, not better. It was her against McKinley, Rathbone, and the two others with them. Her abilities alone should make the fight almost even, even more so if she managed to free Greta and Beth first. She couldn't tell all that to these folks, though. She turned to go since she wasn't getting anywhere with these folks.

"I track," a slurred voice called.

Laughter came from all around.

Marta turned to the man who had spoken. He stood from a table in the very corner of the room. He was an old, frail Indian who looked like he would drop dead at any moment. He stood hunched over in a deerskin tunic and pants.

The old man added, "That much wampum pay for many drinks, methinks. I do it."

Again, laughter sounded from the other patrons. Hell, Marta didn't believe he could track in the state he was in, and neither did anyone else. Was this the best she could do?

The old man lifted a fist. "I tell you, I fit to track. I best tracker around. Medicine woman say I live a long, long life. Come, we track now."

He moved toward the door in a slow shuffle. His arms shook as he moved. It pained her to see the feeble old man declaring himself fit when it was obvious that he had many issues with his health in addition to his drunken state. Hell, the amount she was willing to pay was probably ten times the normal rate.

The old man suddenly tripped and fell about halfway to Marta. She jumped down to help him as everyone laughed again. Before she reached him, she was pushing the healing spell onto him.

When she knelt beside him, he snored, and she found no injury to heal. He was just drunk.

The poker table was close. She asked the closest poker player, "Where does he live?"

The man rolled his eyes and turned away. The player next to him offered, "He lives with his granddaughter in the hut at the north end of

Eighth Street. You can't miss it; it is the only one with Indian crap decorating it."

Marta thanked him as she lifted the old man to his feet. She made it look like she was doing it physically, but she was using air spells. She threw the man's arm around her neck to complete the illusion before walking with him in tow.

Once outside, Marta set the man onto the back of her horse. She didn't know why she was wasting her time with him. Maybe because he had stood up to help her when no one else had. But did that mean she owed it to the man to see him safely home when she had somewhere else to be?

Twenty minutes later, she still didn't have an answer, but now stood outside the hut the poker player told her about. She took the old man off her horse, then put him down beside her so it still looked like she was helping him physically before knocking on the door.

A young Indian girl, around sixteen, answered the door. Marta immediately realized the girl could connect with the magical orb; she was a witch.

The girl's brow furrowed. "What are you doing with my grandfather?"

"I went to the saloon looking for a tracker, and your grandfather offered to help. I'm Marta, by the way."

Marta even held her hand out for a shake. The girl eyed it, but didn't take it.

With some mirth, the girl asked, "How much gold did you offer?" She gave a small laugh. "He couldn't track a bleeding bear over the snow-covered ground with his bad eyesight. It must have been a lot for him to ignore this fact and take on the job."

Marta nodded, but she was embarrassed to say how much. Besides, maybe the tracker gene was passed down through the generations. She still held her hand out. "What is your name?"

The Indian girl still refused to shake Marta's hand. "Wind Rock. How much?"

"Twenty dollars now and twenty per day," Marta stated.

Wind Rock's eyes widened, and the smile slipped off her face. She cocked her head.

"Are you also a tracker?" Marta asked. "If you're any good, I'll pay you the same rate."

Wind Rock suddenly backed away, though she still held the door open. "Put him on the cot in the corner. Then you can leave."

"Please," Marta started. "I need a tracker."

"I said put him on the cot and then leave."

Marta asked. "Where am I to go?"

"I don't care."

The girl's annoyance was clear. Marta walked in, settling the old man on the cot indicated. Even though she was in a hurry, having this girl as an asset in her quest was worth sticking around to convince her to come along. To that end, Marta said, "Would you at least allow me to stay the night? I did just bring your grandfather home, and I have nowhere to go tonight."

"I have no more cots." Wind Rock said.

"I have a bedroll and can make do on your floor." Marta eyed the floorboards of the hut. "It looks more comfortable than the ground I would otherwise be staying on." It probably wasn't, but a little lie never hurt anyone.

Wind Rock's brow furrowed. "You can't stay. You must realize that neither my grandfather nor I will track for you. Got it?"

Marta nodded, but she needed this girl to not only track for her, but also to use her magic in the fight. Surely there was a way to convince her.

CHAPTER 8—WIND ROCK

A scent of something brewing was in the air. It wasn't coffee, but it wasn't off-putting either. On the stove was a pot. It must have been some sort of soup, and it smelled delicious.

"What's for supper?" Marta asked.

Wind Rock eyed her before sighing. "There's some hardtack over on the shelf there if you want some of it." She moved to the pot and stirred it.

"That isn't what I meant." Marta pointed to the pot.

The old man didn't stir despite the women talking normally. She indicated the pot. "What are you making?"

Again, Wind Rock eyed her. Marta was beginning to feel like she was a nuisance here, but didn't know why this woman was being so guarded.

Finally, Wind Rock said, "It isn't food."

"So, what is it?" Marta asked.

"You're just going to tell me I'm too young."

Something in Marta snapped. What did youth have to do with cooking? The fact that her friends were in danger made her not in the mood for this woman's reasoning. "Look here…" Marta began with a little too much venom. She stopped and took a deep breath. "We started off on the wrong foot. I'm sorry to be a nuisance. I'm not trying to be a burden, and I am just inquisitive."

Wind Rock didn't even look in Marta's direction as she spoke. Instead, the girl focused on whatever was on the stove.

Marta's words hung in the air between them, and Marta waited for Wind Rock to flinch first. Maybe she was weighing what she said. Then again, despite the girl showing a very good grasp of the English language, maybe Wind Rock didn't understand everything that was said.

"You seem well versed in English," Marta said. "How did that happen?"

Wind Rock huffed, still focusing on her pot and slowly stirring it. "My father was a white man. Since I was born a half-breed, I wasn't allowed to stay with my tribe. My mother and grandfather moved me here to raise me among the white folk. My mother died when I was young, so my grandfather is the only one I have left. The people here weren't much more accepting than my own, but they did allow me to go to school and learn from them while my grandfather did odd jobs around town."

Wind Rock met Marta's gaze after she was done with her explanation. Marta felt for the girl losing her mother at a young age and being among so much persecution. It was time to change the subject. "So, what are you making?"

Wind Rock returned her attention to her pot. "It's a remedy for stomach aches. My grandfather always gets them after a long night of drinking."

"Ah, so a medicine."

Wind Rock nodded.

"Is it made with magic?" Marta asked.

Wind Rock's stirring faltered for just a second. Otherwise, she didn't react. It made Marta wonder if this girl knew anything about her abilities. "You do know that you are a witch, right?"

Wind Rock stopped stirring, cocked her head, and glared. She still didn't look toward Marta. Was Wind Rock considering the question or playing dumb? "We don't use that word. We are medicine women."

Marta gulped. "Sorry. I meant no offense."

Wind Rock turned her attention to her pot, resuming stirring. "I don't use the power to heal my grandfather when he has done something stupid. I'd rather he learns not to do dumb things. Though, he still hasn't."

"But you can heal?"

"Of course I can heal. I'm quite good at it."

Marta nodded. "I'm also a good healer. Hell, better than good. I've now brought two people back from the brink of death. Maybe I can teach you a thing or two."

Marta was also hoping it would go two ways. Hell, if they formed enough of a bond, Wind Rock would have another ally in her fight to get her friends back. Surely that was worth her time here rather than being on the road after Rathbone.

Wind Rock was shaking her head, though. She said, "I've had plenty of teachers. Despite my exile from the tribe, medicine people are above tribal politics and are even shared between tribes. A number have come to tutor me over the years. I'm sure that I'm more knowledgeable than you are."

The girl looked too young to even know half of what Marta knew. Then again, working with the power tended to slow down aging, especially working with healing.

"Just how old are you?" Marta asked.

"My age has nothing to do with it. I learn fast and am shown things just once before I pick them up."

Marta felt like she was talking to a typical teenager who knew everything about the world so didn't need to know anything else. "There are still things I can teach you as I am sure there are things you can teach me. We can work together."

"I doubt it."

"Just tell me how old you are."

Wind Rock shook her head. "It doesn't matter."

"Probably," Marta said. "I am getting more and more curious, though."

"This is my sixteenth spring," she said.

Marta whistled. Only sixteen and almost as strong in the power as Marta. Surely in the years ahead, this girl would surpass her in strength. That was what happened to Marta. She still didn't think she had reached her peak.

"I'm waiting for you to say something dumb like 'you are too young to know as much as I do.'" Wind Rock said.

Marta shook her head. "If you had teachers, then you might know a good deal."

Wind Rock nodded. "So, how old are you? As strong as you are, I'm guessing fifty."

Marta was surprised at how close the girl was. She would be fifty-three in a couple of months. All she said was, "Close enough."

Wind Rock cocked her head and smiled. "A little low, I take it. You must be a good healer."

It was the first smile Marta had gotten from the girl. Were they on their way to being friends? Hell, Marta would settle for a little sharing of knowledge.

Before Marta could work on the relationship more, Wind Rock asked, "So, what does McKinley want with you?"

Marta's heart stopped. How did this girl know about that? What did she know about it? Marta wanted to fire a million questions at her at once.

What was more, Wind Rock's expression was now serious again. Marta knew that whatever she had gained in their relationship was now lost for whatever reason. She would have to work hard to get Wind Rock to help her. That meant she couldn't just lie about it.

Even more, this sixteen-year-old might know more about McKinley than Marta did. She had to find out what Wind Rock knew so Marta could succeed in her quest to get her friends back. It was time to start firing questions. "What do you know about McKinley?"

Wind Rock blinked a couple of times, but was otherwise a rock. Her lack of emotion was giving Marta a headache. Or was it the fact she was scowling so hard?

Marta stepped toward the girl, then put her hands on her hips. "Answer me. What do you know about McKinley?"

Wind Rock moved until they were toe to toe. Marta had to look down at the girl, but, for some reason, she seemed as tall as Marta was.

In a calm whisper, Wind Rock said, "I asked you a question first. What does McKinley want with you?"

Marta wanted to throttle her, but saw the connection she had to the power. When had she grabbed it? Was this going to turn into a magic fight? Marta was sure she would win since she was slightly stronger, but knew that didn't matter. She needed this girl, and fighting wasn't going to work.

Marta huffed. "This is a waste of time."

She still didn't grab the power. If she were struck, she would have to rely on turning into a skeleton to defend herself. She also didn't back down from Wind Rock, either. Then again, given the girl's age, she probably didn't realize what her lack of taking up the power meant.

Wind Rock cocked her head. "I can see you want something from me. You can't get it until I get my answer."

Marta's mind did a flip. Was this girl offering to help her find Beth and Greta? Surely not. Marta considered Wind Rock's words very carefully.

Before this quid-pro-quo statement, Marta had asked for Wind Rock's knowledge of McKinley since she obviously knew something. Wind Rock, on the other hand, wanted to know what McKinley wanted with Marta.

Sighing, she slumped. This was the exchange Wind Rock referred to. Marta stepped back, removed her hands from her hips, and sat on a cushion that looked to be for that purpose.

"I don't know," Marta finally admitted.

"You don't know?" Wind Rock asked. She also sat on a cushion.

Marta shook her head thankful, that Wind Rock was also backing down. She even released the power as she sat.

"I mean, I did take down Pastor Goodman, who was a warlock and some sort of compatriot of McKinley's," Marta said.

"I know about Goodman since the whole town has been talking about little else for months. But killing a warlock wouldn't have mattered to McKinley."

Marta shrugged. "People tend to try to kill what they are afraid of. If I can take out Goodman, maybe McKinley was afraid he was next."

Wind Rock shook her head. "He has a whole army to protect himself with. You can't touch him."

This surprised Marta. McKinley had an army of warlocks to do his bidding. She had only counted on a few warlocks standing in her way. She was suddenly afraid for Greta and Beth.

"Then maybe it was revenge," Marta said. "Goodman admitted he was a student of McKinley's. Maybe they were close."

"Your friends are the other two medicine women, right? Greta and Beth?" Wind Rock asked.

Marta nodded.

"Have they been killed?" Wind Rock asked.

Marta felt her face contort. The slipper she found on the ground had to mean Greta and Beth were captured, right?

Wind Rock sighed before Marta could answer. "They were collared, weren't they?"

Again, Marta was surprised. "What do you know about collars?"

Wind Rock rolled her eyes. "I'm asking the questions here."

Marta waved a hand dismissively. "I've been forthcoming enough. It is your turn to give me something."

Wind Rock crossed her arms under her budding bosom. Her face was again a mask of no emotions. When she spoke, it was as if she were chanting. "My mother was abducted by McKinley before I was born. McKinley wanted my mother because she was beautiful. She was also a powerful healer.

"The collar controlled my mother. It made her do his bidding. Under his control, she was forced to help him collar other medicine women and convince warlocks to join McKinley's army. My mother spent many moons under his control.

"Then one day, my mother was forced to try to heal a dead medicine woman that they had accidentally killed while trying to collar her. My mother was pushed to her limits, and she ended up being cut off from the power."

Marta listened, trying not to break down. Greta and Beth were in this man's clutches. Were they doomed to share the same fate as Wind Rock's mother? "Then what happened?" she managed to ask.

"No longer a medicine woman, she escaped. McKinley probably didn't care at that point since she was useless. My mother died during my eighth summer, but not before warning me of the dangers of McKinley and his ilk. He hunts for medicine women with certain qualities, and I'm trying to figure out what is so special about you for him to want you."

Marta found her mouth to be drier than the hottest Kansas summer day. So much pain and suffering caused by one person. Her heart went out to this girl who had lost her mother.

"How did your mother die?" she finally asked.

Wind Rock replied, "Madness. Being severed from the power drove her mad. She would have died sooner, but my father came along and saved her. He gave her me before having to move on. Since she was pregnant, she couldn't follow him, but I was enough to have her hold onto sanity for a long time. She even taught me spells."

"I'm sorry for you losing your mother," Marta said.

"It was long ago," Wind Rock said.

Marta was silent for a bit, soaking in all this information. Finally, she asked, "How do the collars work?"

Wind Rock shook her head. "I'm not sure, but I do know that whoever has the token controls the person wearing the collar."

"Token?"

"Yeah, kind of like a coin."

"And the collar works on warlocks as well if you can manage to collar one?" Marta asked.

Wind Rock scrunched her face as she thought. Finally, she said, "My mother only mentioned medicine women wearing collars."

Marta nodded. Of course she couldn't turn them around on a warlock. "Can they be disabled?"

"I don't know," Wind Rock stated. Her eyes bore into Marta as she said, "I'm still trying to figure out what McKinley wants with you."

Marta looked down at herself. She wasn't a gibfaced jollocks. She was a lovely and vibrant woman. Bourne certainly liked her. Plus, she was a powerful witch.

Then again, did it matter why McKinley wanted her? He had Greta and Beth collared. Bourne was either dead or kept captive. What mattered was convincing this girl to help free her friends from this bastard before something happened—like getting severed from the power.

Marta realized that was easier said than done. She studied the strong Indian girl—who was sixteen going on fifty—realizing she had her work cut out for her in making her case.

CHAPTER 9—MISSION

"I may not know exactly what McKinley wants with me. I just know he wants me," Marta said. After a moment's thought, she then added, "He also has my friends, Greta and Beth. Rathbone told my beau that he was going to be my motivation."

Wind Rock cut her off. "That makes no sense. The collar that is put on you makes you do what he wants. I'm not sure what all can be done, but I know it is painful to disobey."

Marta shuddered at the thought of not being in control. Especially not in control of her power. What kind of destruction could be wrought on people?

Marta's heart went out to Greta and Beth. Then something else came to mind, and it made her gasp. "Your poor mother…"

Wind Rock dropped her head. "She wouldn't talk about specifics of what happened to her, but I got the picture."

Marta nodded. Then she questioned, "So, why does he want Bourne?"

Wind Rock lifted her face, squinting at Marta. "He's a warlock, isn't he?"

"Absolutely not. I would know if he were. For one thing, I've been able to make a talisman that can block spells from hitting me."

She fished it out to show Wind Rock. "It went cold when Rathbone showed up. It hasn't reacted one bit with Bourne around."

"I take it you and Bourne are close."

Marta nodded, uncertain where this was going.

"How close?" Wind Rock asked.

"We've been courting for nine months."

"Just courting?"

Marta's cheeks felt hot. "That is none of your business."

Wind Rock nodded. "Probably not, but I wanted to see how deep you were with him. Some of my tutors mentioned that many of their spells don't work on loved ones."

"I've done plenty of magic on him." She knew that wasn't a good stand to take in the argument, so she asked, "Can't warlocks detect other warlocks like witches—er, I mean medicine women—can detect other medicine women?"

Wind Rock nodded with her brow furrowed.

"Then Goodman and Bourne would have known about each other, so Bourne couldn't be a warlock," Marta said, continuing her train of thought.

"Or they were working together."

Marta laughed. "They most certainly weren't working together. For one thing…"

Marta stopped as she remembered Bourne being with Goodman when he had the talisman blocking her to take her to the church for her execution. Then he was the last one to believe Goodman was a warlock. Surely, this was circumstantial.

"For one thing, what?" Wind Rock questioned.

Marta eyed the girl before her. She was hesitant to complete the thought, but timidly said, "They fought each other." She was sure, though, that he wasn't a warlock. He couldn't be. This girl didn't know anything about him.

"Have you fought with Beth or Greta?" Wind Rock asked.

Marta locked her jaw. Of course there had been some arguments, but nothing like trying to kill one another as Bourne and Goodman had. That didn't matter to this argument, though. "I know more about Bourne than maybe even he knows. He isn't a warlock."

Another thought came to her. "I've healed him on multiple occasions. Twice, he was seriously injured."

Wind Rock's face twisted as if she were considering this.

Marta felt like Wind Rock came to the same realization that Marta did, but she said it anyway. "If Bourne were a warlock, he would have self-healed. How do you know so much about the situation anyway?"

"As I said, you've been the talk of the town for months."

"So?"

"So, you tend to listen when it may affect you," Wind Rock said. "At first, I was afraid they would go on another hunt for medicine women and take me out like they tried to do with Beth, but they seemed to calm down after finding out you saved that sheriff."

"So, they know you have magical abilities?" Marta asked.

Wind Rock cocked her head. "I don't think so, but I didn't even know Beth was a medicine woman until she was hauled off by Goodman. I don't think we'd ever met, though."

Marta nodded.

Wind Rock smacked her lips. "Anyway, I've heard a lot about you and the hero who brought down McLeod. I just don't see how he can be used as your motivation."

"But I can break out of talisman blocks. Maybe Bourne is there to make certain I don't even try."

Wind Rock shrugged. "I don't think a collar can be gotten out of like a block to your power. For one thing, the collar isn't meant to block you, but to direct your powers."

Now was Marta's opening to get back to what she wanted from Wind Rock. "Then my friends need to be freed before they are forced to do something bad or are hurt like your mother was."

Wind Rock shook her head. "You might as well forget about them. They should be considered dead to you. They are no longer themselves but are puppets."

Marta noticed there wasn't a spark in Wind Rock's eyes. She didn't care for Marta's friends. "How dare you suggest that?"

Marta looked away then. The old man on the cot slept away his hangover. Wind Rock cared for him, right?

Marta turned back to the girl, forcing a smile since she knew something this girl didn't. "You may act tough by telling me to forget them. I take it that's what the other medicine women did when your mother was taken."

Wind Rock's eyes became beady, her brows furrowed.

"You may say you don't care about other people, but you do." Marta nodded to the grandfather. Determination took over her anger. "It also sounds like you are lonely. You have to imagine what it takes to love someone since I take it you don't have suitors."

Wind Rock was as still as a rock. Marta wasn't done, though. "You can sit here accusing my beau of being a warlock without any shred of proof if you like, but I can tell you are haunted by your mother's disappearance. I can help if you'll only let me in. So, will you?"

Wind Rock huffed, cocking her head. "Get out," she hissed through gritted teeth.

"No," Marta said.

Wind Rock's eyes widened.

"You need me," Marta continued. She paused a moment before adding, "And I need you."

Wind Rock paused before saying, "You need me to track for you."

Marta shrugged. "At first, I came to Council Grove to find a tracker. What I need, though, is an ally in my fight against McKinley. My friends are out there, and I will get them back. You can help me get them back sooner than if it were just me bumbling about on my own."

Wind Rock hung her head.

"Uh, you can track, can't you?" Marta asked.

Wind Rock nodded. She seemed lost in thought.

"If anything, do it for your mother to make sure no one ends up like her again," Marta cajoled.

Still, Wind Rock didn't budge.

"If Goodman is any indication, that man is out there spreading evil. You and I can bring him down. Together, we are a force to be reckoned with," Marta added.

Wind Rock didn't react.

"What happens when McKinley comes for you?"

"He won't," she softly said, not meeting her eyes.

"How do you know?"

Wind Rock slowly lifted her head to meet Marta's gaze. She spoke slowly, but with purpose, "I know." She took a breath before continuing, "I will not be a part of your suicide mission. My place is here taking care of my grandfather." She pointed to the door. "Get out."

Leaving that house was the hardest thing Marta ever had to do, but she needed to regroup before trying again. She felt a tear slide down her cheek as she slowly trudged out of the house into the cool night air. Her horse was still at the hitching post where she left it. Her mind was mush as she made her way to the horse.

Once there, she glanced over her shoulder. Marta had left the door to the hut open when she left and now Wind Rock filled the empty doorframe. She held the power, her hands on her hips.

Marta focused, trying to keep her hands from trembling she checked the horse's tack. Obviously, this girl wouldn't help her. She had to keep looking on her own.

She had a goal, and it made her feel better. She straightened her back, set her jaw, and checked to make sure her bedroll was still securely tied behind her saddle. Mainly, she wanted to be sure the money hidden underneath hadn't been stolen. She also cinched the saddle since she had loosened it before going in.

"Hey," Wind Rock started.

Marta was so focused on her horse that she hadn't noticed the girl approach. Marta spun around to see what Wind Rock wanted.

"What is your plan?" Wind Rock asked.

"I don't know," Marta said, with a bit of venom. "I think Rathbone was heading south, so that's the way I'll go. Hopefully, I'll find a tracker somewhere along the way."

Wind Rock pursed her lips and sighed, but she didn't say anything. What did this girl want from her?

Marta quickly saw that going south was a long shot at best. Surely, there was a better plan. "I could always go to St. Mary's to investigate him from there."

Wind Rock shook her head. "He hasn't been there for at least a decade. That is almost as futile as going south."

Marta crossed her arms and glared. "Then what? How do you know he isn't somewhere south or at St. Mary's?"

"I keep my ears out for news about him. After his exposure at St. Mary's, he went into the wind. My mother was abducted shortly after that, and he took her out west somewhere. I'm not sure whether he is still in that direction, but I do hear rumors of abductions around Salina. I don't think he would go south, though."

Marta glared at Wind Rock. "So, I should go to Salina? Is that your advice?"

Wind Rock shrugged.

Marta closed her eyes. "Where would you suggest that I look?" Opening them back, she blew out a breath in frustration.

"You should go back to the last place Rathbone was and search for tracks there," Wind Rock said.

Marta shook her head and huffed. "I'm not a tracker."

Wind Rock nodded. "You need one, though."

This girl wasn't being all that helpful, and it rubbed Marta the wrong way. She clenched a fist. "Any suggestions on who would be willing to track for me?"

Wind Rock shook her head.

Marta was done. She turned on her heel, untied her reins from the hitching post, then moved to mount her horse.

"Wait," Wind Rock called. "You still haven't told me your plan."

Marta had her foot in the stirrup as she shot a look at Wind Rock. "I guess I plan to find a tracker."

Wind Rock rolled her eyes. "That isn't what I meant."

Marta waited for Wind Rock to continue, but she just stood there. Marta took her foot out the stirrup before turning back to the Indian. "Then what did you mean?" Marta was surprised her tone was so vile even though her blood was boiling.

"When you find McKinley, what is your plan?" Wind Rock asked.

Marta saw the way Wind Rock's eyes sparkled. Marta had hope again that she had her tracker and ally on the line. She needed to reel her in. "He needs to answer for what he did. I'll haul him in front of a judge and see that he hangs."

Wind Rock's brow furrowed. "He can't be brought to justice. I don't even think it is possible to capture him."

Just like that, Marta had lost her again. She sighed. "If I must, I'll kill him, but that is the last resort."

"I don't think you can stomach killing him," Wind Rock said.

Marta's stomach boiled. What did this girl know about what she was capable of? "I've killed before, and I'll kill again if I must."

"You must," Wind Rock simply stated.

Marta shook her head. "It sounds like you need to be the one to avenge your mother."

Wind Rock's head dropped, and she toed the ground. She didn't say anything for the longest time.

Marta hid her excitement. Her anger dissipated. She might have her fish on the line again or at least considering the bait. "You can come with me, you know. You can kill him yourself."

When Wind Rock lifted her head, a tear was sliding down her cheek and her eyes glistened. "I can't kill him. Even someone as vile as him." Wind Rock grabbed Marta's arm. "Please, kill him for me."

"Why can't you kill him?" Marta asked.

Wind Rock shook his head. "I just can't. I've imagined meeting him and the things I'd say, but I can't imagine killing him. Please, do it for me."

Marta's resolve melted in that tearful look and plea. Maybe it wasn't in the girl's nature to kill. "I'll kill him." Marta then added, "But first, I need to find him."

Wind Rock stiffened again.

Damn it! There went Marta's fish again. "Why don't you want this?"

Wind Rock just hung her head in response.

Marta turned to mount her horse. She was through with the ups and downs of this.

"Let's wait until morning to head out," Wind Rock started. "I'll leave a note for my grandfather if he isn't up by then to go to the res to be looked after. I'll take our donkey, so we don't have to ride tandem."

Marta's jaw dropped. Her arms trembled with excitement as she turned to the woman who stood before her. No longer a girl, Wind Rock had aged considerably with just one statement.

"A night's rest would do us some good, but we should hurry every chance we get," Marta stated.

Wind Rock turned on her heel, then headed back inside. Marta's heart was in her throat as she was sure Bourne, Greta, and Beth were as good as rescued with this medicine woman on her side. Then again, with Rathbone and the other warlocks McKinley had under him, they could be on the suicide mission that Wind Rock prophesized. Was there any way to avoid that fate?

CHAPTER 10—DEATH CURSE BLOCK

The donkey, which Wind Rock rode, dictated the pace. It irritated Marta that they were going so slow, but Beth and Greta's horses were stabled at Marta's neighbor's. One of them would work better than this stupid donkey, so that swap was going to happen. She thought about offering to have Wind Rock ride tandem again, but that would be complicated now that they were underway and had nowhere to put the donkey.

They were heading for Marta's house as Wind Rock had to have a good place to pick up the trail. It was the closer of the three places Marta had seen Rathbone, so the logical choice to start.

Thinking of Rathbone made her remember the first time she met him. "Is there a way to block a death curse?"

Wind Rock eyed her while keeping the donkey going. Marta's horse slowly walked while the donkey huffed and puffed. "Are you thinking about killing my donkey?"

Wind Rock healed the donkey for the umpteenth time since they set out. "No," Marta said. "I issued one at Rathbone, but it didn't land."

Wind Rock inhaled deeply. She seemed tight-lipped on the journey. Not that this was anything new. The girl hadn't been all that expressive since Marta had met her.

Wind Rock finally said, "I know shields, transcending, and the counter curse can't block the death curse. Nor can they block a healing. You'd need a totem against the curse."

Marta wondered what a totem was, but there was also something else more interesting to ask. "What is transcending? I know about shields and the counter curse, wims, but I don't know about transcending."

Wind Rock sighed. "From what I've heard, Goodman got stuck after transcending. He didn't go back to human form until right before he died."

The realization hit Marta. "You mean the skeletal state."

Wind Rock rolled her eyes. "Yes, you are a skeleton when you transcend. It prevents injury to the medicine woman or warlock."

"Got it. What is a totem? Goodman had five talismans in his possession, and now Rathbone has them."

Wind Rock nodded. "I think that is another translation between our worlds. What I call a totem is probably a talisman to you."

"That's what Goodman called them. I like the word 'totem' better."

"And five would be overkill to block the death curse," Wind Rock said.

Marta nodded. She didn't let her know Rathbone only had one the first time around.

Marta could tell that Wind Rock still mulled things over. "From what I've heard, though, you can't issue any magic when you are around a totem."

Marta finally found a subject that she knew, and Wind Rock didn't. She thought about lording it over her, but she was finding it more pleasant the more the girl talked. "You can work with another medicine woman to have them push you to obtain the magic. We've also discovered that if you calm and center yourself in a void, you can then reach the power by repeatedly punching through the block. Or at least I can. Beth and Greta haven't been able to master that one yet."

"I've done linking with other medicine women, which sounds like the first thing you described. I'm amazed you were able to get around five talismans."

Marta knew they could learn from each other, and this was an example. This partnership would work because they were going to free Bourne, Beth, and Greta.

Wind Rock cocked her head and squinted. "But if you had gotten around the talismans, how did your death curse get blocked."

Marta shrugged. She didn't know all that much about talismans. Everything she knew came from Goodman. Where was he when she needed him?

Marta had gotten Wind Rock's curiosity up. That was the key to their relationship. Maybe that was the whole reason she had agreed to this trip. Marta would impart what she knew to see if that got her curiosity up even more. "Maybe I had only partially gotten around the block to where I could issue magical spells, just not the death curse."

Wind Rock sighed. "That doesn't seem right. Totems shouldn't be able to discriminate between spells."

Marta winced. "Well, maybe Rathbone had another talisman that just blocked the death curse," Marta said.

"That may be, but I'm still not convinced. Something seems off. Maybe linking, or the pushing as you describe it, limits a person's ability to issue the death curse."

Marta found herself nodding until she realized something. "I've healed while linked. Isn't healing and issuing death about the same?"

"Well, except for them being opposite." Wind Rock started before pausing a moment. "When a medicine woman is linked, she is giving her life force over to the other woman. You'd almost need to do a reverse link to give your death force over to do a death curse. I don't think that is possible."

Marta was disappointed. She wasn't figuring out how to defeat Rathbone the next time she saw him as she hoped.

Wind Rock piped up. "But if you can disable the totem, or in this case, totems, then you don't need the link. Then you can issue the death curse."

Marta perked up. "How do we disable a totem?"

Wind Rock shrugged. "I'm just throwing out whatever comes to mind here. I don't even know if a totem can be destroyed."

Marta felt like they had been so close to a solution here. Now they felt just an inch closer on a journey of a thousand miles. If only Greta, Beth, and herself had worked to destroy the talismans last summer rather than bury them to allow them to fall into someone else's hands.

That was the past. She needed to figure out a way to disable the talismans before she ran into Rathbone again. She just didn't know how soon that would be.

For the rest of the ride, they talked and mused over magic. It was as if they had somehow bonded, but Marta wasn't sure how. Maybe she had passed some test or something.

CHAPTER 11—HOME AGAIN

After swapping the donkey for Beth's horse at the Olson's farm, they finally made it to Marta's house. Seeing the ruins of the house again brought a tear to Marta's eye. For some reason, she lost focus of everything else in the world but that.

The new room had withstood the fire better than the rest. Part of the walls for that room still stood. There was nothing worth salvaging to rebuild, though. Marta wasn't sure she even wanted to. What was tying her to this house and this piece of land?

"Did you hear me?" Wind Rock asked.

Marta looked away from the destruction. She tried to pull herself together. They had a job to do, and that was to save her friends.

Wind Rock pointed down the hillside to the west. "A good set of wagon tracks go that way." She then pointed north. "A better set goes that way. I'm still trying to figure out which is coming and which is going. You stay here while I search a bit to try to determine that. Okay?"

Marta nodded. "The track to the north should be the coming since that is from town."

Wind Rock stiffened. "That's assuming they hit Bourne's place first. We can't assume anything. I'm here to track, so let me do it."

"Just trying to help," Marta called to the departing Wind Rock. She was so touchy. Why was that?

Marta dismounted her horse, still avoiding the ruins of her home. She felt a bit queasy, more than likely due to the smoke. The outhouse still stood a few feet behind the house, but she didn't want to get sick in there.

A noise from the outhouse drew her attention, though. She made her way toward it to investigate. Marta approached cautiously and as silently as possible, straining to hear the noise again. She held on to the reins, so her horse followed behind her.

She didn't hear anything new in the outhouse, but she stopped about twenty yards short. "Is anyone there?" she called.

The outhouse door burst open. A man was pulling up his trousers as he locked eyes with Marta. "I thought I heard people out here. Who are you?"

Marta, in surprise, grabbed the power in case she needed to defend herself. She didn't recognize the man. Despite him still getting his pants buttoned up, Marta watched him to see what his next move was. He had no visible weapons, so that was a relief. "Who are you?" She put up a shield up in case he tried anything.

"I asked first," the man gruffly said. "Who are you?"

This was her home. What gave this man the right to dictate who answered who first? Hell, he was using her outhouse without her say, so it was only right if he were a little more courteous.

Now that his pants were up and he even had his suspenders over his shoulders, he came out of the little building. He was young, but a year or two older than Wind Rock. Unlike most youngsters, though, he walked and talked with an air of authority that most people didn't get until later.

The man cocked his head, still waiting for a response.

Hoofbeats like thunder drew Marta's attention north. On Beth's horse, Wind Rock flew up the hill from the trees. Behind her, two men on horseback, in long coats and ten-gallon hats, gave chase.

"They're warlocks," Wind Rock shouted.

Wind Rock didn't have a hold of the power, which was odd.

Marta returned her attention to the man in front of the outhouse. Was he also a warlock? It would make sense he was with the other two, but she didn't want to strike without knowing for sure.

The man shot a fireball toward Wind Rock. Marta easily blocked it, then issued the death curse to the man in front of the outhouse since he was the only one in range. It seemed obvious now that warlocks would be waiting for her in case she returned.

Marta issued the death curse two more times at the warlocks coming up the hill. Wind Rock rode flat out until she was behind Marta's shield before stopping her horse. She still didn't grab the power, and she slumped over in the saddle. Marta had to extend her shield to protect the new occupants in it.

Her death curses failed to land on the other two warlocks. Instead, they just dissipated a few feet away. They rode on, though they were now just ten yards away from them.

The medallion Marta wore went cold, and she flipped into the skeletal state. The death curse must have been issued at her, but had failed due to her own talisman. She hurled fireballs back at the riders.

This got the men to stop their horses. They must have had shields as the fire just dissipated in midair in the same spot each time. They also turned into skeletons as they returned fire. Marta still had her shield up, so these stopped short of the mark. The horses danced in place as the battle raged.

Marta glanced at the warlock who had been in the outhouse. He was down and unmoving, so she didn't have to worry about him getting into the fight.

Since fireballs weren't working, Marta sent down lightning from above. Unfortunately, though, the warlocks had their shields blocking there, too, as the lightning stopped just short of hitting them.

And still, Wind Rock did not get into the fight. Marta became concerned Wind Rock was injured, but she focused on the fight.

Not wanting to continue, Marta released a magic bomb against the warlocks' shield. She called it a bomb as that was the best description she could come up with. It was just a monster ball of energy—an orb of lightning, fire, and lava. It hit the shield, and the shield flashed white as it absorbed the energy and then seemed to rain down all around the warlocks. She was ready for it, but the warlocks weren't.

They fell backward off their horses. The horses turned and ran off without their riders. The two warlocks weren't hurt in their skeletal state, but they weren't returning fire.

Marta went back to fireballs since the bomb took a lot of stamina. There was no longer a shield blocking her, so the rain of fire was making it through. The men's clothing burned as they staggered in their attempts to get up. Soon, they had a shield back up.

They got their fires put out in short order, but Marta kept up her onslaught. She even readied another bomb. She became conscious of the smell of burned grass and ozone. Ignoring it, she focused on her adversaries. With the fires burning some of their clothing, it exposed the small talismans they each wore.

Then a bomb went off against her shield that made her teeth chatter. Unlike the warlocks, though, she was prepared for it. Her shield weakened, but she quickly reinforced it. The only thing it impacted was that she didn't fire any fireballs for half a second. She even delayed the bomb she was preparing since she had to expend power to stabilize the shield.

She continued the onslaught of fireballs, lightning, and even the bomb. Again, the bomb took down their shields, but only for a moment. The men backed away, though. They were losing, and they knew it. They were putting up a good fight, and Marta wondered just how they kept up with her.

Marta was also conscious of her fatigue. She wanted it over sooner than later, so she marched forward as they backed away. Marta wasn't done yet, though. She wanted a chance to overwhelm those talismans so she could issue the death curse.

The warlocks stopped issuing magic. They turned to run, their shields still blocking her, but they were going down every time Marta issued another bomb. Even though she was exhausted, she hitched up her skirt to give chase.

"Marta," Wind Rock called weakly.

Confused, Marta turned to the girl. She was hunched over in her saddle. It was the first time Marta had gotten a good look at Wind Rock's right arm. It had been hit by a fireball before she made it to Marta's protection. Blood dripped from her fingertips, and her arm was badly burnt and mangled. The bone was even exposed. She was in bad shape.

Wind Rock's head swayed, and her eyes fluttered before rolling back. She fell from the saddle. Marta quickly caught her in a bed of air with the magic before safely lowering her to the ground. She was even careful of the wound.

How had this happened? Marta gave a glance over her shoulder at the fleeing warlocks. Her blood boiled at them hurting Wind Rock, at their escape, and at them being here to trap her. Add to it the fact they could now report back to Rathbone and McKinley that Marta had help.

Marta turned to the unconscious medicine woman. She winced, imagining the pain the girl must have felt. How had she not turned into a skeleton or blocked the curse with a shield? Marta hoped she had enough strength left to heal Wind Rock. It wasn't something Marta had considered when she had gone all out to fight three warlocks, but she couldn't lose this girl's help. At least not yet. And could Marta live with herself if she lost the girl at any point in the journey? Marta didn't know, and she didn't want to find out. She went to work to save the girl's life.

CHAPTER 12—HEALING

It took every ounce of energy Marta had left to push the healing spell onto Wind Rock. Even then, the power flowed through her at a trickle rather than the full breadth she normally used for this spell. It went to work, but it was taking longer than it normally did. Marta steeled herself so she wouldn't succumb to exhaustion and drop the spell.

Wind Rock bucked when the magic hit the wound. She didn't call out in pain, but a tear slid down her cheek. She closed her eyes as the spell worked.

Marta watched as the muscle reattached itself from the deepest part out. It was like the tendons had grabbed hold of each other to pull the wound together. It took a lot longer than it should have. There was a lot of blood lost, but that couldn't be recovered by the spell alone. Wind Rock would need to hydrate in the coming hours.

Marta knew if she had this wound, she would have passed out long before Wind Rock had. This woman had some strength.

How easily Marta had forgotten Wind Rock was a young girl. Such was her demeanor and wisdom. If this didn't heal right, the girl might be crippled or, worse, dead.

Marta strengthened her resolve, trying to grab even more power. She had to fight for the amount she currently had, not to mention any extra. She was determined to heal Wind Rock or die trying.

Despite the extra power, the wound didn't heal any quicker. It still slowly closed. Marta's hands shook as she worked the magic. A tear slid down her cheek as exhaustion and pain addled her. Whatever had done this seemed to have cauterized the wound, or the girl would have lost even more blood than she had.

Finally, the skin sealed. The magic reverberated, reassuring her that it was healed. She let go of the spell and then the magic. The magical orb suddenly felt like it was too far away to reach. She would need to rest before doing any more magic.

She glanced up at the sun. It wasn't as bad as when summer came around, but it would still be a bear if she didn't get some shelter from it. She looked down the hillside at the trees. That would do.

Wind Rock was still out. Marta barely managed to lift her. The entire way down the hill, Marta's knees shook and threatened to buckle. Again, she was determined, so she pressed on. Wind Rock couldn't have weighed more than seventy-five pounds anyway.

Where the wound was, the girl's arm was red and puffy. There were the beginnings of a scar as well. Wind Rock did breathe easily as she was carried down the hill. She'd live, assuming no other warlocks came around.

    Marta barely had Wind Rock set down in the shade before Marta was also laying on the ground next to her. She had half a thought to stay awake and keep an eye out for warlocks, but she finally gave in to the welcoming embrace of sleep.

CHAPTER 13—BREAKING

Bourne watched as the four-foot spike went into the ground. He was tethered to it by a heavy-duty chain and a shackle at his ankle. The ground shook as the spike hit home. It wasn't pounded multiple times like a railroad spike. It just slipped into the Earth with one giant heave.

A warlock was nearby, but Bourne knew he wasn't doing the work. He commanded Greta with a coin he held.

When the spike was settled, she turned to the warlock. "Is that good?"

The warlock nodded. "All except for your tone and questioning me at the end. You speak only when spoken to."

Bourne hadn't thought her tone to be rebellious. Hell, she did what was asked of her.

Suddenly, she bucked as if struck by something. She fell to her knees, trying to catch her breath.

"What did you do to her?" Bourne asked.

The warlock held up the coin. "I can do anything I want while in control of her medallion."

Bourne eyed it. "Can anyone control her, or do you have to be a warlock?"

The warlock cocked his head. "You wouldn't be trying to escape, would you?" He chuckled. "Strike him, deary. Give him a painful whip for such a thought."

"I meant no disrespect," Bourne said while Greta spoke over him, pleading not to dispense pain.

The warlock gave them the stink eye. He pointed to Bourne. "Only warlocks can handle a medallion since we need magic to control the slave."

He turned to Greta. "You don't get a say anymore."

She screamed in pain, and it made Bourne jump. Another scream and another. He heard a whip that he couldn't see repeatedly flick. After about a dozen screams, they finally stopped.

"Don't disappoint me further. I can whip you to near death, heal you, and then do it all over again. You don't know torture until you've seen me do it. That's why I've been tasked to break you." The warlock then huffed.

He eyed Bourne before turning on his heel. "Come on, deary. We have work to do."

Bourne took a deep breath to steady himself. He hadn't realized he had been shaking. If only he could get his hands on that man's throat, he would throttle him.

The two set off down the hill back to the main camp. Bourne was being put outside on the hillside overlooking it. It was opposite from where the mansion sat. Nobody told him why he was staked here.

Soon, Bourne spotted Beth. A warlock trailed her. Between them, a bunch of canvass, ropes, and poles glided over the ground without ever touching it. One moved it with magic, and Bourne suspected it was Beth.

When they came abreast of Bourne and his spike, the warlock said, "Here is good."

The materials fell to the ground. "Start putting up the tent, devil spawn," the warlock commanded.

Sighing, Beth slumped.

"Don't give me no gruff, heathen," the warlock sneered.

Beth called out in pain like Greta had when she was whipped. Bourne wasn't sure if that was the actual reason for the outcry, but it seemed likely. These warlocks liked inflicting pain. Bourne gritted his teeth to keep from saying something he would regret.

The warlock moved closer to Bourne as the tent began erecting itself. "Is there something else I can do to make your stay more comfortable?"

Bourne examined the spike, chain, and shackle on his leg. "Removing this restraint would be great."

The warlock cocked his head. Finally, he gave a burst of laughter. "That's a good one. It'll make McKinley chuckle when I tell him."

Bourne hadn't said it to be funny. He wanted the hell out of here. If he could take a few witches to their freedom as well, that would also be great. Even if he couldn't, he'd be back with Marta. Together, they could surely free everyone.

"How about a cot?" the warlock asked.

"Excuse me?" Bourne inquired.

"You know, a cot to sleep on. Would you like this devil spawn to bring you one?"

Bourne eyed the warlock. Just who was he to be calling her devil spawn? "Sure," he finally drawled.

"Excellent," the warlock said. He then turned back to Beth. "We used to make them work naked in the beginning."

Bourne did a double-take. What kind of animals were these men? Finally, Bourne mustered an, "Oh?"

"Yeah, but the women were getting raped. It meant the vow of chastity wasn't being followed. So, this was curtailed."

Bourne nodded like it made sense. It didn't, but he played along.

"It made breaking the devil spawn easier, sure, but we couldn't have commandments being broken. I do miss them being naked, though," the warlock said.

Bourne gulped. He couldn't imagine a beautiful woman like Beth running around naked while tons of men leered at her. He realized the warlock was waiting on something. "I bet," he said to fill the void.

The warlock nodded. He still watched Beth work. She was nearly finished, just had a few ropes to stake down. She circled the tent as she used magic to accomplish this.

"Well, we better get to work somewhere else. Someone will be along with your cot soon."

The warlock turned and walked off. Once the tent stakes were in place, Beth ran after him like a puppy who had lost its master.

Bourne's mouth went dry. He had seen men with their slaves back in the day before the war and the Emancipation Proclamation. He'd been glad when those days were over, but here it was all over again. Except in many ways, this was much worse. How could good Christian men act like this?

He scanned the camp before turning and retching in the bucket that was left there to be his latrine. He had to get out of this hell!

CHAPTER 14—MORE HELP

Marta woke with a start when something popped. She grabbed the power to defend herself from an attack. Why had she fallen asleep with danger around?

"Easy there," Wind Rock said. She stoked the fire, holding a stick in one hand and a canteen in the other. She took a long pull from the canteen.

Marta dropped the power. Twilight ebbed, so she had to have been out for over twelve hours.

"Thank you for saving my life," Wind Rock started. "You did a fine job of healing me."

Marta examined Wind Rock's arm. The scar she had feared was pretty unattractive. It was half-formed, but there was nothing that could be done about it. At least the redness and puffiness were down.

Then what Wind Rock said hit. She'd said, 'fine' as in better than good. It was a rare compliment. "You're welcome," Marta returned, basking in the praise.

Something about the situation felt off. "How did you get injured if you knew about the skeletal state?"

Wind Rock scrunched her face, then took another swig of water. "They had totems that blocked my powers before I could transition. I also wasn't paying attention to my surroundings, so I didn't know they were there until it was too late. I was too focused on tracking."

It still didn't make sense. "Why did they attack you when they were waiting for me?"

"They saw us approach and were mounting up when I came upon them in the trees. I heard one say something like, 'So much for that lardass letting us know when Marta was coming.' That's what alerted me to their presence. The thunderbolt hit me and knocked me from my horse. My dress caught fire, but the flames went out when I hit the ground. With no access to magic, I couldn't retaliate. The other one said, 'With her squaw gone, we should be able to take her three to one, no matter how powerful she is.'"

"They thought you were dead," Marta interjected.

Wind Rock nodded. "I remounted the horse, then set off up the hill to warn you. They didn't know how powerful you are."

There was another compliment on Marta's skill. She must have been doing something right to get this much praise.

"Since I already held the power, they couldn't block my access. You couldn't get it once you were behind my shield?" Marta said.

Wind Rock hid her face. "I tried your trick of calming myself in a void to reach the power, but it wasn't working. I don't know whether it was those damn bombs or my injury, but I couldn't calm down."

Marta nodded. "I don't think I could have if I were you, either."

Wind Rock took another drink from the canteen. She didn't seem any less embarrassed.

"I wonder about the range of those talismans. When did you feel like you could access the power again?" Marta asked.

Wind Rock shrugged. "They were a good way down the hill before I could have grabbed the power. Probably fifty yards."

Marta whistled. Maybe the range increased since there were two of them, but she didn't think it worked like that. "In any case, I was able to drive the warlocks away. I even killed one."

Another thought occurred to Marta. "Why were they waiting for me today and not yesterday?"

Wind Rock cocked her head. "Maybe they were here yesterday, but asleep from their overnight raids. Those guys weren't exactly the greatest watchdogs. One in the outhouse while the others were down the hill resting."

Marta shrugged. "Or they were supposed to be hiding, and one didn't know what I looked like. The two who came after you looked familiar. I'm fairly sure at least one was Bourne's abductor."

Wind Rock eyed Marta. She didn't say anything for a long time. She just drank from the canteen now and again. Finally, she said, "I think we need more help."

Marta cocked her head. What was this girl proposing? Did she want to give up and return to Council Grove? "We can't waste time gathering medicine women. Especially now that those two can report back to McKinley."

"There are other ways to communicate with medicine women."

She said it so matter of fact that Marta was beyond intrigued. Communication with other witches would be awesome. "How?"

"In the dream realm, the medicine women hold meetings. You need to be at the next one," Wind Rock stated.

Marta was overwhelmed. She had a million questions, but she couldn't focus on just one. Finally, she said, "Why does it have to be me?"

Wind Rock indicated her arm. "I am in no shape to walk the dream realm. I need rest, and walking the realm doesn't allow for that. You need to do it."

Marta felt excitement fill her. She would gather more people to help rescue Bourne, Greta, and Beth while experiencing something new. "Okay. How?"

Wind Rock scowled. "You have to realize there is a danger in dream walking. Once there, other's dreams may try to pull you in. Then, you are at the mercy of the dreamer. If you die in the dream realm, you never wake up."

"How can a person die in a dream?"

"Not sure, but some people don't wake up. It is believed the dreamer can kill a walker if they dream it so."

"So, I make sure I don't die there," Marta said with a forced smile. Inside, her stomach churned and her chest constricted. It sounded like there was no way to prevent it, and she wasn't ready to die.

"Tell me what to do," she prodded.

Wind Rock gave instructions on the spell, the dreams Marta might see, and how to navigate in the realm to find the other medicine women. Marta listened intently, but she was scared to death. She knew she had to do it—the risk was worth the reward. She just didn't know what the hell she was doing. Would she wake up in the morning?

CHAPTER 15—DREAM REALM

Since she wasn't going to get much rest tonight, it was a good thing Marta had slept the day away. Though, she needed a bit more after the massive use of power earlier.

From her bedroll, she eyed Wind Rock, who watched her with half-closed eyes. She was going to be sleeping soon herself. There would be no one to watch over them, but it was a risk they had to take.

Wind Rock smiled encouragingly. At least that was how Marta perceived it. She didn't think Wind Rock would mock Marta, not with as nervous as she was. Then again, she didn't know Wind Rock all that well, so it was better to believe the positive.

Marta didn't know why she'd even suspect Wind Rock of being anything but sincere here. This would work, and Marta would wake to see a new day. She had to.

Marta took a deep breath before grabbing the power. She didn't know how to weave the five elements for this spell, so she uttered, "Shree voygone."

Her subconscious directed the magic to flow through her. It shot upward a few feet before falling on her in a dispersed, fluttering fountain. She closed her eyes as instructed, and…

Nothing happened. She waited a few seconds, but that didn't change. She needed to see what was happening with her spell before she asked Wind Rock, so she opened her eyes.

Stars were as far as the eye could see. Thousands, if not tens or hundreds of thousands, floated around her. All different shades of yellowish-orange. Wind Rock had said that the redder the ball, the more of a nightmare it was.

"Amazing," Marta muttered. Her voice echoed a dozen times. She wanted to reach out and touch one of the balls, but Wind Rock had advised her not to. The stars represented the dreams people were experiencing right now.

If only she could find Bourne's. Just to make sure he was still alive to give her hope that the journey she was on would bring him back alive.

Marta made a paddling motion with her hands and feet. She wanted to look around, but she knew she needed to find the meeting place the medicine women used. Swimming wasn't moving her, so she stopped her movement.

Apparently, she needed to use magic to move. She was still connected to the power and the spell she was using to be here. She manipulated the spell to push her to the left.

Marta stopped as her heart rate spiked. She then manipulated the power in the opposite direction. It was working!

Now to find the gathering of medicine women. The spot would look much like the other stars, but Wind Rock had said it was blue since it wasn't an actual dream.

Marta flew through the stars, searching for a blue one. How was she going to find a single ball in this giant mess? Everywhere she looked were yellow and orange balls. None were blue.

She kept moving, feeling her breathing increase. She tried to calm her mind. It wasn't time to panic—not yet.

Suddenly, a red star hurtled toward her. She changed direction, but it gave chase. Why would a dream be after her?

Marta felt like she was being sucked in by the red star. She thought about giving in to see what happened, but Wind Rock's advice to avoid the balls at all costs stuck in Marta's mind. She had said nothing about balls chasing her, though.

She glanced back to find the ball closing in. She couldn't outrun the damn thing forever. Sooner or later, she would succumb to it. She decided to meet it on her terms.

She turned to face the dream orb. It was on her in an instant, enveloping her. There was a flash of white, and then...

Bullets flew all around her. Men shot at each other, but most seemed to be aiming in her direction. Bullets curved through the air to pass right by her. A couple even ruffled her hair. Suddenly, a hand grabbed her and pulled her down behind a rain barrel.

"Marta, keep down," Bourne called.

His voice was a bit sing-songy, but he was alive. Marta's heart threatened to beat out of her chest. Her beau was alive!

She rushed to hug him, but he pushed her back. "I said to stay down!" It was said more gruffly than before.

He peeked over the barrel, getting a couple of shots off with his revolver. Then he ducked again. That drew more fire from the enemy, whoever it was.

Marta tried to see who Bourne shot at. "Stay down," Bourne yelled. "I can't do my job if you keep putting yourself in danger." Her glance allowed her to see the street of Kent, though there seemed to be dozens of items upended to give the shooters protection. Behind Marta and Bourne was the trail out of town. She'd also spotted Rathbone, though he seemed a bit taller than she remembered. There was also a ten-foot man with a full beard and long hair. In all white, he was an imposing figure to say the least, whoever he was.

Bourne arched around the side of the rain barrel, popping off shots from there. He must have hit someone as Marta heard a groan of pain. Then another volley of bullets hit their rain barrel and all around them. No matter how many holes were shot in the rain barrel, allowing the water to flow out, the barrel remained full.

Marta shook her head. It would only take a second to end this fight. She reached for the power in her mind's eye. The first try whiffed. She tried again, but it wasn't there. It wasn't out of reach like when a talisman blocked her. It was simply gone. She was a witch without powers now. How could that be?

Marta didn't know what to do. She had never been without the orb. It gave her more than power. It was her life, her constant companion. Even blocked or when she was exhausted, she still could see the power in her mind's eye. Having nothing made her mouth go dry. What was she without her magic? Marta Farragut, ordinary pioneer?

A shot kicked up dust next to her foot. She was powerless to stop the fight or even return fire.

She eyed Bourne's second gun. He hadn't needed it yet. Had he even reloaded? She could grab the second one and shoot, but she'd never fired a gun. She'd never had to.

"They're closing in," Bourne said after one of his peeks around the rain barrel. "We may have to make a run for it."

They were at the edge of town with only prairie grass surrounding them, which wasn't adequate cover. They were doomed to die.

For some reason, Wind Rock's voice echoed in Marta's head. "If you die in the dream realm, you never wake up."

CHAPTER 16—TRAPPED

Marta's hands shook, and her chest tightened. She crossed her arms, a chill snaking through her. Each shot made her jump. She was as good as dead. Why couldn't she figure a way out of this?

"Run," Bourne bellowed as he shot ten times in a row. How had he, though? Shouldn't his gun only hold six or seven bullets? Nothing made sense.

Her feet didn't comply with the directive they were given, either by Bourne or by her brain. She was doomed. Her mouth was too dry to vocalize her certain death.

An apparition in the shape of an old Indian woman appeared before her. Marta's mind failed to comprehend the woman's existence, let alone what it might mean. The woman said something.

Marta shook her head, trying to concentrate on the apparition. She already feared this place, so the woman only slightly added to her unease.

"*What* are you doing here?" the Indian asked.

Marta stared at the apparition. What *was* she doing here? She didn't know. How could she tell the woman something she didn't know herself? Marta continued to jump at each shot. Finally, she asked, "Where am I?"

The Indian rolled her eyes. "You're in his dream," she huffed. "How did you get here?"

Marta shrugged as she continued to shiver. "The dream chased me down, then I was here."

The Indian woman glanced at Bourne. He still shot over the rain barrel from time to time. Fewer shots came from the enemy, so maybe he was picking them off. Could he win?

"He's handsome, I'll give him that," the Indian woman started with. "He also seems keen on protecting you, so he must be good."

What did that have to do with anything? Marta didn't need a social commentary. She needed to be rescued.

"Do you want to remain trapped here?" the apparition asked.

What kind of question was that? Marta clenched a fist. "How do I get out of here, and who are you?"

"You need to stop thinking about him. It is unfortunate he was dreaming about you when you were thinking about him, but that can't be helped now. Clear your mind, and come with me. I am Runs With Does." She reached a hand out for Marta.

Just how the hell was Marta supposed to stop thinking about him when he was shooting a gun beside her, she didn't know. She wanted to ask this crazy old kook how to when the answer came to her. Wind Rock had told Marta to void her mind of everything except for the meeting place with the other Indians. Like how she calmed herself to get through a block by a talisman. She could do the same in the dream realm. It would help if the others didn't shoot, though.

She closed her eyes to help block out everything around her. Bourne started another volley of shots, so she quit listening. Next, she turned off her sense of smell. Bourne so close made it harder to forget touch, but she managed it. There was nothing around her. She visualized a flame and burned her anger, fear, and any other emotion she felt. She was one with the flame. Marta *was* the flame.

She focused on only the blue star Wind Rock talked about. That was what Marta needed to do. That and to go with the Indian who appeared in the dream.

"That's better," Runs With Does said, breaking into Marta's forced silence.

Marta nodded, then started doing a breathing exercise to continue to keep her mind clear. She needed to repair the break in her sound buffer.

"Hey, make sure you pay attention to me. You might want to open your eyes now."

Marta complied. A dozen women stared at her from where they stood among ancient ruins. She struggled to place the ruins from her reader as a kid with its columns and missing roof. Wasn't it called the Parthenon? It had a blue tint to it rather than the white stone she remembered it being described with.

Runs With Does stood beside her. Still a ghostly version of herself, though she was now full-bodied rather than just a floating head.

Marta looked down, realizing she was the same way. It was like she was here in spirit rather than in her body. She was a ghost!

As she scanned the area, she realized there was more like forty, with more coming. Most were Indians, but some rivaled her in white skin. There were even a few blacks. All were women.

They all wore cloaks. Some even covered their head. She couldn't tell who or what they were. Then again, did it matter if they weren't all Indians? It came as a surprise, though, as Marta thought Wind Rock would have mentioned it.

The next thing Marta noticed prompted her to speak. "Not all of you can do magic!"

"Correct," the woman who had appeared in Bourne's dream said. She couldn't do magic, or at least Marta didn't sense any abilities in her. "Magic is only one way to get here. Some people are born with the ability to visit the realm on their own."

What other secrets had Wind Rock kept from her? She wanted the girl here to answer this and so much more. Hell, a friendly face among so many hostile stares would have been nice.

"How did you know about this place, anyway?" Runs With Does asked.

"Wind Rock told me about this and how to get here," Marta stated.

"Is Wind Rock okay? We were expecting her tonight," Runs With Does said.

"She's recovering from wounds she got in a warlock attack. I've healed her to where she is fine but needs her rest."

The old Indian muttered something under her breath. "Tell her that Runs With Does says to be careful of who she keeps as company."

Marta cocked her head. Was this woman saying Marta was bad company? Should she call this woman out on it? Her fear kept her from saying anything in the heat of the moment.

"Why are you here?" someone else asked.

Runs With Does raised a hand. "Remember the decorum, ladies. Even though this woman doesn't know our custom of only talking when you have the peace pipe, we must keep with tradition." Runs With Does looked to be the eldest person here and either that commanded a huge amount of respect, or she was in charge due to some other factor.

Runs With Does handed Marta the pipe that she spoke of. "So, why are you here?"

Marta took the pipe and a deep breath. "First, let me apologize for not knowing the customs of this place. Wind Rock told me the essentials about how this place worked. I should have inquired further as to what to expect, though. Sorry about that."

Runs With Does gave a nod. With her stony expression, Marta wondered if that was to accept the apology or to move her along.

Marta tried to remain calm. "My name is Marta Farragut. I'm here to ask for your help in fighting evil. This is a matter of life and death. Two nights ago, my boyfriend and two of my medicine woman friends were taken by a warlock named Rathbone. He is associated with the warlock, Bishop McKinley."

A few gasps sounded from the crowd.

Marta took that as a good sign. "I need my boyfriend back. I am lost without him. I don't want my friends to share the same fate as Wind Rock's mother. We need help.

"Today, Wind Rock and I encountered three warlocks. I killed one. We need to take down Bishop McKinley's forces, free all the medicine women under his control, and rescue my boyfriend." She sniffled. "Nobody else should have to suffer this kind of outrage."

Marta tried to gauge the crowd of hard faces. Some had

sympathetic eyes while others stared stonily.

The one who spoke out of turn earlier snapped her fingers. The peace pipe flew from Marta's hand to the woman. It wasn't magic that made the pipe fly. It was an ability of the dream realm. "McKinley has probably a hundred magicians under him, including captured medicine women. We have never dared to move against him for fear of killing our kind since they would be made to work against us, and we'd need to defend ourselves."

Many people nodded. Marta's heart sank. Was there any way to change these women's minds?

Another woman snapped and got the peace pipe. "Plus, we could be captured in the attack, adding to his army. We are better off cutting our losses."

Marta snapped her fingers, catching the pipe as it flew to her. She was proud of herself for learning the new trick so quickly, but the loss of her friends and the way these women reacted replaced that feeling. "We can't think of captured women as acceptable losses. What if you were the next one to be captured?"

"We'll be captured or killed if we move against him," Runs With Does said after snapping for the pipe. "Only someone who is truly pure of heart can move against him. This has been foreseen."

This gave Marta pause. She heard of vision quests, especially among Indians. She didn't think they were the most reliable. Could Runs With Does truly foretell the future?

Then she thought about the purity of her own heart. She wasn't religious or that good of a person. She thought that if she saw a wrong and she could right it, she would. There just wasn't always a way to right all the wrongs in the world. Or was it that she wasn't pure of heart.

Marta snapped her fingers without really meaning to. She could have reached out and taken it from the woman next to her. Then again, she had called it from Marta. She stared at the pipe for a moment when she caught it.

She sighed, not wanting to get into a heart purity discussion. "Like most any battle, there are losses. Some losses are even innocent ones." She met the gazes of some of the women near her. "You have to decide if this cause is just and worth those loses."

She held up the pipe. "This is supposed to represent peace. Well, I say there is no peace while McKinley can abduct people. He is gathering an army, and you must realize that he means to use it in some capacity. Will he move against you? Probably not, but it will be too late to stop him if you wait for him to make the move."

"Wind Rock and I are moving against him. Please join us."

She had people's attention. Marta could see the wheels turning in their minds. Some, at least, were on her side. Could the rest be convinced?

A snap from beside Marta whisked the pipe from her hand. Since she ran this place, Marta turned to hear what the old woman said.

"You are a foolish child for going after McKinley. Even more the fool for endangering Wind Rock."

"But I need to rescue my friends."

"And now you speak out of turn." Her eyes narrowed. "Be gone." Runs With Does flicked her wrist and…

The next thing Marta knew, she was in her bedroll under the trees near her house. The fire was dying, and Wind Rock snored from her bedroll.

Marta clenched her teeth. She had failed to get the medicine women on her side. Did that spell disaster for the mission?

CHAPTER 17—SLAVE LABOR

Bourne awoke with a start. In the dream, there had been a bullet heading right for his forehead. He'd been powerless to stop it. He tried to slow his breathing, reminding himself that it was just a dream. A bizarre one, but still a dream.

He thought about the people he'd been shooting in the dream. McKinley, Rathbone, and some of the other warlocks he'd met had been there. Everyone was larger than life with McKinley being bigger than everyone else, but they didn't use magic against him. Instead, they fired revolvers at him and Marta.

Marta hadn't used her magic to fight. She'd had no gun, relying on Bourne for protection. That was certainly a switch.

Then there was her behavior. First, she was the damsel in distress, then suddenly domineering. She'd acted like she was going to put a stop to everything. So pretty much as she did in real life. Then she'd gone into a deep depression and anxiety. He'd never seen her like that. When she started talking to herself, it freaked him out.

Then she was gone for a few seconds before returning. Her demeanor was back to being the damsel in distress. This had to mean something, but Bourne couldn't fathom what. It was probably just that he missed her. He wondered where she was now and how she was coping with his kidnapping.

Bourne realized he was much calmer than when he'd first woken. He was wide awake, but he thought if he laid here a while, he'd become groggy and sleep some more.

He stood from the cot and stretched. The tent was at least eight feet tall at its peak. It was made from green canvas that would have been an officer's tent at one time. Bourne tried not to think about how such a thing had fallen into McKinley's hands. He hoped it was bought, but he didn't think so.

In the corner was a bucket and he used it now to relieve his bladder. Someone would be along at some point to take it and dump it. The chain shackled to his right ankle made him move a bit funny, but he made it to the bucket.

Once done with his business, he moved outside. He was twenty-five yards from the nearest tent. He wasn't sure why he was being segregated from the tent village, and he hadn't gotten an answer when he asked. Probably nobody except for the man running the show, McKinley, knew.

Bourne turned and inspected the spike. It went through rock, so there was no way to remove it. The head was a good foot in diameter, and it stuck out of the ground a few inches. He'd have to break the chain if he wanted to be freed. The problem was the chain was heavy-duty. The links had to be an inch and a half long with quarter-inch piping. In the whole ten yards of chain, he couldn't find a single weak link.

Movement coming up the hill drew his attention away. Greta, Beth, and a warlock headed his way. Beth held a chair, and Greta carried a food tray and a cup. The warlock was the same one who had beaten Greta and controlled her the day before.

Wordlessly, Beth set the chair down in front of the tent.

"Fetch his pail and empty it in the usual spot, deary," the warlock said. He turned to address Bourne. "The bishop noticed you spent a lot of time watching the camp yesterday. He thought a chair would allow you to do that more comfortably."

Beth grabbed his bucket, moving off toward the creek. Greta stood there, holding the food and coffee. The warlock waited expectantly.

It took Bourne a moment to get what the warlock waited for. When he sat in his new chair, Greta handed him the tray.

The warlock patted Greta's bottom. "You can head back to the cooking tent to help serve others as they wake up."

Greta complied without a word. She had flinched at the pat on her bottom, but otherwise kept a stony expression. She was broken. Bourne wished she had a bit more backbone, but then he couldn't figure out how he could make a move with so many warlocks around.

The warlock watched her leave. "Man, I wish I hadn't made that vow of premarital celibacy. She is a pretty one, that's for sure. Maybe I'll have to wed her just so I can get my jollies."

Bourne clenched his fists. He wanted to strangle the man for even thinking of such a thing. Finally, he said, "She'll never marry you."

"It'll take her a while to agree. Probably twice daily beatings, but she'll eventually do it. They always do. Sometimes, it takes a lot, though."

The warlock sighed. "But I think that one is taken anyway. The bishop likes her and Greta, so they'll probably end up as his next concubines."

Bourne saw an opening to cause a rift. "So, he doesn't have to marry to get his jollies?"

The warlock shook his head.

"And you're okay with that?" Bourne asked.

The warlock cocked an eyebrow. "Why wouldn't I be? The bishop provides us with the light in this dark time. Witches are killing us off, and we're supposed to let it happen? No, we're going to take the fight to them. There are some rules that we must follow to accomplish that, but it is a small price to pay. Besides, I'm extremely picky about who I marry. There are a few guys who have taken multiple wives because they weren't completely satisfied with the first. I don't want that to happen to me."

It was said in one huff. Bourne had struck a nerve, which was the goal. But he hoped to cause a rift between the warlocks and McKinley. That hadn't happened.

"My apologies," Bourne began even though he didn't feel like serving up the platitude. "I know so little about this place, and I'm just trying to understand. Just like I watch the camp to understand."

The warlock nodded. "You'll come around eventually. Speaking of the chair, would you like me to deliver back any comment?"

Bourne glanced at the chair. The sun was beginning to rise, and there was one thing he'd need. It was too hot in the tent during the day, and he needed shade. "Yes. Can I get an umbrella?"

The warlock frowned. "I meant anything regarding appreciation."

"Oh. Yes, send along my thanks in addition to my request for an umbrella. It doesn't have to be a big fancy one that sticks in the ground, just a little something to offer some shade. There aren't near as many trees around here as back home."

The warlock pursed his lips. "I'll pass along the message."

He turned to leave, but then stopped. "There is no use looking for weaknesses in your chain. There are none. Relax while you are here, Sheriff. Enjoy your vacation."

The warlock left then. Bourne thought about asking what there was to enjoy, but he didn't think pissing the guy off more would help anything. Then again, what if he did piss these people off? What would happen? They wouldn't kill him as he wouldn't serve as bait if he were dead. They could beat him to within an inch of his life, then heal him, before beating him again. It would be pure torture. Better to avoid that.

Beth returned with his bucket. "I've even washed it for you, Bourne."

He nodded. He didn't like to think about her doing shit work like that. He stared off at the camp as he sipped his coffee.

Beth put the pale in his tent, returning in just a second. She stopped before him. "I've been asked to take you to bathe later. When would be a good time for that?"

Bourne saw a chance. "Right now would be great. I take it you are going to remove me from my chain, right?"

Beth cocked her head. "You'll be unshackled from the chain, but you won't be able to escape."

Bourne shook his head. "All you have to do is look the other way. I'll be gone in half a heartbeat. I can even knock you out if you want so you won't be blamed."

"You don't understand. My leash won't allow for that." She pointed to the collar at her neck.

Bourne put down his food and coffee as he stood. "Then I'll have to take it off," he said.

She backed a step. "Please don't touch it. It can only be opened with magic anyway."

"Just let me look," Bourne called.

As he reached out, she blocked his hand. The force pushed Beth's hand to the collar, and all hell broke loose. Her eyes rolled up, she fell to the ground, and she began convulsing. Bourne had seen a grand mal seizure before, and it had looked minor compared to this.

A feeling of helplessness washed over him. He wasn't a doctor or healer, so what could he do? He yelled, "We need some help over here!"

A few witches and a warlock were up the hill in a matter of moments. It felt like an eternity to Bourne, but it wasn't. They stabilized her.

"She should know better than to touch her collar by now," a warlock said.

Bourne watched as Beth was carried off. She seemed fine, just sleeping now.

Well, not fine. As long as she wore that collar, she wasn't fine. She needed that thing off, and the sooner the better. Bourne just didn't know how that was going to happen. Hell, he didn't see how they were going to escape. He could watch, though. Surely, he'd spot a weakness and be able to leverage it. It was a long shot, but he didn't know what else to do.

CHAPTER 18—ON THE ROAD

Upon waking, Marta tried to rouse Wind Rock, but she wasn't having any of it. She needed her rest after the healing, so Marta left her to sleep and instead thought about what her dream journey had meant.

All she could think about was the night Bourne had been abducted. It was her fault she hadn't been able to stop it. She'd been knocked out instead of saving him. Now instead of going after him, she was watching an Indian girl sleep the morning away.

She was soon fuming that Wind Rock hadn't wakened at her prompting. Marta ground her teeth and munched on a bit of hardtack. She tore a piece off with a little too much vigor. Then she slowly chewed it as she considered ways to make up time once they left here. Their speed was going to be determined by how fast Wind Rock could track.

After a few extra hours of sleep, Wind Rock finally stirred. Marta was left with the task of breaking camp while Wind Rock looked for tracks. She had a heck of a time finding the trail left by the wagon. It was the two warlocks who had escaped Marta's curses that tipped off where it was.

The delays in finding the trail, added to the fact Wind Rock needed more sleep, had put them behind. After mounting and heading down the trail, they moved much too slowly for Marta's taste. She wanted to get to Bourne as quickly as possible. Finding those who had escaped along the way would be nice as they wouldn't be able to report back to McKinley. Although, that was a long shot at this point since they had departed fast, and Marta and Wind Rock were going slow. She surveyed the terrain around them as they tried to find the spots where two warlocks might hide.

As they rode, Marta filled Wind Rock in on what happened during her trip to the dream realm. Wind Rock pursed her lips the entire time, focusing on the trail she was following without commenting.

When Marta finished recounting the events, Wind Rock said, "The next time a dream draws you in like that, don't succumb to it. Think of something other than the dreaming person. A specific animal is safer as it is still a living thing, but not a human."

Marta found this advice fairly obvious now that she had experienced it, though the tip about an animal sounded good. She had planned to use the emotion-consuming flame to block out thoughts in general. It also helped she now knew what the meeting place looked like.

There was much about the dream realm she wanted to know, and the person beside her had some knowledge. "Why didn't you tell me that before?" There was a little more heat to that question.

Wind Rock spared a beady-eyed glance in Marta's direction. "I didn't think it would come up."

Marta steamed. It didn't help that she didn't know what she didn't know. "What about the finger wave Runs With Does used to kick me out and wake me up? Is there a way to block that?"

Wind Rock rolled her eyes. "That trick only works on the young or the naïve."

The butt of that comment wasn't lost on Marta.

"You just have to fight the will to leave," Wind Rock continued. "You have to realize you are in control of your presence in the dream realm. Once you do, it'll go much better for you."

Marta nodded. She was in control. She'd remember that. Some old Indian woman was not the one in control. Right. "This is good advice." Again, there was some venom to her words. "What else can you tell me?"

Wind Rock shrugged. "I'm not sure there is much else. But speaking of control, you can control what you have around you. The meeting place is created and manipulated by Runs With Does or whoever is the first to arrive."

"So, why the Parthenon?"

Wind Rock scrunched her face in thought. "I'm not sure. I think it has always been that way, so the tradition continues. Either that, or it has some significance to someone."

That wasn't the most helpful to Marta, but at least it was something—unlike what was changing around her. She scanned the horizon for potential attackers, realizing they hadn't made it far on their journey today. "Can we go a little faster?"

Wind Rock shook her head. "Only if you want to risk losing the trail. The wagon wheel marks are tough to spot as it is an older trail. The horse pulling the wagon has a significant nick in its shoe, but that only helps in differentiating the trails. The warlocks who injured me left a better trail as they were in a hurry and it is a fresher track, but that is assuming they are going the same way your friends were taken. We could be following them somewhere else. So far, though, they've been going the same way."

Marta sighed. Wind Rock had an answer for everything. Marta felt this urgency to rescue Bourne, Beth, and Greta sooner than later. Like there was more danger the longer they stayed in McKinley's control.

"I'm also watching out for an ambush," Wind Rock added. "They surprised me once, but not again."

Marta scanned around them again. "I've been watching for warlocks as well. You can focus on the tracking while I focus on protecting us."

Wind Rock gave Marta a sidelong glance. "I appreciate you also keeping an eye out, but we both need to watch for danger."

"But we need to move faster." It came out as an angry plea.

Wind Rock grunted. "You can't hurry this type of work. You've got to be patient."

Patient. Marta was patient. She was being beyond patient for this little girl to insult her and insinuate so much. There was only one child here. Patient. She'd show Wind Rock how to be patient.

"Besides, the warlocks are long gone," Wind Rock continued. "They don't have to rest their horses as they can be healed. We have no real hope of catching up to them unless they are lying in wait somewhere. We've lost about a day due to my injury, so they could be anywhere. Maybe they'll get tired and rest on their own, but if they are motivated enough, they'll drive straight through to their goal."

Marta glowered at Wind Rock, who rode oblivious to the angry eyes on her. Marta didn't need the reminder of the lost time or the reason why. She knew exactly why they were behind.

She reminded herself that it wasn't Wind Rock's fault she had stumbled upon those warlocks or been injured in the surprise encounter. Marta wanted to blame the girl, but she couldn't. Well, she could do anything she wanted, but it wasn't justified in this case. They had both stumbled into trouble at the get-go. Did this mean the entire expedition was doomed?

The warlocks now knew of Wind Rock, so Marta's secret weapon was revealed. They didn't know Wind Rock was a tracker, but they could probably guess as much since they had seen her looking for a trail. This meant they knew Marta planned to come after them. She had lost the element of surprise, which was the only thing they'd had going for them.

Was there something else that could give them an advantage? Marta studied Wind Rock, noticing how she searched for tracks around them. Both Wind Rock and Marta were powerful, there was no doubt about that. But were they strong enough to take on an army of warlocks?

"Do you have any ideas on how we can attack McKinley and his followers when we find him?" Marta asked.

"I'm not sure there is much point in planning an attack without the details of what their compound looks like."

Marta nodded. "See, that is a plan in itself. We scout the camp once we find it, and then plan our attack."

"Well, I think you need to be the one to come up with the plan. I've got no experience fighting, but I saw you fight. You have the experience and a good head for tactics," Wind Rock said.

It was a rare compliment, but one Marta was certainly not going to refute, though she didn't feel all that receptive to one. She'd been lucky in killing the one warlock the day before. Hell, she'd gotten lucky in getting Goodman in the first place. She couldn't rely on luck, but there might be something she could get. "Maybe we'll have some help by the time we find them."

Wind Rock shrugged. "Only if you do better on any other trips to the dream realm."

Marta blew up. "I'm no meater. I know I need to do better, but you don't seem to want to be forthcoming on anything. Tell me something I don't know."

Wind Rock stopped her horse. Marta did the same, scowling at her compatriot.

Wind Rock stared straight ahead. "So, that is your problem with me. I thought you were just jealous of my knowledge. I didn't realize it was your frustration at what you're lacking."

Marta grunted. She thought it obvious she was frustrated.

"I'm sorry I can't just impart everything I know in one mind dump. Just like you can't impart what you know to me," Wind Rock said rather sweetly.

The apology surprised Marta. She realized Wind Rock was also frustrated with Marta for being frustrated with her. "I'm sorry, too."

Wind Rock cocked her head. Did she want an explanation? Was one owed?

"This is all my fault, this whole thing," Marta added. "I couldn't prevent Bourne and my friends from being kidnapped. I'm sorry I want to rush to get them back. I think that has clouded my judgment. I appreciate you coming on this journey with me."

Wind Rock scrunched her nose. "How is McKinley unleashing his evil your fault?"

Marta didn't know how to respond.

"Look, you can't do everything for everybody. You just need to do your best wherever you can. Right now, both of us have been put on the course to stop the evil that is McKinley."

Suddenly, Marta saw this girl in a different light. She was here for her reasons, not for Marta. Correction, Wind Rock was a woman. That was sometimes easy to forget.

Marta grinned at Wind Rock. "Come on. Let's get that bastard. Best speed ahead."

Wind Rock shot her a smile back. Wordlessly, she moved her horse. Her eyes fell to the ground in search of the trail.

Marta also moved forward. With their mission renewed, she scanned the horizon, scrutinizing every crevasse and clump of tall grass that could hide a person. There was no sign of an impending attack, but who knew what was around the next corner.

CHAPTER 19—ABILENE

Marta spared another glance in Wind Rock's direction. Her normally stony expression had been replaced with pursed lips and a squint. She seemed more focused on what was ahead instead of looking all around for danger like she had been the rest of the day. "What's wrong?" Marta asked.

Wind Rock shook as if startled. "Who said anything was wrong?" She tried to put back on her stony facade, but it was obvious something wasn't right.

"Come on," Marta started. "We're doing this journey together. We need honest, open communication between us if we have any hope of succeeding. I can tell you're nervous about something."

Wind Rock cocked her head. Finally, she sighed. "I am worried we are going to reach the Abilene Road only to lose the trail. We won't be able to follow them on the road as their tracks will be lost among so many others."

Marta nodded. She knew tracking was going to be tough. It was part of the reason they were going so slow. "You think they are going to turn on the road?"

Wind Rock shrugged. "It'll be easier going. If they continue this west-northwest route, they'll need to cross the Smokey Hill River sooner or later. Abilene is the easier crossing due to the bridge."

Marta saw an obvious flaw in this. "They wouldn't go through Abilene as there are too many people there."

Wind Rock pointed to the ground. "Those are wagon tracks I'm following. You can cover a wagon so people can't see."

Marta frowned. "Surely they wouldn't go to Abilene with Hickok there."

"Why do you say that?"

Marta furrowed her brow. "I would think criminals in the middle of committing a crime would avoid Hickok."

"Bah," Wind Rock answered. "He is blind to most crime. He won't question a covered wagon passing through in the middle of the night."

Marta recalled all the glowing reports Bourne had on the improvements in Abilene since Hickok went there. "I don't know what you've heard, but crime is way down since Hickok became city marshal."

Wind Rock blew a raspberry. "Crime is down because his reputation as a no-nonsense, rough son-of-a-bitch keeps things in order. Not him."

His reputation was still him, wasn't it? Marta thought it better to not question that aloud. "All I know is he helped Bourne in the past, and Bourne respects him. In my book, it makes him a good lawman."

Wind Rock nodded. "I don't have any firsthand experience, but he is a topic of conversation for the dream realm council from time to time. He worries them, so it worries me."

Marta didn't know what to say to that. She rode in silence while continuing to eye the landscape for an attack. Finally, she said, "They would have taken a more northerly angle if their goal was Abilene. We're far too south, still."

Wind Rock shrugged. She just followed the trail, which was invisible to Marta, and glanced around from time to time.

The sun was hanging low an hour later when Wind Rock broke the silence. "Should we camp here or try to make our way by moonlight?" The moon was just a few days from being full.

Marta gritted her teeth. This journey was going way too slow. "Can't we go a little farther?"

Wind Rock shrugged. "The dimmer the light, the more likely I'll miss something. Besides, we can't see an ambush in the dark."

Marta whistled as she thought. They were in a valley that would be out of the wind. She just didn't want to stop.

She thought about making camp up the hill so they could see their surroundings better. No matter what, they couldn't have a fire since they couldn't hide it. She decided here was better since being on a hill would make them visible to others. "Let's stop here to stay out of sight."

Wind Rock nodded. "There's an abundance of groundnuts around here. How does that sound for dinner?"

Marta's stomach grumbled. Something fresh was better than jerky and hardtack in the saddle. "Sounds good. After dinner, can we go to the dream realm together so you can show me some tricks before we meet with the council?"

Wind Rock stopped her horse. She didn't look in Marta's direction. "It isn't good to go to the dream realm on back-to-back nights. You need real sleep. Nobody from the council will be there."

Marta rubbed her forehead. Of course nobody would be there. She needed another chance to explain herself. Why couldn't she catch a break?

Oh right, because she was Marta, and the world conspired against her. She couldn't get out of the clutches of a rogue pastor who'd tried to kill her, failed, and ended up bar-b-que. Then she had to kill him because he was a warlock bent on using her before killing her. And now her friends were being held against their will.

She sighed. "I guess we can talk a bit about the realm and the council over dinner. Then I'll know how to get into their good graces."

Wind Rock nodded. "Yes, we can do that. I don't know if you can change Runs With Does' mind, but I'll talk you through some tips. Promise me that you won't go to the dream realm tonight, though. I'd hate to have a dream swallow you with no one there to help."

Marta slowly nodded. For some reason, she thought Wind Rock's plea meant something going on, and she didn't want Marta there. If that were the case, then there was no way in hell she wasn't going. She would just have to hide from Wind Rock. "With no council tonight, I don't see a good reason to go," Marta said to throw Wind Rock off her trail.

It was half true given she might not have a good reason, but a little practice couldn't hurt in addition to making sure she wasn't being left out of anything. She wouldn't go for long, just long enough to get a feel for the place, try some of the stuff she'd learned so far, and whatever else she learned over dinner. She was determined to not be a child at the next meeting she had with Runs With Does.

Wind Rock gave no indication she suspected anything from Marta but a normal night of sleep.

CHAPTER 20—DREAMING

One trick Marta had learned in the last few months was spell masking. It made the spell even more difficult to do, but it hid her magic from other witches. If she were attacking a witch, like Greta or Beth in practice, then they couldn't see what she was attacking with. Right now, she was using it to secretly perform the spell necessary to get into the dream realm. Not that Wind Rock was paying attention. She was asleep as soon as she crawled in her bedroll, leaving Marta alone to do as she wanted.

Once in the dream realm, Marta was again among a constellation of glowing balls. As improbable as it was, it looked like there were more here tonight than the previous one. She was in awe of the sheer magnitude of it. Just how many people were out there dreaming?

She was lost in her head. Thinking of the dreamers of the world, she felt tiny and alone. How big was the world?

More, who were all these people? She wondered if she could spy on some to figure out if she knew the dreamer or if there was some way to find out who they were. She had stumbled upon Bourne the previous night. She wondered if she couldn't direct herself to him.

Marta recalled it was bad luck Bourne had been dreaming about her while she thought about him. That combination was what got them into contact. Should she even try it again? Better would be a way she could tell it was his dream out there. She'd be able to reassure herself he was still alive without endangering herself in the process.

She choked back a sob. He had to still be alive, didn't he? She thought hard about him in the hopes his dream would draw her in again. Surely, he wouldn't be fighting his captors this time, would he? From talking with Wind Rock, Marta was ready for a fight should she need to.

Minutes went by, but no dream drew her in. Her heart beat faster with every passing moment. He had to be here. He just had to be.

She forced herself to swallow. What if his captors had done something to him? She had been working on the assumption that Rathbone needed Bourne alive to be bait for her. Surely, that was a valid assumption. To think otherwise was too hard for her to face.

From nowhere, a yellow ball approached. Bourne! She found him. He was alive. Even better, he wasn't having a nightmare tonight.

She wiped the tears she hadn't realized had fallen down her cheeks. Now that she had her proof, she had a decision to make. Should she succumb to the dream or get the heck out of there before it drew her in? Was there any harm in a little peek? Bracing herself, she allowed the dream to draw her in. She would meet him in…

Hell. She was in hell. Fire and brimstone flamed all around her, burning the world. Bourne was nowhere to be found. She felt the heat enter and consume her. Death was here, and she was death.

She had been expecting a good dream due to its color, not this hell. She needed to pull Bourne out of this, but he was absent. This was his dream. Why was he dreaming this?

A tall figure with long hair and a beard rose from the flames. The flames didn't touch him while they burned her.

"Quiet," the figure bellowed.

Marta realized she'd been screaming. She stopped, clenching her teeth to bear the pain. She recognized this man as a smaller version of the tall man in Bourne's dream.

"I'm coming for you, Marta," he said, pointing at her.

She shuddered. Who was this guy, and how did he know who she was?

She was done with all of this. Closing her eyes, she thought about the waking world. She wanted to go there, and she wanted to go there now.

"You can't escape me," the man said. He then laughed maniacally.

This wasn't working. Marta wasn't in her bedroll. She was still stuck here.

She took a deep breath. Flicking a hand, she said, "Be gone."

She felt her spell, which allowed her to be in the dream realm and mask that fact, dissipate.

***

Marta awoke in a sweat. She bolted upright in her bedroll, gasping for breath. Her pulse threatened to race beyond control. She choked back a sob.

"Wa-ta-li!" Wind Rock yelled, startling Marta. "Go to actual sleep!" She didn't bother opening her eyes.

That caught Marta off guard. Did that mean Wind Rock knew Marta had gone to the dream realm? She calmed herself before saying, "Sorry for waking you. I had a nightmare."

Wind Rock huffed. "Whose nightmare were you in?"

Damn. She did know Marta was in the dream realm. For some reason, lying came easy. "Bourne's."

Wind Rock turned to her. She eyed Marta. "That wasn't Bourne." She cocked her head. "Why did you lie?"

Marta's heart stopped. How did Wind Rock know? Did this girl have some ability to read people? Or was Marta that transparent?

After a moment to consider lying, she finally said, "I don't know."

Wind Rock cocked her head.

Marta rushed on with, "I don't know why I lied. I don't know who it was. I don't know why I even try to hide things from you. I'm sorry."

Wind Rock arched an eyebrow. "At least you're honest now." She laid back down. "How many times do I need to tell you not to let yourself be pulled into people's dreams?"

Marta gulped. "I thought I was in control, this time."

Another thought came to her. "The dream was yellow, so not a nightmare. Yet it was hell in there."

"One person's hell is another person's favorite place."

Marta sighed. It was that man's pleasure. "I was thinking of Bourne. How did I end up in someone else's dream?"

"Bourne must not have been the only one you were thinking about."

Bourne had been the only one. She wanted to find him safe from… She gasped. "One of his captors was dreaming of capturing me."

Wind Rock laughed. "That makes sense. Remember that any dream can hold nasty consequences."

Marta didn't need to be told that. She knew the dangers but decided to ignore them. "So, how did you know I was in the dream realm?"

Wind Rock sniffed. "You aren't the only one who knows how to hide your magic."

Marta shook her head. Of course Wind Rock had followed her. Nothing else made sense. "Did you pull me out of that dream?"

"No," Wind Rock said in a near whisper. "You must have gotten out yourself."

Marta laid back down. Maybe she was learning a few things, but she knew there was much more to know. "Can you please teach me how to navigate the dream realm?"

Silence answered her for the longest time. Finally, Wind Rock sighed. "I'll show you around a bit."

Marta's heart lifted in glee. She had won something from the stone.

"Just not tonight," Wind Rock continued.

"Why?" Marta asked. It came out in a rush, which didn't hide her disappointment.

"You don't get actual rest in the dream realm. That is why the council doesn't meet every single night. We'll go early tomorrow so you can meet Runs With Does with a little more experience."

Marta found that her excitement returned, but it was a little reserved. Wind Rock had agreed to help, but not when Marta wanted. It would eventually come.

Then Marta could meet with the council and get their help. Runs

With Does wouldn't find her to be a child this time.

CHAPTER 21—TRAIL JUNCTION

Much to Marta's relief, they were up early and on the trail as soon as there was enough light to track by. She hoped this was a sign of the new norm. Unfortunately, they still were going at the same slow pace, but it couldn't be helped.

As was anticipated, they came to the junction with the road running to Abilene. At the moment, there wasn't a cattle drive going through, but there were divots on and near the road and cow patties here and there. Even Marta could tell a herd had gone through fairly recently.

Wind Rock slowed her horse to a dead crawl, watching nothing but the ground. She was concentrating hard. Did this mean Bourne's captors had gone through before the herd came through? Surely that was Marta's fear talking.

Marta glanced around for an ambush. Not that she anticipated any such thing near a highly traveled area, but with Wind Rock otherwise occupied, she needed to keep watch.

"Stay here," Wind Rock said sternly.

Marta had already stopped where she was. Wind Rock then kicked her horse to move it along. She went to the far side of the road, then started looking there.

"I've lost the trail," she muttered.

"You what?" Marta asked in a sudden rage. Wind Rock's job was to keep them on the trail, and now she couldn't even do that.

"I'll find it again. Give me a minute."

Marta tried to calm down. All wasn't lost yet. She watched, hoping Wind Rock found the trail there. She stopped her horse a little way off the road, dismounted, and looked around in a slow arc. Marta tapped the pommel of her saddle as she waited.

Wind Rock turned and walked a good thirty yards to the left before stopping again. She did another look through once she stopped.

Marta sighed while watching. They were losing valuable time. It might be time that Bourne, Beth, and Greta didn't have.

While Marta waited, she did another sweeping search for an ambush. Wind Rock soon moved back in the other direction about sixty yards, without even sparing Marta a glance. When she stopped, she did another arc.

When she finished, she shook her head, mounted her horse, and rode back to Marta's position. "I'm not seeing the trail here. They must have gone either south to Wichita or north to Abilene. You decide where we go."

Marta shook her head. "So, now we are guessing?"

"Do you have any better ideas?"

Marta closed her eyes to not scream. "They wouldn't have been heading nearly due west for a reason. If they were going to Abilene, they would have gone more of a northerly route. The trail has to be here." Marta opened her eyes at the end of her tirade.

Wind Rock shrugged. "It was dark. Maybe they couldn't be sure how to get there, so they took a more southerly route as they couldn't miss this trail. They didn't want to hit the river and not be able to cross it."

"I don't buy that for a minute. Why would the warlocks who ambushed us go the same way?" There was venom in Marta's words, but she didn't care.

Wind Rock huffed. "Well, why does the trail end at the road?"

Marta shrugged violently. She didn't know, but didn't want to say so. She glanced to the west to see if anything provided a clue. The landscape looked about the same as it had for miles now.

Marta turned the way they'd come. "Why don't you show me what you have been following?"

Wind Rock grumbled, but she complied. She even dismounted to point at a divot in the ground. "This nicked shoe is one of the things I've been following. The wagon and horse have also disrupted grass and left other marks, but this is easier to spot."

Marta examined the shoe print. It was like all the other upside-down "U" shapes around, but it did have a distinctive gouge in the two o'clock position.

Still in the middle of the road, she had to decide where to keep searching. For some reason, north pulled at her. She turned in that direction, eyes on the ground.

Several times, she thought she spotted the distinctive track, but couldn't tell for certain with all the cattle that had gone through. There were so many tracks, it was overwhelming. She just noted there were no shoes on the cattle, so their tracks were pretty much divots without much detail. Ruling out the cattle tracks narrowed down which ones were potentially the distinctive nicked track.

Soon, Wind Rock was riding at her side, looking like Marta was. Yard after yard, they carefully made their way while studying the ground. They'd gone a couple of hundred yards before Marta realized she hadn't scanned the landscape for an attack. She stopped to do that.

"Did you see something?" Wind Rock asked.

"No," she retorted, still grumpy. "Just checking for an ambush."

Wind Rock nodded before continuing her task.

The only thing that seemed a bit ominous was a dirt cloud behind them. Marta's heart leaped at the thought this was a bunch of warlock activity, but she soon realized it was probably another cattle herd being taken to market in Abilene. The cloud was just too big to be anything else. In any case, it meant they would need to find the trail soon and keep ahead of that to not lose it again. Then again, it might be a lost cause.

"There," Wind Rock said, pointing.

Marta stared at where Wind Rock indicated. Sure enough, the nicked horseshoe was there. "Oh, good. We need to stay on it quickly if we have any chance of continuing to follow it." She then indicated behind them.

Wind Rock said, "I see what you mean. Are you sure they are heading this way?"

Marta glanced back. She wasn't sure if the cloud was any bigger. "Abilene is a logical destination to get the cattle on trains."

Wind Rock nodded. "For now, let's assume they are coming this way. We know which way the warlocks are going, so we can each watch one side of the trail for the track to see if they turn."

Marta liked the plan, and she began to breathe easier since it appeared she had picked the right direction. "I'll take the west side." She was on that side of Wind Rock, anyway.

"I think not. You aren't the professional tracker, and they are more likely to turn that way."

She moved off in front of Marta's horse, cutting her and any more discussion off.

"Now you think they'll head west."

Wind Rock shrugged. "You make a good point."

Marta grumbled. The track probably would go all the way through Abilene before turning, but it was good to watch.

Marta moved to the east side of the trail, wider than the widest cow track. She didn't want to miss in case they did turn back that way. Their destination might be coming soon.

Marta also occasionally glanced up for any sign of an ambush, but it was hard to watch for the gouged horseshoe track while on the lookout for warlocks. They moved at a slow pace. The only good thing was that they were moving a little faster now. Even at this pace, they weren't going faster than the cattle coming up from behind. Eventually, they would be overtaken, but it hopefully wouldn't be until right before they hit town.

A whistle turned Marta's attention to Wind Rock. She waved her over. Marta had fallen a little behind Wind Rock, so Marta took care to see where she was should she have to return to her side, but she hoped this meant Wind Rock found something.

Marta rode the thirty or so yards to where Wind Rock waited. She was at a path junction with one heading due west. It was much narrower than the Abilene Road, that was for sure. She pointed to the path. "There haven't been any cattle on this road, so it was easy to spot their track."

Marta didn't see anything but nodded as if she could. "They turned on the Abilene road to get to this road and have an easier way west."

Marta looked back to the east side of the road. There wasn't even a well-trampled path going that direction, so this was only a three-way junction. Thus, Bourne's captors couldn't have gone north at any point before now to pick up this road.

She let a breath go she hadn't realized she'd been holding. "We're getting close, I think."

"Or this is just a road these people knew well."

Marta set her jaw. Wind Rock's pessimism was dragging Marta down. In any case, they could now travel together with Marta resuming her role as a lookout instead of an amateur tracker.

She looked west. Bourne was somewhere down this trail. She hoped there were no more surprises to come.

CHAPTER 22—PHANTOM

The road they now traveled was well used, but Wind Rock indicated that there didn't seem to be many users since the nicked horseshoe had traveled it. This meant they could travel at a faster pace. Marta was glad even though she was getting a little saddle sore.

This road went through more trees than what they had been going through. Marta wondered just how close they were to the Smokey Hill River. The trail made several slight curves as they went, but, in general, they kept going west. All the while, Marta kept an eye out for an ambush and only occasionally looked where her horse was going. It was a mundane task at this point, but necessary. Hell, it was the only thing keeping her from falling asleep in the saddle.

Suddenly, a fat old Indian wearing only a loincloth appeared in the middle of the road about ten yards ahead.

Marta stopped her horse as her heart skipped a beat. "Phantom! What are you doing here?"

Wind Rock also stopped her horse, but she seemed calm in comparison to Marta's reaction. "You know Phantom?"

Marta nodded, not taking her eyes off the being from the Western Sky. "He sort of muddied the water with Goodman last year."

Phantom raised a finger to his lips.

Marta rolled her eyes. Every time this being came around, it led to more questions than answers. Now he wasn't going to answer her.

Phantom pointed at Marta, then at the ground. He did the same thing to Wind Rock.

Marta wanted to ask why, but looked to Wind Rock instead. She shrugged before dismounting. Marta sighed, but she followed suit as silence seemed necessary for whatever reason.

Phantom turned, waving them forward. He led the way down the trail.

They were coming on another curve before it went up a hill. Inside the curve, there was a dozen trees with a thicket of bushes filling out the area. It was a good place to hide.

From out of the bushes, fireballs were launched at Phantom, making Marta jump. Instead of blocking the fireballs or retaliating, Phantom disappeared again, pissing Marta off. She connected to the orb, calming a little as she went to work. The first task was to block the fireballs, and she did that by cutting through the spell.

Wind Rock grabbed the magic and had a shield up in an instant.

Marta slipped into her skeletal state. She couldn't see the magic producing the fireballs, so the attacker had to be a warlock.

Fireballs were launched in rapid succession, so probably more than one attacker. With Phantom gone, they were now directed at Marta and Wind Rock. Marta let the fireballs fall against Wind Rock's shield so she could free herself to launch a counterattack. Each fireball hit with small pop as they were snuffed out. The residual heat from them warmed the air another twenty to twenty-five degrees. Marta looked for the attackers.

The horses pulled back at first. They realized pretty quickly that they weren't in danger. They were used to this sort of stuff by now. They did stamp their feet some, but Marta didn't have time to calm them.

Marta put her bomb spell to use in the middle of the trees. Dirt, trees, bushes, and other plant matter flew in every direction. Some of the trees and branches came at her, so she pushed them aside with magic. Where the copse used to be was now a crater. Three men occupied that crater—Rathbone and the two who had gotten away from her house the day before yesterday. Marta gulped as she readied another attack. She didn't like the odds of three against two.

Wind Rock let a dozen fireballs fly at the men, but those stopped just before hitting home. The warlocks were shielded and ready. Their shields had even withstood Marta's huge explosion, which was the reason they were still alive. Some of the grass and trees burned with the fury of the fight. Marta didn't have time to worry about that. She had three warlocks on her hands.

The three moved forward like snakes as they continued to rain fireballs on Marta and Wind Rock. Marta fought back with bombs and lightning. They didn't seem to faze the men as the attacks hit shields. They wore talismans around their necks. They must not have been in range when Marta and Wind Rock tapped into the magical orb. Now that they were connected, they couldn't be pushed out. At least, Marta didn't think so from the training her, Greta, and Beth had done over the winter.

Marta's conversation about talismans with Wind Rock came to mind. Their conclusion was to overload the talisman. Their shields would prevent Marta from gaining access to those talismans.

A funny thought hit Marta. She would have laughed if not for the serious nature of the fight. Marta started doing the healing spell. She could feel it reach the three men before her, so it got through their shields. Then it stopped. While it didn't reverberate like when the spell was done, it just ended up not doing anything. This must have hit the talismans.

"What are you doing?" Wind Rock asked.

Marta waved dismissively rather than answer. The death curse was the opposite of healing in every way. Healing was perpetual, giving life, and making things right. She needed to alter it. She wiped the sweat from her brow.

Another thing Greta, Beth, and Marta had messed around with was blocking people from the orb of power. It was similar to the healing spell. Since the healing spell didn't seem to be working, she stopped it and tried the block. Again, it got through the warlocks' shields, but it didn't hit home. Something did happen, though.

Marta held her breath as the gems on each of the talismans lit up. What did that mean? Did that mean she was blocking the talismans?

She issued the death curse to see what would happen. Again, it did not strike home. It was only blocked by the talismans.

Issuing two spells at once was a little bit of work, but Marta was used to it. She was tired, though, especially since issuing the massive detonation and now these hard spells. Her vision blurred. Somehow, the two spells she issued became one. It became a blocking death curse or something like that.

The effect was twofold. The first was the talismans quit blocking her spells. Right after that, since she hadn't stopped issuing this new one, it worked on the men. She could see their shields go down as Wind Rock's fireballs finally hit home, which apparently surprised her as she quit issuing them.

Rathbone dropped to the ground with a shriek as soon as he was hit, then rolled away. The other two screamed and screamed as fire consumed them. Rathbone's rolling had snuffed out his flames, and he got up and ran. Marta noted that the man's talisman was left behind on the ground.

Marta's breath caught. She looked at Wind Rock, finding her staring back with wide eyes. "What did we do?" Marta asked.

Wind Rock shrugged, wiping the sweat from her brow. "That was a nifty spell." She returned her attention to the men, and Marta did the same.

Cautiously, Marta and Wind Rock walked forward, horses in tow. "They didn't even turn into skeletons, which makes me suspect you severed them from the magic," Wind Rock commented.

Rathbone certainly wasn't doing any magic as he crawled, and then ran, away. He didn't even try to save the other two warlocks, who were now silent. Marta spared the smoldering, burnt flesh-smelling corpses a glance. More death in her wake, but she pushed down her remorse.

Marta thought about issuing the death curse on Rathbone, but she wanted answers from the man. She continued to walk after him. He was a mouse, and she was the snake. Besides, she was a bit unsteady on her feet because of all the complex magic she wielded. She would need some rest soon.

"Are you going to kill him?" Wind Rock asked.

Marta shook her head.

"Why not?" Wind Rock asked.

"He has answers. I have questions."

Wind Rock sighed. "You're going to torture him, huh?"

Marta nodded.

"Well, are you going to capture him or just toy with him?" Wind Rock asked.

Marta rolled her eyes. It felt good to mess with him, but Wind Rock had a point. That wasn't her goal. She was unsteady as she mounted her horse.

The trail had another bend. Rathbone rounded it, hiding himself. Marta got her horse going at a trot to catch up to the man on foot. Wind Rock inspected the two men she'd killed.

By the time Marta got to the bend, she found Rathbone mounting a horse. Marta hadn't accounted for this eventuality. Rathbone spared her a glance before urging his horse up to full speed in three strides going due south.

Marta took a deep breath, in part to wake herself up fully again. She ground her teeth to fight for the strength to go after the man. Hell, how did he have this much fight after losing a battle as he had? She wondered if Wind Rock's assessment that he was severed was correct. Now a horse race would determine whether the man got away or not. Was she up for it?

CHAPTER 23—RATHBONE

Turning after Rathbone, Marta spurred her horse up to full speed. Rathbone wasn't following a trodden trail, but was instead quickly weaving through trees, faster than what Marta could get her horse to go. She wasn't going to give up, though.

Blinking away her tiredness, she urged her horse to go faster. She didn't want to lose the man. Yard after yard, Rathbone's horse seemed to pull away just a little more. With his twenty or thirty-second lead, Marta didn't know if she had anything in her arsenal of magic to reach him, especially with how tired she already was. While she was adept enough to create huge shields, that wouldn't affect him this far away. In the training over the winter with Greta and Beth, she could hit something at one hundred yards when fully rested. Maybe even two hundred, but it would have to be with something lobbed inaccurately or the simplest of spells. As tired as she was, she couldn't throw a fireball with any accuracy at ten yards.

Marta rode on in sheer determination. She might fall off and break her neck riding this hard in this state, but she didn't care. Rathbone knew where Bourne was, so when she caught him, he could divulge that information.

The yards stretched into a mile with the trees giving way to pastureland. Her horse slowed a bit, getting tired. Rathbone's horse must be exhausted, too, as it had slowed a bit as well. It still was going at a faster pace and its rider kept looking over his shoulder, but they were now only a minute ahead.

Marta had let go of the power when the chase started. Even holding it would wear her out even more. Now she needed it for one more quick spell. Grabbing it was like trying to tame a bear, but she got it. As hard as it was, she healed her horse and restored the beast's speed.

She let go of the power once more with her maneuver done. It sucked even more life out of her, but it was worth it, though it was imperceptible at first. It took about half a mile for her to tell that Rathbone's horse was no longer faster. After that, she caught up quickly. In another half a mile, she was only ten yards behind him as they approached a line of trees.

This was it. She was now close enough to do something. She had to grab the power again. It was even worse this time. Before, it had been a bear, but now it was more like taming a tornado. It took numerous tries, but she finally connected with it.

The simplest of all spells was the air one. She \ didn't have enough strength to lift him from his horse, so she just batted him in the shoulder. When he started to go over, he kicked free so he could try to land on his feet. He failed miserably, coming down on a knee and then rolling clear of his horse.

She stopped her horse so suddenly it skidded to a halt next to the man. Marta then tried to put a shield between the man and his magic, but it didn't want to form. He no longer had a talisman to block her spells, but her tiredness prevented her from doing more.

Rathbone crawled backward about a dozen feet until his back was against a tree trunk. He seemed to freeze. "It's gone."

"What?" Marta asked.

"The magical orb."

Marta cocked her head, waiting for the man to continue. Her spell hadn't worked, so how was he disconnected? Then she recalled what Wind Rock had said about them being severed. "Did I sever you from it?"

Sweating profusely, Rathbone gulped before nodding. "Please, give it back to me. This world is darker without it."

Marta shuddered at the thought of losing the power. He was suffering a tremendous loss. Burnout was always a real possibility, though. Several times, she had pushed herself past the point where other witches had burned out. At least that was what Beth and Greta said.

Marta shook her head. "Even if I knew how to restore the power to you, I wouldn't."

He became a sniffling mess. "Please," he cried. "I can't live without the magic."

Marta's skin crawled. Maybe she would take things easier in the future to avoid burning out and ending up like this man. She didn't wish this on anybody. This was worse than torture, and she didn't know if she could do it to anybody else.

She snapped her fingers a few times. "Hey," she called, trying to get his attention. He looked up. "Is Bourne alive?"

He cocked his head, squinting, but he stayed mute.

She stamped her foot. "Where's Bourne, Beth, and Greta?"

His eyes brightened. "If I tell you, will you restore the power to me?"

Marta sighed. "I've already told you that I don't know how."

Rathbone shied away, clamping his jaw shut to keep it from quivering. The light disappeared from his eyes.

Marta waited, but he didn't say anything. He wasn't going to. "Tell me where he is," she screamed.

Rathbone sniveled. "No," he said firmly. "Go to hell, witch."

Marta rolled up her sleeves. She might be okay with a little torture after all. When she held her hand out, a ball of flame sprang up in her palm. "Tell me, or else."

"Or else what?" Rathbone sneered.

Marta held up her other hand with another fireball. Her mouse still didn't react. Now what? "I'll…"

What could she do that was worse than burning him? She could offer something else. "I tell you what. If you tell me where my friends are, I'll not only not burn you, but I'll try to fix your connection to the power."

Rathbone rolled his eyes. "You sound desperate. You've admitted you can't fix me."

"I'll figure it out. I know I can," Marta sputtered.

He shook his head, closing his eyes.

Suddenly, Rathbone's hand came up, clutching a dagger. Marta snuffed out the fireballs as she put a shield around herself to block the attack. Rathbone opened his eyes, screaming as he shoved the blade into his ear with a mighty thrust.

Marta dropped her shield as Rathbone fell over from the momentum of the impact. "No!" she raged.

She ran over, yanking out the knife. The blade was five inches and hard to pull free. She desperately started the healing spell even before it slipped free.

The healing spell instantly reverberated, which told her there was nothing to heal. Rathbone was dead. She dropped to her knees. "Why?" she sobbed.

Marta stood, staring at the dead man. She still held the bloody dagger, lost as to what to do next. If only she hadn't said she couldn't restore his power, even though it was the truth. He said he couldn't live without the magic. No wonder he wasn't afraid of her fists of fire.

There was nothing else she could do but turn back to the road and resume the tracking of Bourne. Killing the man who took him had been a hollow victory. If only Rathbone had told her where he had taken Bourne, she'd feel better. Hell, even if he'd confirmed Bourne was still alive. Now she was tired, still lost, and no closer to finding him or her friends.

She mounted her horse, heading back toward Wind Rock. There were now three fewer warlocks in her way, so at least they had that. They could keep going and eventually get to their goal of eradicating McKinley and his followers. For now, they could just keep chugging along. Hopefully, there were no more surprises around the next corner.

CHAPTER 24—QUESTIONS

Marta could hear snoring before she reached the road again. The smell of burnt flesh still hung in the air even though the corpses were nowhere to be seen. Instead, Wind Rock tended a small fire that Phantom slept next to.

Marta dismounted next to the fire, doing her best to hide her unsteadiness. She then stepped over to the spirit lying on his back on the ground. She gave him a sound kick in the ribs.

He grunted but didn't stir. The snoring stopped, though.

"What are you doing here?" Marta asked, pissed he had disappeared during the fight.

"You're welcome," Phantom replied.

"For what?" Marta asked.

"For saving your life," Phantom said before rolling on his side.

Marta waved her hands dismissively at that bullshit. "Wind Rock and I saved our own lives. You disappeared." There was more than a little venom in her voice. "You didn't even use your magic against them. That would have been a ton of help."

"He means he saved our lives by showing us where the ambush was," Wind Rock said.

She cooked a stew of some kind that smelled wonderful in Marta's hungry, exhausted state. "You sure having a fire is such a good idea?" Despite appreciating Wind Rock's food, Marta's anger showed in her voice.

Wind Rock glanced toward what used to be a line of trees, some still smoldering from Marta's bomb. "I think people know we're here. I also burnt the corpses to ash and buried them."

Marta nodded, glad the stew wasn't made from human flesh. She took a deep breath to calm a bit. "So how do you know Phantom?"

"I think he tends to show up when you least expect it. I thought he only visited other natives, but, apparently, I was mistaken," Wind Rock said.

"A steak sounds good, but don't miss it," Phantom said. He sounded half-asleep.

"What are you even talking about? What is going on?" Marta sat, hoping that would stop her head from reeling. She glared at the being, but he didn't answer her.

"Did you get that other warlock?" Wind Rock asked.

Marta nodded with clenched teeth. She might as well talk to someone who would answer. She loosened her mouth to say, "He committed suicide before I could question him, though."

"Sorry about not letting you question the other two. I was more worried about defending ourselves."

Marta waved a hand dismissively. "It's fine. Your stew more than makes up for it. We'll just have to continue tracking."

"That's a waste of time," Phantom said.

Marta's jaw dropped. Now the jerk spoke, but he was still cryptic.

"What is?" Wind Rock asked.

"Questioning the warlocks," he said as he scratched his bum. "Or even tracking them."

"But I'm trying to find my friends—Sheriff Bourne, Greta, and Beth!" Marta exclaimed. She knew the Phantom couldn't death curse someone living, so she was sure she couldn't do the same to him even though she wanted to right now. Another kick in the ribs would do them both some good.

"I know where they are," Phantom said.

Marta waited for only a second before realizing the spirit wouldn't continue. "Where?"

"McKinley's encampment."

Marta groaned since she already knew that. "Where's that?"

"Near Lincoln Center," he said in a matter-of-fact tone.

"What do you mean the center of Lincoln? Lincoln is north in Nebraska, and they've been going west!" Marta was near tears as she yelled at him. Marta groaned again and looked at Wind Rock in askance.

"Do you mean Lincoln, Kansas?" Wind Rock asked. She seemed calm right now.

Phantom nodded.

"Where's Lincoln, Kansas?" Marta asked, suddenly hopeful.

Wind Rock shrugged. "Northwest of Salina, somewhere."

Marta's heart sank. At least they had a direction. They could ask people along the way, but she would feel better if they knew exactly where they were going.

"I will take you there," Phantom said.

Marta's chest lifted from all the weight pulling off it. "You will? You won't disappear?" she asked. She'd thought the spirit would disappear again once he was done with his nap.

"I already said I will take you there," Phantom said.

"My friends, are they okay?" Marta asked in a fevered rush.

Phantom shrugged. "Don't care."

"Why not?" Marta asked as her heart sank.

"They aren't important to my goal," he said.

Marta sighed. "What's your goal?"

Phantom propped himself up on an elbow to gaze directly at Marta. "McKinley needs to die. That'll restore the balance of power in the Western Sky. As long as he lives, my powers and the powers of those in my realm are threatened."

Marta studied Phantom, trying to figure out just what he was offering here. "So, you'll help us kill McKinley?"

Phantom shook his head. "I can't kill him, but you can. I take you to his encampment then you kill him."

"Then what?" Marta asked.

Phantom shrugged. "Then you can free your friends." He looked at Wind Rock. "And you can free yours."

Marta looked over at Wind Rock. She continued to ignore her. Was there another reason why Wind Rock agreed to this venture?

"How big is McKinley's army?" Wind Rock asked.

Marta thought it was at least practical enough of a question. Marta suspected she wouldn't be able to question Wind Rock on her motives.

Phantom shrugged. "I think these latest kills put the number of warlocks under his command down to around fifteen. There are at least forty captured medicine women and witches, though. They will be forced to do whatever is asked of them, including killing us."

Marta's heart skipped a beat. She wouldn't be able to kill any of the women in that camp. They would have to free them to take down the warlocks, including McKinley. Though Marta and Wind Rock had killed four up to this point, and this new curse of Marta's seemed like a winner. If Phantom helped them, then they could have a chance.

"What is your plan?" Phantom asked.

It took a moment for Marta to realize he was talking to her. "We are going to have to come up with one once I see how the camp is laid out. I was hoping to free the women to hit the men together, but you make it sound like that isn't possible."

Phantom shrugged. "Anything is possible. Just not always probable. I can get you to a nice overlook of the camp, though."

Marta nodded. "That sounds good." She indicated the stew. "Is it ready yet? I'm famished."

Wind Rock nodded. "Yes, then we need some real sleep before we meet with people in the dream realm."

"Ooh, can I come?" Phantom asked.

"You know you aren't welcome," Wind Rock hissed.

Marta thought there was a good reason why he wasn't welcome, but didn't want to bring up what might have been a sore subject. She did have another thought, though. "Where do you go when you disappear?"

"Elsewhere," Phantom said.

Why did she expect a helpful answer? She needed to put thoughts like this out of her mind and count her blessings. She was glad to have the help she had, though she did wish the being had more interest in saving people. Both Wind Rock and Phantom wanted McKinley dead, and there seemed to be good reasons for both to be here. She didn't want others hurt in the crossfire. At least Phantom and Wind Rock were still letting her call the shots and helping, so she could wait before bringing up the need to save lives when she came up with the plan to get McKinley. Then, she should be able to get them on board with what she wanted. She was sure she could. Otherwise, there was no hope for their quest. Marta had to hold out for all the hope in the world. Now she just needed to get more allies in the dream realm tonight to make her quest have a better chance of succeeding.

CHAPTER 25—DINNER WITH MCKINLEY

There was no sign of Bourne's dinner, and it was getting late. He continued to watch the camp, seeing a few fires shared by people with tin plates. Some of the food aromas drifted his way, making his stomach grumble in complaint.

Finally, Bourne spotted a warlock heading his way. Upon closer inspection, disappointment filled him at finding the warlock approaching without a plate. It was always a witch who brought his food anyway, so maybe Bourne could complain to this guy about the missing meal.

The shackle around his right ankle suddenly sprang open. Bourne's eyes widened as he gauged the distance between him and the warlock. Ten yards. Was it enough?

Bourne sprang to his feet, then bolted right. He made it four steps before he was bound in the air from head to toe. Even his open mouth was held in place. He wasn't going anywhere right then, and it irked him that his attempt was so feeble.

"McKinley has requested your presence to dine with him this evening," the warlock stated. There was no indication he was upset by Bourne's escape attempt.

Bourne was turned toward the man. The warlock eyed him, and Bourne suppressed a shiver.

"You can walk, or I can torture you as you are carried. Your choice," the warlock said.

Bourne's jaw was released, and he worked it out as he considered his reply. If he could walk freely, he could find something to distract the warlock and run away. Also, torture didn't sound all that appealing. "I'll walk."

They didn't say a word as they passed the outskirts of the camp. Every noise and movement was ignored by the warlock. Nothing fazed the man.

Right before hitting the porch, Bourne turned his head to the right in a quick motion and stopped. "What was that?" Bourne excitedly asked.

The warlock stopped, but he didn't even look the way Bourne was. He was on Bourne's right, staring at him. "I wasn't born yesterday."

A shock hit Bourne's keister. It was like a discharge of static electricity, but a bit more powerful. "Ow," he said as he grabbed his rump.

"Keep moving," the guard said.

Disappointed, Bourne trudged the remaining few feet to the steps leading up to the porch and in. The door was closed behind him before he realized he no longer had the warlock on his heels.

Bourne whirled back to the door, then tried to turn the knob. It was locked, and there wasn't even a keyhole there to unlock it. Still, Bourne tried the door a few times, trying to get it to open.

"Sit down at the table," a booming voice called. It seemed to come from everywhere and nowhere. Bourne searched for the source of the voice, but he couldn't find it. Was it McKinley who spoke?

A sweep of the parlor gave him views of the front sitting room to the right and then a dining room to the left. Neither room had doors, and both were marked by huge archways. Ahead was a pair of closed double doors leading to who knew where. Escape wasn't possible from anywhere that Bourne could see.

He slowly made his way into the dining room. It held a long table that could easily accommodate twelve. He didn't think he'd ever seen a table this big so ornately done up with reeded carved legs and matching chairs. This was a well-done piece and expensive to boot.

At the far end of the room was another door on double hinges where scrumptious smells came from. Along the wall was a large buffet table with glass door cabinets on top. Different-colored liquors were displayed there. The ornamentation of this piece even matched the table. Either the same craftsman did both or they were done to match. Again, expensive to come by. McKinley must have been wealthy. The wood didn't even look like it was local.

Bourne heard one of the double doors open behind him, so he turned to face the parlor. McKinley entered the room, the door closing behind him without him touching it. "I thought I asked you to sit down."

Bourne glanced at a chair. "I thought it was rude to sit before the host arrived."

"Ah, but you are the guest of honor. There cannot be any impropriety on your part."

Bourne shrugged. "I was also admiring the craftsmanship of these pieces in here."

McKinley bowed his head. "Yes, the witch who carved these did a great job. Completely done with magic, and everything matches to a tee. You won't find a single mistake on these. I even had the wood brought from California. Redwood."

Bourne didn't know what to think about this. So not some master crafter. "Magic, huh?"

McKinley nodded. "The whole house was built with magic. In fact, I was directing the witches as they made everything. I burnt one out while putting this place together, but it was worth it."

Bourne mouthed, 'burnt out,' as he mulled it over. He'd heard Marta, Greta, and Beth talk about that danger to their abilities with an accident, but he didn't want to be in the same room with someone who had driven someone to that fate.

"And expensive, too," McKinley added. "The wood was one thing, but shipping was atrocious. Not that I care about money, but still."

Bourne rolled his eyes. Yeah, this bastard was loaded.

McKinley ignored Bourne. "I'm parched. How about you?" He snapped his fingers, and the noise magnified tenfold. It made Bourne jump.

Greta burst into the room from the kitchen. Bourne's mouth dropped open at the sight of her—she was *naked*. He averted his gaze, his cheeks going hot. He was pissed to see her reduced to such a manner as doing labor without clothes on.

"Two whiskeys," McKinley hollered.

From the corner of his eye, Bourne saw Greta go to the buffet and retrieve glasses. Since Bourne wasn't looking in Greta's direction, he caught sight of Beth walking into the room. She held two bowls, not wearing a stitch of clothing either. Bourne shifted his gaze to the ceiling to avoid both women.

"Don't you think beauty should be enjoyed?" McKinley commented.

There was a place setting at either end of the table. Beth put a bowl at both. Greta finished pouring drinks, then handed them to the two men. Bourne found himself blinking a lot, doing his best to look in safe directions while seeing things from the corner of his eye. McKinley openly stared at Greta.

Beth headed for the kitchen as she said, "The veal will be ready in about five or ten minutes."

McKinley's face turned red, and the sound of a horsewhip sounded. Beth yipped. Goosebumps formed on Bourne's arm at the thought of magic whipping someone.

"Devil woman, only speak when you are spoken to," McKinley yelled.

Beth grabbed her bum as she hobbled the rest of the way to the kitchen. "Yes, Your Holiness," she called.

"That's better," McKinley said. He turned to Bourne. "Sometimes, these witches take some time to train properly."

Bourne's eyes bugged out at this point. He wanted to shrink away from the insane man.

"Why are you okay with hanging out with witches, especially ones who kill?" McKinley asked.

Bourne took a slow breath as he thought about the question. He couldn't just not answer. Not if he didn't want to be tortured. "Well, Greta killed that soldier in defense of someone else."

McKinley shook his head. "I don't care about mere mortals. I'm talking about Goodman, Rathbone, Monteray, Waincraft, and O'Rourke."

Bourne didn't know who Monteray, Waincraft, and O'Rourke were. He did allow himself a small smile at hearing the demise of his captor, though. "I hadn't heard Rathbone had died. Except for Goodman, I don't know the others. Should I?"

McKinley cocked his head. "Given your connection to Marta, I would have thought you would since she had a hand in their deaths. Monteray's death was a couple of days ago. Rathbone, Waincraft, and O'Rourke were today. You felt nothing?"

Bourne shook his head. "Should I have?"

McKinley cocked his head again. "Well, that is something." He harrumphed. "No matter. I felt their deaths."

"How?" Bourne asked.

McKinley smiled. He lifted a finger to his lips. "Another time," he simply said.

Bourne suppressed a shudder as he took a step toward his chair before a hand stopped him.

Suddenly, McKinley's face went stern and unsmiling. "By the way, I mean to destroy that witch, Marta, when I'm finished with her. She has cost me some fine warlocks."

Bourne's breath caught. "What are your plans for her?"

McKinley smiled again, removing his hand. He'd been so gabby, but now he refused to answer. What the hell was going on?

Bourne found he was shaking. "What are your fucking plans for her?" he repeated louder.

McKinley's smile never waned. He still didn't answer.

Bourne tried again. "Why even have me here if you aren't going to talk? You should have just left me in my tent. Why am I here?"

McKinley shrugged. "We have plenty of time to talk. You also intrigue me, Sheriff. I think you hold a key to something, but I could be wrong. I'll contemplate that before we meet again. For now, we dine." He turned on his heel, then headed for the other end of the table.

Bourne watched the man walk with a clenched jaw. Someway, somehow, Bourne was going to get the upper hand on this madman. If he didn't, Marta would end up just like Greta and Beth or even worse.

For the moment, Bourne was another toy for McKinley. The man would try to get in Bourne's head. He would have to be careful going forward or he might end up dead before Marta did.

CHAPTER 26—MEETING IN THE DREAM REALM

"Wake up," Phantom called.

Marta opened one eye. It was now dark. She didn't feel fully rested, but better. She was surprised Phantom hadn't disappeared on them again. At least he roused them in time for the meeting in the dream realm, but she still wouldn't fully rely on him.

Wind Rock also stirred. "Ugh. I need more sleep."

"I know," Marta said. "We can sleep in tomorrow, but we need help tonight."

Wind Rock nodded. "Let's go."

She then cast the spell that got her into the dream realm. Marta followed suit.

"I'll stand guard," Phantom said.

Marta closed her eyes, and...

She opened them to a sea of stars, careful not to think of anybody besides Wind Rock. While she waited, she searched around for her, unsure what direction she would be coming from. It was surprising they weren't right next to each other to begin with, but Wind Rock had explained that the dream realm existed outside of the physical world and couldn't manipulate it. Distances didn't matter here.

Marta felt a pull in a direction, so she allowed it to take her. Still thinking of only Wind Rock, Marta searched for the young girl. After about a minute of moving, she found a figure heading toward her. With all the bright lights of the dreams, it was hard to make her out until they were close.

"Good," Wind Rock said as they stopped about a yard apart. "Now change your appearance."

Marta glanced down at the brown riding dress she almost always wore. Well, what she wore in the physical world. She imagined the most elegant evening dress that a lady of some finance would wear in Paris or some such place away from the hard, rugged frontier. She felt her waist pinch in as a green dress replaced hers. The bodice hugged her curves while the skirt flowed out into a huge bell.

"A little much, isn't it?" Wind Rock asked.

Marta shrugged while eying Wind Rock's deerskin tunic and skirt. Still, Marta mimicked it, but took some liberties with a bearskin sash and a coon hat. She felt a bit more like Davy Crockett in a dress than an Indian squaw, but it didn't feel bad.

Wind Rock nodded. "Very good."

Marta wasn't sure if that was a compliment of her skills or her style of clothing. She didn't inquire about that. "Can I change my appearance?"

Wind Rock cocked her head, looking at Marta's tunic.

"I mean like my face. Can I look like you if I wanted?"

Wind Rock arched an eyebrow. "Why would you want to?"

Marta shrugged. "Maybe to walk around incognito or something?"

Wind Rock nodded. "Yes, you can change it if you like, but it is advisable not to in council meetings. Some people wear hoods to hide their faces—usually white folk so they aren't discriminated against—but that is the extent of it."

That was good to know. She had nothing to hide. So what if she were white? "What's next?"

Wind Rock shrugged. "Just remember that you are in control of yourself here, and I think you'll be fine."

Marta didn't know if she agreed with her. Sure, they'd talked about how things worked in the dream realm for the last couple of days, but she needed some practice. "Surely there is something else I can try."

Wind Rock nodded. "It's time we went to the meeting place to familiarize yourself with it and test out some of the abilities you have there."

Marta hesitated. "Won't the council be there?"

"Not yet. It's still a little early. We'll have some time to test out a few abilities. You remember how to get there?"

Marta rolled her eyes. She then visualized the blue Parthenon structure. In just a moment, she was whisked away and standing in the middle of a circle of women, most sitting, but some standing. In another second, Wind Rock was beside her.

"Wind Rock," Runs With Does exclaimed. "That white girl isn't allowed here." She then flicked her wrist in Marta's direction. "Be gone."

Marta gulped, fighting the urge to wake in her bedroll. Instead, she concentrated on staying here. It was hard to do since she wasn't expecting people around.

"You've been teaching her, I see," Runs With Does said. She was wearing the same garb she had the first time Marta met her.

Wind Rock snapped her fingers, and the peace pipe floated in her direction. She caught it. "I think a stubborn mule is easier to teach, but yes, I've given her a few pointers along the way. She is desperate, and would have killed herself to get here without my help."

Marta took a long look at the girl beside her. Who was the stubborn mule? Then again, maybe Wind Rock was stretching the truth to be on Runs With Does' good side. A little mutual picking on Marta was practically expected. Wasn't it?

Runs With Does snapped for the pipe. "She seems the type of person willing to run headlong into danger, and get others killed. Are you being careful?"

Wind Rock huffed as she snapped for the pipe. "Why ask a question you know the answer to? We've run into four warlocks, and Marta has found a new way of defeating them. She can sever them from accessing the magical orb."

There were murmurs and gasps around from the onlookers.

Wind Rock wasn't done. "She can teach us all the severing curse, and we can finally defeat McKinley and his army."

Without really meaning to, Marta snapped her fingers. The peace pipe appeared in her hand. She stared at it. When she spoke, it was just above a whisper. "Wind Rock shows a lot of faith in my abilities, and I want to thank her for that. Defeating McKinley is only one of my goals. I need to free my friends." She looked around at the medicine women. "Nay, I need to free all of our friends. Please, I beg you all for your help."

There were no murmurs now. Nobody said a thing or even moved. They just watched her with stony stares.

Runs With Does snapped, and the pipe was whisked from Marta's hand. "You can't barge into our meeting and ask for our help. This is a sacred place, and your worth must be proven to even be here. Wind Rock represents her clan, which is why she is allowed. You don't belong to a tribe of any kind and act on your own. No, we will not help you."

Marta was outraged at being talked down to. She heard someone snap near her, or she would have gotten the pipe to speak her mind.

The pipe ended up in Wind Rock's hand. "How dare you talk about my clan when I am not welcome at any tribal fires. My clan consists of my grandfather and me. I'm allowed here because of my abilities and who my mother was. She was also a victim of McKinley's, or have you forgotten that? Marta has done more for her honor than any of you ever have. She wants to free the women captured by McKinley, unlike what any of you tried to do for my mother. Since you didn't help her, you need to help Marta now."

Runs With Doe just glared. Some of the other onlookers gaped at Wind Rock with open mouths. Marta was impressed with the girl for standing up to the leader. It was awesome to see.

"Oh, and another thing," Wind Rock continued. "Phantom has shown up again. He is now guiding Marta and me near Lincoln Center, Kansas, where McKinley's camp is."

There were several groans at the mention of the spirit's name.

A younger medicine woman near Runs With Does snapped for the pipe. "The news of Phantom does help your cause as we now have a location. We also see that you two are resolute in your convictions to go after McKinley."

When the woman paused, Marta nodded enthusiastically to get her to say more.

She sighed. "Very well. We will consult with our clans and discuss the possibility of joining your quest. We'll then talk at the next meeting to make a decision."

"But that isn't for two more days," Marta blurted out.

"Tradition!" Runs With Does shouted as others tsked.

Marta snapped. She thought about apologizing, but just went into why she was angry. "We'll be in Lincoln before the next meeting. I don't know how long some of you will need to travel, but we can't wait long for you to make up your mind. We need an answer tonight so you can be on the move tomorrow. The more time wasted means the less chance we'll get my friends back without irreparable harm."

Marta stopped for breath before launching into more of a tirade, but Runs With Does snapped for the peace pipe.

Runs With Does visibly tried to restrain herself. "Patience," she called, then took a breath. "You two will need to scout McKinley's camp. We need to know what we are up against."

Marta felt like this was just a stall tactic, and the answer was going to be an eventual 'no' anyway. It was a waste of time. Or if there was going to be help coming, it wasn't going to be in time.

Runs With Does smiled, though it looked like a snarl with her anger. "Everything will work out as it should, child."

Marta wanted to voice her concern that it wouldn't, but the medicine women started leaving. They just winked out like a flame getting snuffed out. It had to mean they were done with the council meeting. Runs With Does was one of the first to leave.

Before tonight, Marta thought she had a real chance with these women. Now she knew better. Maybe she would have to find another big spell to take down an entire encampment of warlocks. She'd have to if she were to have any chance now since it seemed like there wasn't going to be any more help.

Dejected, she also winked herself back to her physical body, and…

Marta rolled over to face away from Wind Rock and Phantom. She didn't want to talk to anyone.

"I wonder why the council was early tonight?" Wind Rock said.

Marta was glad to know Wind Rock hadn't set her up, but it was too late to ask that question. Instead, Marta focused on what she could do. She needed some rest so she could think of a way to victory tomorrow.

CHAPTER 27—TRAVELING WITH A PHANTOM

It was midmorning before Marta woke to the smell of brewed coffee. Wind Rock had been up well before her, so she was able to down a cup to wake up and then savor another while breaking camp. It had been days since she last had a cup, so this was a pleasant treat. Phantom spent his time meditating rather than helping the girls with their "corporeal things." As he didn't eat, drink, or even need belongings, he didn't feel he had to help them with that stuff.

As they got going, Phantom started skipping up the trail into an outright run. Marta was glad to see someone was in a hurry, and thought they would have no problem keeping up with that speed.

"I wonder why he doesn't just instantaneously transport?" Wind Rock asked as she mounted her horse.

Marta shrugged. She would have to kick up her horse to match Phantom's speed.

"Let's take it slow and easy," Wind Rock said.

Marta hesitated. She wanted to get a move on. "We'll be behind Phantom."

Wind Rock gave her a sidelong look. "What's your hurry?"

What did she mean? Marta pointed ahead. "I want to keep up with him."

"If he instantaneously transports, there is no keeping up with him. He'll wait for us to catch up. He's always doing stuff like this," Wind Rock said.

They moved their horses to the middle of the trail, leaving the remnants of the campfire behind. It was at a slow walk, though.

"Well, he isn't instantaneously transporting, whatever that is. Let's keep up with him," Marta said.

Wind Rock shook her head. "When he disappears from one place and ends up in another, that is instantaneously transporting. We'll have to ask him why he isn't doing it."

"How do you know about these things, anyway?"

"I've had teachers who explain them. I've encountered Phantom twice before as well. He checked in on me on those occasions, but the teachers I had at the time weren't happy he was around due to his odd antics."

Marta could relate. But there was still something she didn't have an answer to. "So, why are we going so slow and easy now?"

Wind Rock turned to her. "Look, we could get to Lincoln by midnight if we ride full out and heal the horses from time to time. Then we'll have an entire day to kill before we scout McKinley's camp and report to the dream realm council. We might as well take it easy so we are rested and can expend our full energy on planning. Plus, we'll be better in a fight if we are rested, and the horses aren't overworked."

Marta sighed. "But the sooner we get there, the more time we have to come up with a plan."

"Is your plan to forge ahead without the medicine women?"

Marta furrowed her brow. What kind of dumb question was that? "Noo," she slowly answered. It was almost a question.

"Then we need to limit our exposure the best we can and that is to get to the camp just before nightfall tomorrow night. Then we scout before reporting what we find in the dream realm. Besides, we'll have another night until the full moon, so the moon will be in our favor the longer we wait to scout."

Marta found the girl's rationale to be sound even if she didn't like it. They should plan to get there just before dusk tomorrow night. At least it wasn't a total loss, traveling at a moderate pace. She could rest while they rode and have more time to come up with what to say to finally convince the dream council to help.

About a half-mile up the road, they found Phantom sitting under a tree meditating. As Wind Rock and Marta came abreast of him, he jumped up and took off at a run again.

"Why aren't you instantaneously transporting?" Wind Rock called.

Phantom stopped. He didn't turn around as he answered her. "Warlocks can now sense me instantaneously transporting."

"How can they do that?" Marta asked. She couldn't sense any of his abilities.

"Something with the upset in the balance with the Western Sky. They have breached my powers and can sense them," Phantom replied.

"Any warlock or just the ones at McKinley's camp?" Marta asked.

They were coming abreast of him again, so he started skipping. "I think all warlocks. That's how I could feel those warlocks about to ambush you."

Marta had been keeping an eye out for an ambush since they broke camp. "Can you sense them, then?"

Phantom nodded. "I can sense them within a fifteen-minute walk. None of them are near here."

Marta arched an eyebrow as she did the calculation in her head. A fifteen-minute walk was about half a mile. But there was a way to breach that distance instantly. "Can warlocks instantaneously transport?"

Phantom was still skipping along, happy as could be. "Of course they can. You could, too."

This was news to Marta.

"How?" Wind Rock asked. It must have been news to her as well.

"My magic and your magic are different. Even if I could explain how to do the spell, it wouldn't work for you. I think it is lost in the corporeal realm."

Marta was dejected to hear this. This lost ability would have come in handy about then.

Ever since meeting Beth and Greta, she'd learned all sorts of spells that weren't in her book. Not that her book was comprehensive since she had figured out some stuff on her own, but it did have a ton of spells. Beth, Greta, and even Wind Rock had teachers. There were things those other witches and medicine women didn't know, or it was too advanced for them to do.

"Besides, we don't want to instantaneously transport right now," Wind Rock said.

"Oh?" Marta questioned.

Wind Rock nodded. "The women in McKinley's camp would feel us. Then the warlocks there would see their reaction and know we were there. We'd lose our ability to scout them."

"We could invert the spell," Marta said.

"You can't invert instantaneously transporting. That, and they'd feel me anyway," Phantom added.

"I know that," Marta started. "I'd just like to know how to instantaneously transport. Just like how I accidentally flew when Rathbone tried to capture me. Not that I would like to fly, but I hate I can't remember how I was able to."

Wind Rock arched an eyebrow, studying Marta. "You flew?"

Marta didn't feel comfortable being looked at in that manner. She nodded meekly.

"Excellent. Yeah, I hope you figure that out."

There it was again. This was the second time Wind Rock had shown faith in Marta that she didn't necessarily feel. Something had shifted in their relationship, she could tell. Then it hit her that it had started when Marta had come up with that severing curse out of nowhere.

Marta wondered if she could trust this shift in Wind Rock's attitude. It was too early to tell, but it seemed like the girl now looked up to her. Like Wind Rock respected her. Something to keep an eye on, that was for sure. She hoped the respect was warranted, and she could live up to it in the future.

Phantom still skipped a little ahead. "Yes, flying is fun. That spell you could invert. Too bad it is a lost spell among both males and females. At least it isn't lost to us spirits."

With that, Phantom quit skipping and started running.

"Why are you running ahead?" Marta called.

Phantom slowed. "So I can have time to meditate."

"Why do you meditate?" Marta asked.

"So I can stay in tune with the Western Sky." With that, he ran ahead of them until he was out of sight. After each half mile or so, he would pop up from meditating alongside the road and then sprint ahead again.

Marta and Wind Rock kept a steady pace, talking about lost spells. Some were noted in Marta's book, which had been lost in the fire. Wind Rock shared what some of her teachers had taught her. They weren't sure how spells got lost. Maybe a lack of teachers and no one recording them. That was soon exhausted since it was hard to discuss what they had only heard rumors to go from. The conversation then shifted to what stronger performers of magic could do that those weaker couldn't.

Every time they came to a trail junction, Phantom would be there to point the way to the correct path, which was straight west until they got to the Solomon bridge heading over the Smoky Hill. He stayed with them as they crossed over it.

Traveling with two Indians—well, one Indian and a celestial being—they avoided the town of Solomon since that was easy to do. It held far too many people with inquiring eyes. They skirted the edge until they were on a road heading west. A marker indicated this would lead them to Salina, which would also have to be avoided.

One thing about it, this path was well used and garnered a lot of curiosity from passersby. Marta just smiled and nodded. She knew they weren't warlocks since Phantom wasn't reacting to them, but Marta didn't like being seen. Phantom quit rushing ahead and actually stayed with them. Both he and Wind Rock ignored the people they passed and just stared ahead. Some, men in particular, did look at the Natives with a little more scrutiny, but left them alone.

After being courteous to the tenth group, Marta grew tired of this. "Is there another way we can go?" Marta asked.

Phantom pointed to the river they were coming upon. "There is a decent trail we can take that goes a bit more north here in a few minutes. It should be void of people, other than the farmers and ranchers who use it. We'll go on that, but this road is on an easy fjord over the Solomon River, so I wanted to take advantage of that. The trail we'll be on kind of follows the river for a while."

Marta was glad for this as she was anxious to get away from so many eyes. She also had a better feeling about this new trail since that would take them more northwest toward Lincoln. Most of the day was gone, but they had plenty of daylight to travel by. Even after the sun went down, they could make light to travel by. Having a road with fewer people on it would make it easier to do such magic.

Another trail came into sight after going up the riverbank just like Phantom said there would be. Marta felt like they were getting closer to their goal, and she would find some way to reach the council along the way. She had to or all was lost.

CHAPTER 28—SOLOMON RIVER

This new trail had no people and there weren't many junctions, so Phantom ran ahead again. Marta and Wind Rock continued at their easy pace to allow the spirit time to meditate. It was well past noon, but there was still plenty of daylight hours to travel before making camp. Then another easy day before they arrived in Lincoln, Kansas.

Around the first bend after Phantom took off, Marta spotted him just standing in the middle of the road and gazing down at the riverbank. Marta hadn't expected this, so she kicked up her horse to see what was going on. She halted her horse behind Phantom, peering in the same direction.

"She's upset," was all Phantom said.

She could see who he referred to. A woman in a black dress sat on a log just across the river. Marta's enhanced eyesight could easily see this woman had been crying. The gun in her hand was also concerning. What was a woman in an expensive, silk dress doing in a place that could tear or soil it?

Marta linked up with the magical orb, then began looking for danger in the area. Maybe she had been robbed, her horse stolen, and she scared off her attackers with the gun. Marta searched for evidence of such a deed. After a minute of not finding any danger, she decided she better go and find out what had this gal spooked.

Her horse barely moved before Wind Rock stopped her with her horse. "You are sure we have time to get into other people's affairs."

Marta shrugged. "We've been going so slow, we can easily pick up the pace a bit if we need to, but this won't take long."

Wind Rock nodded and backed her horse. Marta directed her horse down the embankment. She didn't hear Wind Rock and Phantom follow her, which was a good thing considering the woman might be spooked by an Indian and a spirit of the Western Sky, even in human form.

Whether it was the babbling water or the woman being so engrossed by the river, she didn't see Marta approach. She stopped her horse in the middle of the river. The water was barely up to the horse's knees at this point.

"Where's the danger?" Marta asked.

The woman met Marta's gaze with red, puffy eyes. She squinted. Marta wasn't sure if it was due to the sun being behind her or what.

The woman cocked her head. She slowly stood from the log. "There is no danger." She wiped her cheek with her free hand.

Marta pointed at the gun. "You look upset and ready for a fight. Or did you already win the fight?"

The woman slowly moved the gun behind her. Something about this situation wasn't right. The woman's disheveled blonde hair added to that feeling. Her unkempt hair was at odds with how fine the dress was.

Marta nodded. "I'm here to help. What's wrong?"

The woman looked around and sniffled. Her one arm was still cocked behind her back to keep the gun hidden. "Nothing's wrong!" she shouted.

Marta shook her head. She needed to be careful, so she decided to try a different angle. "What's your name?" she asked.

"What do you want it to be?" the woman asked.

Marta was taken aback. What kind of answer was that? What the hell was going on?

The woman rolled her eyes and blew out a long breath. "Forgive me," she started before pausing a second. "I'm not in the best frame of mind. My name is Chassidy."

"Tell me what's wrong, Chassidy, so I can help."

"Who says anything is wrong?" Chassidy murmured.

"The gun you're hiding behind your back is an indication. Your appearance is another."

Chassidy grabbed a lock of hair and pulled it to where she could see it. She dropped her hand to her side, exposing the gun again. Her voice took on a distant tone. "Men seem to like my hair, and I spend a lot of time making it look good for them. Then some asshole says a few nasty things about it in the paper, and I'm now ashamed of it."

She seemed to suddenly remember that Marta was there. "Or maybe I'm just ashamed of myself. The article said some awful things about me in general. Do you like my hair?"

Marta tried to picture the hair if it were properly brushed. "It looks good to me. Why would someone print bad things about you in the paper?"

Chassidy huffed. "Ignorant Salina prudes have taken to badmouthing madams in the paper. Hell, the writer probably visited a few in his youth, and he can't get it up now."

Marta's eyes bugged out. "You're a whore?"

"Madam!" Chassidy shouted.

Marta raised her hands. "I meant no disrespect. Forgive my naivety."

Chassidy eyed Marta before finally nodding. "You look to have an easy life."

Marta shook her head. "I guess looks can be deceiving. Life is what you make it."

"If you can live with it." Chassidy paused, then drew in a short breath. "Or if you can live with what people print in the paper about you."

The gun in her hand took on a new meaning. Marta wasn't naïve about people willing to take their own life as she'd had a few unlucky neighbors succumb to the darkness of the harsh frontier. Some neighbors had hidden their depression well, and she hadn't been able to help them. Others, she was able to get them to see that all wasn't lost. She hoped to have another success here.

Marta gauged Chassidy to see if she would follow through with her threat. Marta came down here looking for the danger to Chassidy, but it seemed like Chassidy was that danger. "You don't want to kill yourself," Marta whispered. She readied a spell to knock the gun away.

Chassidy's brow furrowed. "Really? Why do you say that?"

"Because it is a permanent solution to a temporary problem."

"That crap about me is in print. How is that temporary?" Chassidy pointed the gun at Marta. "Why don't you move along and leave me in peace?"

Marta backed her horse a bit, showing her hands. "Whoa, Chassidy. You don't want to harm me. I'm here to help. I can help."

"How can *you* help *me*?"

Marta was in the middle of rescuing Bourne, Greta, and Beth. She couldn't exactly stop to help this woman land on her feet. She made a shield in case bullets started flying. "Well, I can help you realize your full potential. You don't need that newspaper. If you don't like what they are saying about how you make your living, then make your living a different way. If you don't think you can have a fresh start in Salina, start fresh somewhere else. Other places would love to have a madam of your caliber if you still wanted to do that type of work. But as upset as you are, I think a different profession is in order."

"Being a madam is all I know," Chassidy said.

Marta nodded. "All that you know to this point. You can do other things. What else do you like to do?"

Chassidy shrugged. "I never really thought about doing other things or even what I enjoy doing."

Marta nodded with enthusiasm. "Well take some time and think it over. Eight years ago, Kansas State Agricultural College opened its doors to women and men equally. You can learn a new trade there if you want."

"All my money was used for beauty products and beautiful dresses. It's expensive to make my hair look this good. Any other bright ideas?"

Marta couldn't see how Chassidy's hair was all that much better than hers. The gun being pointed at her made her not respond. "I'm sure a bank will loan you the money to take some classes. You can find a way."

Chassidy shook her head. "I don't think I can."

"Of course you can. If you don't, the alternative is spending eternity six feet under while the worms eat you."

Chassidy spoke in a near whisper. "Or I can go home to heaven and live in my forever home with God."

Marta didn't know what to think about a Christian prostitute. Surely there was a conflict between those two ideologies. Again, the gun made her hold her tongue. "You're better than this, Chassidy. You're better than what that person wrote in the newspaper." Another thought came to Marta. "They probably are just jealous of your good looks and fantastic hair."

Chassidy stood a bit straighter.

Marta had her. Now to put things over the top. "When you show them that you've gotten a new life, they'll be even more jealous."

Chassidy slumped. "Or they'll parade around in victory that they've gotten a madam to take a new job or move out of their perfect community."

The gun started to turn and move back. "Well, I better give them what they want."

Marta still had hold of the magic. She shot the air spell before the barrel end could make it to Chassidy's temple. The gun fell from her hands, bounced off the log, and ended up in the river. Marta readied another spell in case Chassidy had any other weapons.

Chassidy stared with bug eyes. For the longest time, she didn't say anything, only breathed in gasps. "You're a fucking witch!"

Marta rolled her eyes. She thought about calling her a 'fucking whore,' but thought better of it. Instead, she said, "At your service."

Chassidy glanced downriver before turning and running as fast as she could. She screamed all the while as she bolted across the river toward the trees.

Marta turned her horse, staring up the hill. Wind Rock was still waiting, but there was no sign of Phantom. Just as well since things hadn't gone the greatest down here.

"I'm going after Chassidy," Marta said in a normal voice.

Wind Rock nodded. She had been connected to the magical orb the whole time to listen into Marta's and Chassidy's conversation. She could even hear this last bit.

Marta turned toward the woman who was now scrambling up the bank to higher ground. Where was she going and how was that going to save her? If Marta had been an evil witch, Chassidy would have been toast already. People did stupid things when they were afraid. Did Marta have what it took to calm Chassidy and give her something to live for?

CHAPTER 29—TIME

Marta couldn't follow the woman directly as there were too many brambling trees with low-hanging branches for her horse to safely navigate. She had to find another way up the embankment.

Once on top, Wind Rock headed Marta off and asked, "Do we have time for this?"

Marta rolled her eyes. Since when had Wind Rock been the one to get them going faster. "Surely we do. Besides, I want to be sure she'll be okay. Not only with me frightening her, but also with her own internal struggles."

Wind Rock cocked her head. "Why do you care about this woman you don't know at all?"

Marta glared. "Why don't you care? She is someone who needs help, and I can offer help. I don't just give up on people."

Wind Rock squinted at her hard before glancing to the west. "That you don't. I guess I don't care about someone who doesn't want to live."

"Well, that is just sad. How can you say a thing like that?"

Wind Rock took a sudden interest in the ground. She took a deep breath. "Because my mother didn't want to live," she whispered. "That is how I know this woman will kill herself no matter what we do." Done talking, she closed her eyes and her lips quivered.

Marta thought back to what Wind Rock had said about her mother's death. Madness was the reason she had given. There were only certain ways that madness could be a killer. Marta had just assumed Wind Rock's mother just wasted away, unable to eat while out of her mind.

A tear slid down Marta's cheek. She closed her eyes. "You can't just close your heart to someone because they didn't know how to function with the pain they felt." She opened her eyes.

Wind Rock's lids fluttered, tears welling in her eyes. Wind Rock's grip on the reins was also tighter, but she still trembled.

Marta moved her horse closer. "I can't imagine the pain your mother felt, but I can imagine yours. I lost my brother, and there isn't a day that goes by that I don't miss him. I know what you are going through, and I'll help any way I can."

Wind Rock nodded, her eyes hardening as she huffed.

"What was your mother like?"

Wind Rock shrugged. Apparently, now wasn't the time for her to talk. That was fine. Marta could talk.

She suddenly pictured Brandon falling out of a tree. "There was also a boy I cared for named Brandon. He couldn't comprehend my magic after I used it to save his life. He then took his own life after being coaxed by Pastor Goodman."

Wind Rock cocked her head. "Is that why you are so eager to find this woman?"

Marta nodded.

Wind Rock looked again at the ground, but differently than before. She pointed as Marta's eyes drifted in that direction. "The woman went that way," Wind Rock said.

Marta couldn't see what track Wind Rock had picked up, but she didn't need to. She just needed her tracker to track. Wind Rock led the way, and Marta fell in beside her. Wind Rock studied the ground while Marta looked ahead for any signs of the woman. Just how far had she gotten in this short amount of time.

They were soon going down into a creek bottom that fed into the Solomon. Near the bottom was a plum thicket. Wind Rock circled the thicket before stopping in the creek. She studied the far bank. "I've lost the track." She turned her head upstream, but she pointed a thumb behind her. "She either went upstream or..." She turned her head toward the river. "...back to the river." Her thumb still pointed behind her.

Marta took a quick look in the thicket. Only a witch or a medicine woman's enhanced vision would have spotted the person hiding in those brambles. She turned her horse to not scare Chassidy off. Marta sighed. "Let's leave the poor woman alone."

Wind Rock arched an eyebrow.

"You heard me. We have people who want our help. Besides, can you imagine how strong that woman is?"

Wind Rock shook her head. "Stronger than me if I were in her shoes, that's for sure. I mean, running from a witch even though she could reach out and stop her with her powers?"

Marta put a little gruffness in her voice for this mock argument. "Hey, I wouldn't do a thing like that."

Wind Rock nodded. "I know you wouldn't hurt a fly. I'm talking about her, though, and her perception."

"Oh," Marta put in, feigning understanding. "You're right. I wouldn't hurt anybody, but she doesn't know that."

Marta glanced back to be sure Chassidy was still there. She was. Who knew if she was listening, though? She had to be, right? "And can you imagine how tough it would be to be a madam in this day and age?"

Wind Rock shook her head. "You'd have to be a lot stronger than me and I'm a stone-cold Indian."

Marta thought back to the tears that had almost fallen from Wind Rock's eyes while talking about her mother. So much for being stone cold, but, again, this was to play into Chassidy's perceptions. She wouldn't have been able to hear that conversation. "Yeah. As an Indian, I'm sure you've had to put up with a lot of discrimination and persecution."

Wind Rock nodded. "Yes, and madams go through similar situations." Wind Rock then indicated Marta. "What about you being found out to be a witch? I live hours away, and I've heard everything about you and the exaggerations."

Marta nodded before dropping her head. "It isn't easy living in a small town with people who hate me. Nobody cares about the good I've done or how I can help them. All they see is a monster in their midst."

"All lies," Wind Rock said. "All these people are only feeding the fires with lies. You aren't a monster. Your heart is so big, and you want to save the entire world. The world needs more people like you."

Marta shrugged. "I can't help people who don't want my help, though. Ugh. I just wish I could tell Chassidy that she is strong and can ignore the lies being told about her. Just like you have ignored the lies about you to become a strong young woman."

"Thank you," Wind Rock said as she cocked her head. "I can tell you mean it. I'm glad you've ignored the lies and have chosen to be my friend."

Marta was taken aback by this. They had become friends, hadn't they? When did that happen?

"Well, don't look so shocked about me saying you are my friend." Wind Rock rolled her eyes.

Marta smiled weakly. "I just hadn't realized we had become so close on this journey. We are good friends, aren't we?"

Wind Rock nodded, then glanced back. It was then Marta realized they still had a performance to put on—their audience was still there. Where could they go from there?

"I know what you are doing," Chassidy called from the thicket. "A blind man could see that you two found me when you stopped your horses in the stream."

Marta turned so she could see Chassidy. "Oh?" She didn't bother to hide that she had known where she was the whole time.

"Yes," Chassidy said. "You are hitting me over the head with everyone having problems due to people's perceptions, and that you two are strong women to handle such crap."

"Well, and also that you are a strong woman. All women are strong. It's our nature," Marta said.

Chassidy sighed.

"And don't forget, we won't hurt you," Wind Rock added.

Marta nodded. She waited for Chassidy to rebuff her again, but nothing came. "So, is our act working?" Marta asked.

Chassidy huffed. "Maybe."

Marta nodded. "Do you need anything else from us, or would you rather we were on our way?"

Chassidy sighed. "Can you make me invisible?"

Marta shrugged. "Yes, but then I'd have to follow you to keep the spell going for as long as you require."

"I take it you two have somewhere else to be."

"We do. We have other people to save," Marta replied.

"Then you better get going," Chassidy said. "You've done your job here. I'll be fine."

Marta turned, but she saw Wind Rock staring in Chassidy's direction with furrowed brows and pursed lips. "What's wrong?" Marta asked.

Wind Rock shook her head. "Nothing," she said before turning back to Chassidy. "Do I know you?"

Chassidy didn't say anything for a minute. "While I do get female customers from time to time, I have never given my services to an Indian, let alone a female."

Wind Rock shook her head. "There isn't any other way I would know you?"

"Not unless you've seen me around Salina," Chassidy replied.

Wind Rock sighed. "I've never been this far west before. Maybe we met in another lifetime."

"Maybe," Chassidy said.

Marta didn't know what to make of this. How could these two know each other? Surely, they didn't. Maybe Chassidy merely reminded Wind Rock of someone.

Marta and Wind Rock took their leave of Chassidy. There were no thanks from Chassidy, but Marta could tell that she was much better off than when Marta had found her. Now, Marta had more lives to save, and it was time to get down the road so she could do it.

CHAPTER 30—ANOTHER DINNER

Bourne wasn't too surprised when a warlock came around at suppertime without a tray of food. It looked like McKinley was buttering him up for something, and Bourne was being treated at his house.

The shackle was removed from Bourne's leg, and he was walked to McKinley's. This time, Bourne didn't even try to escape. He would go willingly a few times, acting resigned to his fate, so he could catch his guard unaware when he made his escape. While it was hard to be patient, he knew he had to be for his sake.

McKinley greeted him at the door. "How are you doing this evening?"

Shrugging, Bourne made his way to the table without being told to go. He couldn't help being hungry, and it was a bonus to not stand for McKinley's bullshit.

"Can I interest you in a whiskey?" McKinley asked, not commenting on Bourne's cold shoulder.

It would have been nice to get to the man, but Bourne could see right through McKinley seeing through Bourne. Bourne sighed, weary of the game he was playing.

"You look like you need a strong one." McKinley turned to the kitchen and bellowed, "Two whiskeys, gals."

Bourne closed his eyes as he heard the kitchen door open. He wasn't sure if it were Greta or Beth who entered and followed the command, but he didn't feel like seeing a naked girl doing McKinley's bidding.

He heard the glass being set in front of him, then waited until he heard the kitchen door close again before opening his eyes. McKinley hovered nearby with glass raised. "To peace on Earth."

Bourne rolled his eyes. He didn't care what the man did to him, but he wasn't going to give McKinley the satisfaction of bending to his will. Bourne raised his glass to his lips and drank, not bothering to touch his glass to the bishop's.

McKinley slowly moved his glass to his lips and drank. He didn't seem fazed by Bourne's game. He even seemed to take a little enjoyment in it.

"Let's play a game," McKinley said.

Bourne couldn't help doing a double-take. Was he talking about the war of wits they were already in, or did he mean a card game? "I can play Pinochle with the best of them, but we'd need another player at the least."

"Not cards. I'll answer any question you have with the truth, but then you'll return the favor."

Bourne cocked his head as he considered the game. "It's only a game if there is some way to win."

When McKinley smiled, it made Bourne's skin crawl. "If played right, we both win key pieces of knowledge."

Bourne scoffed. He wasn't sure he wanted to allow McKinley to win even if it meant Bourne gained something as well.

McKinley raised his glass again as if he were making a toast. "I tell you what. You can ask the first question. If you are unsatisfied with the answer, you can refuse to answer my question." He then sipped his whiskey.

Something had been nagging at Bourne ever since dinner the previous night. "How do you know where Marta is?"

McKinley tsked. "Such a bad question to start this game. Are you sure you want it answered?"

Bourne shrugged. He couldn't think of any reason not to ask. Hell, McKinley's refusal to answer might mean something in Bourne's favor. "It's been asked, so answer it."

McKinley drew in a deep breath, eyeing Bourne. Had he struck a nerve? Finally, McKinley said, "Marta is traveling with something that belongs to me. I have a connection with it, and I can feel it. It crossed the Solomon Bridge this afternoon, and it should be here in another day."

Marta was going slow. Why? Unless she wasn't sure of the way, so she was randomly going in a direction. But McKinley seemed sure she was on her way here.

"My turn," McKinley said.

"Uh…" Bourne interrupted. "You haven't fully answered my question."

"I haven't?" McKinley chided. He furrowed his brow.

Bourne nodded. "You were vague as to what was in Marta's possession that you have a connection with."

"I see," McKinley said, putting his elbow down on the table and then resting his head on his fist. He just stared at Bourne.

Bourne took the opportunity to sip at his whiskey. He didn't back down from his request. "You said if I wasn't satisfied with the answer…"

McKinley grunted. "The item traveling with Marta isn't a what, but a who."

"Go on," Bourne said, starting to not like all this prompting.

"You know of Phantom, don't you?"

Bourne slowly nodded. "He visited Marta."

"He's visited her again."

"And what role does he have in all this?"

McKinley sat up. He put his hands out in front of himself, palms toward Bourne. "Whoa. My turn to ask a question."

Bourne sighed. He still wasn't sure his answer was totally answered and truthfully to boot, but he'd better let McKinley have his question. "Proceed."

"If you were a warlock, would you be interested in joining my army?" McKinley asked.

Bourne thought this hypothetical was the biggest waste of a question imaginable. "No," he simply answered.

"Oh, come on. Why not?"

"That's a new question," Bourne pointed out.

McKinley arched an eyebrow. "No, it is a clarification of your answer. I'm not satisfied with a simple, 'no'."

Bourne shook his head. He didn't think there was much more he could do to resist answering it fully and in truth. "I wouldn't follow a madman to my doom."

McKinley chuckled. "Your doom? You do know that you would be invincible as a warlock, right? Plus, you would have my protection and the protection of the others in this camp."

"My soul isn't invincible, now, is it?"

McKinley cocked his head. "But I'm a religious leader. I could save your soul if you were in my army."

Bourne wished he could laugh, but he didn't see anything funny about his situation. "The answer would still be no."

McKinley shook his head. "You do know that once Marta is here, you'll have outlived your usefulness… unless you could make yourself useful some other way."

This made Bourne stare into his drink. What the hell was McKinley's game? What madness was he offering here? "Can you somehow make me into a warlock?"

McKinley rolled his eyes. "You previously asked a question and a question asked must be answered, so I'll answer that one. You asked what Phantom has to do with all this. I recently figured out how to combine my power with Phantom's, and now I just need the right witch to steal from as well. The witch must be powerful beyond those I've already accumulated. Once I have all three powers, I'll be able to rule the world as the one true God. I am the second coming of Christ, and all I need is Marta in my grasp to prove it to the world."

Suddenly, Bourne's mouth went dry. He finished his whiskey, but that didn't help. McKinley was madder than Bourne thought. Just what the hell was going on? Was there any way Marta could stop him?

"My turn for a question," McKinley said, breaking Bourne's reverie. "Once I am all-powerful, would you follow me then?"

Bourne shook his head, and it caused McKinley to stiffen.

"What? Why?" McKinley asked.

Bourne closed his eyes. He didn't like this game and needed it to stop. "Humans are flawed. They can't be trusted with as much power as you are describing."

McKinley nodded with a scowl. "And in answer to your question of if I can make you a warlock, I can't. You must be born with the ability to perform magic. Some aren't aware of their powers until late in life, but most of my followers were tapping into the magical orb as children."

Bourne was a bit relieved to find out he wasn't a warlock or could be made into one. "Marta was doing things as a little girl," he muttered.

"I'm not surprised. My question is…"

"Wait," Bourne interrupted. "If you can't make me a warlock, why are you asking me what I would do if I were one?"

McKinley cocked his head. "You'll have to ask that on your next turn as that isn't a clarifying question."

Bourne pursed his lips, glaring at McKinley. "Yeah, but I'm not satisfied."

McKinley shook his head. "Oh come now. Play the game fair. I did completely answer your question. This *is* a new question."

Bourne huffed. "Fine. I withdraw it for now."

McKinley nodded. "Why do you think I am some evil being when, once I have complete control of all three powers, I can do so much good for this world?"

"Abducting people and keeping them chained up is the very definition of evil," Bourne spat.

McKinley shook his head. "Not when it is for the greater good."

"I've given my answer, and I grow weary of the game. Now answer me. Why are you asking me about being a warlock if you can't make me one?"

McKinley smiled. "I have my reasons."

Bourne crossed his arms. "Either tell me the reasons, or end the game."

McKinley knocked on the table. "Then we'll end the game."

Bourne was surprised at this turn in events. He thought he would get McKinley to answer.

"Well, since you were a good sport in my game, I should still treat you to dinner. Maybe we can do more tomorrow," McKinley said as he stood and walked to the other end of the table. He clapped for the ladies, so Bourne shut his eyes again.

The meal was spent in silence, but Bourne couldn't help but

wonder what he would have done if he was a warlock. Given that he was once on the wrong side of the law, he might have given into McKinley's way. Now, he was a different individual than he once was, but with the corruption of power, he might never have gone straight.

He was glad he wasn't a warlock, or he might have drawn Marta's ire instead of her love. He hoped she was stronger than McKinley thought, and he could be defeated. He also hoped she was not used to make the man all-powerful. He almost wanted her to turn back and stay as far from McKinley as possible, even though it would leave Bourne to die as he wasn't useful to the bishop and his plans. This madness had to stop somehow, and he didn't see any other way with a clear path to victory.

Bourne was prepared to sacrifice himself to serve the greater good. He had been since becoming a deputy and then a sheriff. It looked like it was about time to do his duty, but he would find a way to take McKinley with him.

CHAPTER 31—OUTLAWS

Shortly after leaving Chassidy, they took a trail almost due west, leaving the Solomon River valley. When they reached the Saline River, they made camp for the night. It was a peaceful spot, and Marta appreciated its beauty. She wished Bourne were here with her.

After a good night's sleep, everyone was up before first light. The camp was silently broken down, though Phantom just sat around, watching everything. Now that they were no longer in a hurry, Marta did her best to not be so antsy. She reminded herself that going easy would be beneficial, assuming they could get help from the dream council.

Marta admonished herself for not thinking more positively. They *would* get help from the dream council. She just needed to focus on the here and now as she packed up.

"Halt!" Phantom called out. He was meditating on a rock with his eyes closed.

Marta was about to tie her bedroll, but she didn't move a muscle as she gave him a sidelong look. She wasn't sure Phantom's command was even directed toward her, so she raised a brow at Wind Rock.

Wind Rock just shrugged as she saddled her horse.

Marta turned back to Phantom. "What's..."

"You are not welcome!" Phantom opened his eyes wide, but they didn't seem to focus. "Go away, McKinley!"

Marta mouthed the name as she mulled over what Phantom was struggling with. There was something sinister afoot, but she didn't know if she should snap the spirit from the Western sky out of it.

Wind Rock grabbed Marta's arm. "Let him fight his demons. There is nothing we can do for him anyway."

Marta nodded. She finished with her bedroll and went to tie it to her saddle, but spotted men at the edge of the clearing they were in. Marta's jaw tightened. How had anyone got this close to her without notice? Grabbing the magical orb, she put a shield around her in case they were warlocks. Wind Rock did the same.

One of the men cocked his head. "You're a medicine woman, aren't you, squaw?" He seemed to be the leader of the group. A scar ran from his forehead down to his left cheek. His left eye was white from whatever injury it had sustained.

Wind Rock huffed as she turned to the men. Phantom didn't react, still locked in a battle inside his mind. It was Marta's turn to calm her friend, and she did so by placing a hand on her arm. "Remember to not use magic unless we have to," she whispered. "We don't want to draw attention to ourselves as we still have the advantage of surprise."

Marta then spoke up. "How do you know she is a healer?"

White-Eye pointed toward Wind Rock's head. "Her headband has the mark for a healer. Never seen one so young, though."

Marta rolled her eyes. "You've been around Indians before, that part is obvious, yet you have no idea what she is capable of."

White-Eye shrugged. "What concern is it of yours, Injun lover?"

Marta took a step forward, feeling the heat rise in her cheeks. Wind Rock caught her arm.

"I'm a healer," Wind Rock said.

The man turned to the others in his party. "Told ya." He then turned back to Marta and Wind Rock. "We've got a sick man in our camp. You will see to him and fix him."

Marta noted the lack of politeness in the order. "My friends and I are in a rush to be off. We have business elsewhere. We wish your man well, but we can't stop to help."

White-Eye put a hand on the holstered revolver at his hip. "I wasn't asking you. I'm telling you. You will fix him or else."

Marta glanced at Phantom. At least he wasn't staring at nothing. Instead, he looked on with interest. His connection with McKinley must have been at an end. Marta wanted to ask him about his episode, but they needed to get the men out of the way.

Wind Rock whispered, "We can either make a scene to scare them off, or we can help them. Shouldn't take long to help them, and saving someone would be a good start to the day. We've got the time."

Marta sighed. Wind Rock was right that it shouldn't take long. "Scaring these guys is tempting, but I'd rather not risk having news get around that we are in the area," she whispered. "Something might get back to McKinley, but the locals are getting restless to contend with as well."

Wind Rock nodded.

Louder, Marta called, "Let me finish saddling my horse, then you can lead the way."

A few minutes later, they followed the men deeper into the valley to the shore of the river. Hidden by a copse of trees just a few hundred yards from their camp was another full of ruffians. Marta counted twenty or so men. Both her and Wind Rock kept their shields up.

The men led them to the riverside where a man was lying with a river of blood flowing from a wound in his abdomen. "I thought you said he was sick," Marta said as she stopped her horse.

Wind Rock handed her reins to Marta as she dismounted, grabbed her pack of herbs, and went to the dying man's side. Marta remained mounted to have a better perch to watch from.

White-Eye shrugged. "He is sick. It's a form of lead poisoning."

The other men laughed. Some of the others from nearby campfires came closer to see what the commotion was about. Phantom didn't stay still, surveying the camp with interest. Marta estimated about twenty to twenty-five men were in this camp.

Wind Rock started making some sort of poultice with some ingredients she pulled from the pack. Marta was glad to see the woman was smart enough to cover her magical abilities. The man breathed shallowly, barely moving. He looked pale as well. He wasn't going to live another hour without their help.

After a few minutes of work on the poultice, Wind Rock readied the healing spell. She then put the poultice on the man's wound. He bucked and cried out as the spell was pushed into him at the same time.

"Fuck," the man who led them here called. "What are you doing to him?"

"It's a fast-acting poultice, but it needs a moment to set," Wind Rock answered. She was still doing the spell while holding the injured man down. Marta could see the spell had also pulled a bullet out of the man before the wound closed, but Wind Rock trapped it in her poultice. "Can one of you spare a shirt or something so I can wrap it around him to hold this in place as he heals? The poultice will need to stay on about ten days before it can be removed."

One of the men complied with her request. Marta hid a smile. Ten days was a good lie. Few would question the wound being healed if it were hidden that long.

"So, who shot him?" Marta eyed the men, but they either looked her dead in the eye or stared at the man on the ground. None answered her.

"Look, people don't just get shot for no reason. Did one of you shoot him?" Marta asked.

"We wouldn't shoot one of our own," White-Eye answered.

Marta nodded. "So, you either attacked someone or were attacked. Since you look like a gang on the wrong side of the law, I take it you did the attacking." Nobody answered, but when she eyed the men again, they didn't seem like they were going to contradict her.

White-Eye was the first one to say something. "What are you going to do about it, Injun lover?"

Marta cocked her head. Maybe she shouldn't have kept her abilities a secret. Then she could trounce these guys with everything she had. Or, at the very least, they'd be scared enough to answer her.

"They robbed someone," Phantom called. He had two saddlebags slung over his shoulders as he rolled a gold coin across his knuckles.

"Hey, that's ours," one of the ruffians protested.

Phantom shrugged, put the coin in one of the bags, where it

clinked against some other coins, and then stopped outside the ring of the gang. "It doesn't belong to you," he simply said.

Marta noted a half dozen unconscious gang members up the embankment. Basically, anyone who wasn't down by the river was out of commission. The ten or so people by the river appeared upset.

"Is stealing stolen goods still considered stealing?" Marta asked.

Phantom smiled. "I don't even have a use for money," he said as he put his hands on the saddlebags. "These people aren't nice, and it is time they learned a lesson." The last part was almost in song, and he laughed to punctuate what he said.

Marta extended her shield to the two horses. Phantom still laughed maniacally as he disappeared. The saddlebags floated in space. and didn't look to be moving.

Everyone had their guns out of their holsters in an instant, but nobody was shooting since their target of what seemed to be a fully human Indian man had disappeared. Marta was sure he wasn't doing his instantaneous transport as she still heard him laughing nearby. Plus, there were the saddlebags still in view, but he could have been holding those up with an air spell. The saddlebags and laughter moved away along the embankment, though.

Marta sighed as she eyed the guns. Some followed the general track of where the laughter came from. Some guns shook. Marta caught the whiff of urine from someone who apparently couldn't hold it with their fear. She tried to think of a way to diffuse the situation. At least bullets could be stopped, so no one was going to get hurt. She just wished the morning had gone a little easier for her.

"What kind of devilry is this?" shouted White-Eye. He then fired the first shot in the direction of the floating saddlebags.

Phantom had his defenses up, and the bullet stopped in midair. Other shots followed with the same result. Most everyone was shooting, and the saddlebags still moved.

The horses in Marta's grasp weren't comfortable with the shots, so they danced. She remained calm so they could feed off her calmness. She pulled them away from the main fray, but they fought her pull and instead stamped their feet at the shots. Little by little, she pulled the horses down into the river near where Wind Rock was. Each shot still made them dance, but they were easing up a bit.

"Let's get out of here," Marta said as she handed Wind Rock the reins of her horse.

She cocked her head toward the ruckus. "What about Phantom?"

Marta groaned. "He started this mess, so he can clean it up himself."

Wind Rock nodded. Quickly, they waded into the river to put more space between them and the gang.

Marta moved to the side of her horse, putting a foot in the stirrup. Before she could mount, she heard a gun cock next to her ear.

"Don't move," White-Eye said. Louder, he called, "Put down our money or your woman gets a permanent headache."

Marta eyed the gun barrel pushed to the edge of her shield, thankful she had it up to protect her. The shield was about an inch thick right on top of her skin.

She thought fast to try to see if there was a way she wouldn't be exposed as a witch. She eyed the other men and Phantom to fully assess the situation. Most outlaws were taking a moment to reload. The saddlebags were stopped at the other end of the throng, and an orb of projectiles hovered around them from Phantom's shield.

Suddenly, the bullets all dropped to the sand as the saddlebags moved straight for the crowd. A few had reloaded and resumed shooting, but their bullets still stopped in midair before falling to the ground.

People were being pushed aside as Phantom walked through the crowd. A few fired, but many were wary of shooting at their fellow gang members. The saddlebags continued straight for Marta and Wind Rock.

"Stop," White-Eye said.

The saddlebags stopped. They were now almost to the river, and most of the men were behind Phantom. Which also meant many guns could be pointed in Marta's direction.

Wind Rock was mounted. She seemed tired. Maybe it was from the healing, but Marta sensed she was weary of hiding her powers. Plus, Marta didn't see any other way clear. She did have to make sure these men were held up so word wouldn't get to McKinley, though.

Marta flashed a smile to clue Wind Rock into her plan.

She looked back up at the encampment. Among the tents, horses, and other supplies, there was an abundance of rope. She used air spells to make the ropes come alive.

Tents, clothes, and other items hanging on rope came down. Ropes fell from their holding places, waiting for the next time the gang rustled cattle. Many were too long for what Marta needed them for, so she cut them with magic.

Like silent snakes, the ropes slithered down the river embankment. When they came upon a person, they jumped and either secured one hand to another or two feet together.

Wind Rock could see what Marta was doing. She gave a wry smile as she turned to watch.

White-Eye couldn't see what she was doing. Instead, he only had eyes for one thing—his precious gold. "Now why don't you put down the money, undo your magic trick, and move over there?" He gestured with his chin.

Marta shook her head. He hadn't even noticed his men going down left and right with their new bonds. She'd even stuffed their mouths with air, so they couldn't call out. It didn't take long before White-Eye was the last one standing. She decided to finish mounting. She didn't even look as the last two ropes bound him, making him drop his gun in the river.

"Hey," he yelled. Marta hadn't bothered to gag him as he fell back into the shallow river with a splash.

"If you'll excuse me, we have somewhere we need to be," Marta said. She watched the man squirm to the shore next to the healed man. Marta assessed him with the magic to be sure he would live.

"He'll be fine," Wind Rock said.

Phantom reappeared, moving to put the saddlebags on Wind Rock's horse.

"What the hell was all that?" Marta asked.

Phantom just turned and started skipping upstream.

Marta took a rock with the power and flung it right at his head. Since he didn't see it coming, it landed a blow.

He stopped and turned slowly back. He didn't rub the back of his head. Though not a big rock, it had hit him with some force. He blinked a few times, but he didn't say anything in response.

Annoyed, Marta crossed her arms under her breasts. She wasn't going to take any more of his nonsense.

Phantom hissed. "If I tell all, you won't learn anything."

Marta cocked her head. "I won't learn anything if you don't tell me."

Phantom rolled his eyes. "That is not how the world works."

"Oh?" Marta's brow furrowed. "How does the world work?"

Phantom shook his head. "You cannot learn the ways of the world from me telling you. You need to go through your trials. Once you have gone through your trials, you will know how the world works."

Marta thought back to everything that had happened since learning she had magical abilities. It seemed like there was no end to the trials she went through. "How many more trials do I need to go through?"

"On this trip, this life, or the existence of your soul?"

Marta huffed. "Let's start with this trip."

Phantom shrugged. "Just a few more, I think."

"You think?" Marta was steamed now. Was she even learning anything from these trials? "So, what am I supposed to learn from this trial?"

"You will see," Phantom replied.

Wind Rock put up a hand to forestall Marta. "What I want to know is what was wrong with you this morning? Was McKinley in your dreams or something?"

Marta was glad for the change of subject, and it was a good thing to change to as she wanted to know this as well.

Phantom eyed Wind Rock. "He is an infection on my powers. He lords it over me, but I will get the last laugh. Not my dreams. I was fighting his connection to me. I think I was successful."

Marta shuddered. "What happens if he completes the connection? Will he know we are coming for him?"

Phantom cocked his head. "He knows I am coming for him like he knows you are. I'm not sure he knows about Wind Rock, and I doubt he knows we are all working together."

Marta sighed in relief. So much could go wrong if the element of surprise were gone.

She heard White-Eye spit behind her. She'd forgotten anyone else was around.

He was eying her when she turned in her saddle. "I will hunt you all down to make you pay for what you have done. That McKinley you speak of is nothing compared to how dangerous I am."

Marta laughed as she put her heels into her horse to urge it onward. It was time they got going anyway.

"You hear me, Injun lover? I'm going to hunt you down and kill you if it is the last thing I do!"

CHAPTER 32—TRADING POST

Marta's stomach grumbled. They were out of hardtack and jerky, so they would need to stop soon to forage for something. She hadn't packed the necessary provisions before setting out for a journey of this length. The sun was an hour from being at its peak.

Phantom stood in the middle of the path instead of his usual meditation alongside. At seeing him, Marta kicked her horse to a trot. Wind Rock followed suit. As they got close, Phantom pointed to the south. "There is a trading post there. Get some food for the days ahead. We have plenty of money."

"Days?" Marta questioned. "We're going to be at Lincoln tonight."

Phantom nodded. "We'll scout the camp, report to the council in the dream realm, then wait for reinforcements. That may be several days' worth of food that you two will need. Then there is your trip home once we are successful."

Marta hung her head. She had only seen the goal of reaching the encampment, not what waited for her beyond it. Phantom was right—they sorely needed supplies.

Phantom pointed to the west again. "I will find a nice place to meditate." With that, he turned and skipped down the trail.

Marta turned her horse to the south. The trading post ended up being just over the hill a few hundred yards away, so not too far from their current path. It sat on a crossroads of sorts. One road was going North-South, and a junction went West. The path they had been on all day circled the hill, crossing the North-South road and fed into the road going West.

The trading post wasn't much more than a shack. A couple of wagons and a few horses were hitched to the front. People ambled about, mainly leaving, but what drew Marta's eye was a preacher standing next to a donkey. A sign that said, "Save First Methodist Church," hung from the burrow.

The preacher saw Marta and Wind Rock approach, so he moved toward them. Marta stopped her horse next to a hitching post. "You look like a good Christian woman," the preacher said.

Marta grunted. "If you don't mind, we're just weary travelers in need of a few quick supplies." She noted the preacher didn't pay any attention to Wind Rock as they tied up their horses.

"Sorry to interrupt your day. I just need a minute of your time."

Marta shook her head. "I'm in a hurry. I'll be passing through again, though. Maybe I'll have time then."

"I can get the supplies, Marta," Wind Rock said. "You can talk like a good Christian woman should." She gave a half-smile as she reached into one of the saddlebags for a few coins.

"Marta, huh? That is such a pretty Christian name. I'm Reverend Hubbard with the First Methodist Church in Salina." The man held out his hand for a shake.

Wind Rock went inside before Marta could say anything. So, Marta turned her sour expression on the reverend and crossed her arms, ignoring his hand. This trading post was a good ten miles to the north of Salina.

"Right. You're in a hurry, so I'll spare you the pleasantries," Hubbard said. He took in a deep breath. "I'm here today asking if anyone is willing and able to spare a few coins for the rebuilding of our church."

Marta cocked her head. "Rebuilding?" she questioned.

Hubbard nodded. "Yes. We were so eager to build, and we didn't quite know what we were up against here in Kansas. The wind is a mighty force. Most of our money was put into the first attempt to build the church. Got one wall of brick completely up before we were struck down."

Marta smiled. "Sounds like God didn't want you to build."

Hubbard arched an eyebrow. "He works in mysterious ways. He wanted us to learn a lesson of some kind, but we don't look at it as an omen."

This was getting interesting. Marta uncrossed her arms. "Why do you think it wasn't an omen?"

"I see the light, grace, and beauty of this world. Omens are for dark forces, Marta. Are you not a Christian woman?"

Marta shrugged. "I walk a path of good, if that counts." Hubbard just stared. She added, "I've been going to church every Sunday for the last year if that is what you mean." She didn't mention it was because she was interested in the fellow she shared the pew with, and she was curious to know if the pastor were a warlock.

Hubbard nodded. "Yes, good for you. Now, back to my problem. We've sought the counsel of more professional builders, and are now ready to build a proper church that can withstand the Kansas wind. We just need good folks to help us purchase the materials for our house of God."

Marta nodded. She'd heard Goodman spout the same sort of spiel before St. Joseph's was built. She hadn't donated to that cause. "I wish I could help, but I don't have any money." It was a lie, and she didn't look at her saddle where her money was currently hidden.

Hubbard frowned. "You don't have an Indian Head to spare? Every cent helps."

Marta shook her head.

"What did you plan to pay for goods at the trading post then?"

Hubbard asked.

Marta stiffened as she remembered all the money Phantom had stolen from the outlaws, which Wind Rock was now using. It wasn't her money, but who did it belong to? She thought a little bending of the truth wouldn't hurt. "My friend is using the only money we have for our needs."

Wind Rock scoffed behind Marta. She was done inside, and started packing what she'd bought into Marta's saddlebags.

Marta turned to the young woman. "What?"

"We have plenty to spare," she answered.

"You don't even know what he wants to use the money for," Marta retorted.

Wind Rock rolled her eyes. "The trading post has thin walls."

Hubbard raised his eyebrows. "So, you are willing to donate to my church? Are you a convert?"

Wind Rock shook her head. "No. I still pray to the gods of the prairie. While I don't believe the same thing you do, a person in need is a person in need."

Wind Rock looked at Marta with wide eyes. "Like a certain woman yesterday."

Marta sighed. Helping someone stay alive was one thing. She just didn't trust churches, not since Goodman showed his true self and his quest for power. Marta turned on the reverend. "What does your church do for your community?"

"Do?" Hubbard questioned. "We spread the word of God, of course."

Marta cocked her head, shoulders slumping. "Anything else?"

Hubbard scratched his temple. After a moment, he said, "Well, we do have fellowship in that we share meals, and I also do some counseling for troubled souls. I'd like to think we are trying to build a strong community, too."

"See, he helps people," Wind Rock said.

Marta didn't need Wind Rock to point that out.

"Yes, we help tons of people," Hubbard said. "Even people who don't go to our church. If we have the resources, we help anyone capable of receiving it."

"And a church will help you do that?" Wind Rock asked.

"And a church will help," Hubbard echoed.

"All right," Marta said. She went over to Wind Rock's horse. She untied the two saddlebags with the money in them, then slid them off the horse. They were heavy, but she managed to not let them hit the ground. "That your donkey?" she asked.

Hubbard took a step toward her. "Here, let me empty those for you."

Marta pulled them back. "You can have the damn saddlebags, too. I'll put them on your donkey."

It could have been the sting to her voice or the venom in her eyes, but the reverend took a step back and let her take the bags to his donkey.

"Thank you both for your generosity," Hubbard said. "We may not all believe in the same god, but you are both good people." He gave them a little bow.

She almost used the power for an assist, but she realized it would be noticeable if she were suddenly able to carry the bags without issue. It wouldn't be smart to get caught using her powers here. She trudged along the best she could.

Marta put the saddlebags on the donkey, wondering if this money was going to help people in the future. She felt a bit relieved to no longer have the stuff. Hopefully, Phantom would have no problem with her giving it away. She quickly returned to the hitching post.

"We need to be off," Marta said as she untied her horse. Wind Rock did the same and mounted up.

"May your journey be blessed," Hubbard said, raising a hand. "I won't forget this or you for that matter."

Marta mounted, giving him a bow from her saddle. "Good luck, Reverend."

He smiled and nodded. Marta put a heel to her horse to get it to walk off. She didn't look back as some other riders approached and Hubbard went to speak to them. He wouldn't know just how blessed he was until later.

CHAPTER 33—FIRE

Marta rode with her head down. Now that she had time to reflect on it more, she realized she should have asked more questions before handing over the money. She wasn't completely convinced the reverend wasn't a warlock. Why had she given all that money to him? Then again, not everyone was a warlock. Assuming they were one wasn't helping. She still had the money for the journey home, anyway.

It was Wind Rock's prompting that made Marta want to do some good with that bad money. Her keeping it was almost as bad as the thieves taking it, but that thought didn't make her feel better. Just because someone was asking for money didn't mean they deserved it, right?

Marta spared a look at Wind Rock. She was riding next to Phantom as he walked. He was sticking around instead of skipping ahead, which was something new. They weren't talking, though. Instead, they seemed focused on a plume of smoke up ahead. Marta hadn't noticed it before. They were heading right for it.

Besides some trees near the river, they were traveling over hilly terrain with prairie grass covering most of the landscape. It reminded her of home but with even fewer trees if that were possible. Around here, as she thought it would be about the same as home, spring was a time for controlled burnings to clear out the old grass, stop any new trees from trying to sprout, and making way for a revitalized stand of grasses for the cattle to graze on.

Watching the smoke, she became concerned about another factor—the wind. It was in their faces today. It felt like it was going to get even stronger, which made controlling this blaze hard. Was this blaze even controlled at all?

They topped another rise, and Marta got a look at what was going on. They were still a couple of miles from it, but it was getting bigger with the wind fanning things. She also spotted several homes between her and the fire. The fire was heading right toward those houses.

"We've got to stop it," Marta called.

Phantom reached out, touching Wind Rock's leg. They both stopped.

"What do we have to stop?" Phantom asked.

Marta pointed ahead. "The fire."

Phantom shook his head. "We do not have to do anything. You may *want* to do something, but it is only a want."

Marta rolled her eyes. "Yes, we do *have* to do something. People and animals will be hurt if we don't. These families may lose everything they possess, if they even escape with their lives. We should have kept the money to help them." She groaned. "Why did we give all of our money away?"

Phantom arched an eyebrow in response. He'd been more understanding than Marta had thought he would be when Wind Rock told him what they had done.

"We don't have to fix everything in the world," Wind Rock said. "If you feel you must do this, then do it. Don't let us get in the way."

Marta crossed her arms. "Back at the trading post, you said that if we have the means to help someone, then we should." She was yelling, but she didn't care.

Apparently, Wind Rock didn't either. Her stony expression remained unchanged. "I did say that. That was about money, though. This is about using your power to control something you couldn't without it. Therefore, you are exploiting your power to change something. Are you sure this is something you should do?"

Marta furrowed her brow. What the hell kind of argument was this?

Phantom turned ahead. "You've also been hesitant to use your power for fear of reports of your usage getting back to McKinley."

"No one is around," Marta said, pointing to the landscape. The few homes she saw had no visible people. "Besides, putting out the fire could be done without people finding out that I am doing it."

Phantom shrugged. "If you feel you must do it, then do it."

Marta grunted. She then gave a "haw" as she spurred her horse to a gallop to the closest edge of the fire. It took her five minutes before she was close enough to start working magic on it, but far enough away that she wasn't feeling its effects. The fire was an ellipsis about a hundred yards long and half that wide.

Marta connected to the orb of power, then pushed the air spell toward the flames and across the top. Her goal was to whisk the fire away like blowing out a candle. The added air only fueled the fire, and the flames grew higher. If anything, she had blown away a bunch of the smoke to allow the fire to breed through more air and grass.

Her horse backed up at seeing the flames surge forward. It quickly expanded to about a hundred and fifty yards long. Marta grumbled in disgust with the fire now closer, and she started to feel its effects. Why didn't her spell work?

She glanced back. A farmer was now out of his home, working on protecting his place. If she sent a river of water through the air to put this thing out, he would see. Hell, everyone for miles around would see such a maneuver. She would certainly be found out then. Plus, the distances were a little much for her to do this.

Wind Rock approached on her horse at a trot with Phantom still skipping along beside her. He didn't even seem out of breath when he and Wind Rock stopped beside Marta.

"I see you've succeeded in making the fire bigger," Phantom said.

Marta set her jaw, returning to looking the blaze over. "That isn't helping."

"Need any help?" Wind Rock asked.

Marta saw Phantom place a hand on Wind Rock's knee out of the corner of her eye.

"Er," Wind Rock started. "What I mean to say is do you need any help with your spell? I'm not going to help put this out."

"You two have the abilities to put this fire out. Why don't you want to help me?" Marta rubbed her forehead as she waited for an answer.

Nobody said anything as the fire spread. The longer they were there, the more Marta wanted to scream. At the current rate of expansion, the fire would reach two hundred yards long in the next few minutes and they would have to move back.

"What have you tried?" Phantom asked.

"The air spell," Marta stated, biting off the sting in her voice.

"Why?"

"Because it's worked for me in the past," Marta spat.

"What else can you do?" Phantom asked in a plain tone.

Marta pointed to the fire. "I could upturn Earth, but that would take forever to get this big of a blaze out."

Phantom nodded.

"I could use the water spell to pull moisture to the fire to douse it out. The amount of water required would need to be taken from more than just the air. It would take a lot of power and a long time to get enough water from the Saline a half-mile away to this blaze."

Phantom nodded. "Go on."

"I can't use spirit or fire as they would be no good here."

"Oh?" Phantom turned toward her, arching a brow.

"Yes, the spirit spell would do nothing since there is no spirit to the fire."

Phantom nodded. "And why not use fire?"

Marta turned, dropped her hand to her side, and stared at Phantom. What kind of nonsense was this?

Wind Rock nodded. "You have to fight fire with fire."

Marta cocked her head. She recalled Goodman saying something similar while they were fighting to swim in the river, only about water. She'd been able to push Goodman and Bourne to the shore with the water spell. She just hadn't been able to push herself.

Marta turned to study the blaze. If she pushed the fire spell into the fire, it should have the opposite effect of the air spell in that the flames would be cut off from the oxygen needed to sustain it. Why hadn't she seen this earlier? Hell, why hadn't these two just tell her this to begin with?

Marta sighed as she started the new spell. Usually, she used this spell to conjure up a fireball or to light something. Now she pushed the spell onto the already existing flames. As soon as she did, the flame would go out and she would go to the next one.

This was much different than launching a fireball. With that, there were other elements than just fire to get it to shoot and shoot straight. This way, she was putting the raw fire element of magic out into the open. With some exertion, she could conjure this basic of a spell from about two hundred and fifty yards away.

After a while of putting out individual flames, she noted that some of the parts she had already put out were starting back up. She had thought she was succeeding, but she wasn't.

She glanced at her companions, but she didn't ask them for more advice. Instead, she made the spell bigger and bigger. She made it as big as the current area if not a little more. The flame fed into her spell, and the spell pushed back. Sweat from the heat and exertion was soon on her brow, threatening to fall into her eyes. Marta felt every single ache and pain in her body, magnified tenfold. She kept at it, though, and soon the entire thing was snuffed out.

She held the spell there in fear that if she let it go too soon, the fire would start back up.

"Great," Phantom called. He started to skip off.

"Hold it," Marta called. For good measure, she encased Phantom in air in mid-skip. "Why didn't you want to put out the fire?"

She looked at Wind Rock to indicate she was included in the question.

Wind Rock shook her head. "Phantom said you had to learn."

"Silence," Phantom called.

"You've already told her this," Wind Rock started. She turned to Marta. "You've got to learn certain things. Phantom called them your trials."

Marta nodded. "Yes, I remember. So, that is why he prevented you from helping me with the spells?"

Wind Rock shrugged. "Yes. Something you'll learn, or maybe everything you'll learn, is needed in the fight ahead."

Marta didn't know what to say. She just watched as Wind Rock moved her horse along the trail. She stopped next to Phantom. "Are you coming?" she called over her shoulder.

Marta dropped the air spell on Phantom, allowing him to skip ahead as he usually did. She still held the fire spell, continuing to hold it until they were past the charred zone. She kept an eye on it as long as she could to be sure it didn't flare up again, dropping the spell after about a hundred yards past it.

The entire time, she thought about what it was she was supposed to learn. She just didn't know what she didn't know. Right now, she didn't know how this was going to help her in the fight to come. She just hoped that Phantom was right, and this would win the day for them. She shuddered to think about what might happen if Phantom were wrong.

CHAPTER 34—WHY BE A SHERIFF?

Lunchtime came and went with no food. It was close to one o'clock when a warlock came for Bourne again rather than a serving witch bringing him food. What did McKinley want with him during the day? Hell, what did the lunatic want with him at all?

Bourne wondered if Marta being due here this evening meant he wouldn't get dinner with the bishop, and this was to make up for it. It wasn't a comforting thought, but maybe this was Bourne's last meal. He wished she would stay away since she was outnumbered here.

He walked the entire way to McKinley's house wondering if there was something he could say to the man to somehow give Marta an edge in the coming battle. He certainly couldn't use her former fight against Goodman or even Rathbone. But there might be something else. He just couldn't see it right now.

This time, the warlock followed Bourne into McKinley's house instead of turning at the door. Bourne went to the dining hall, finding five warlocks in addition to McKinley already seated and eating. Place settings for Bourne and the warlock that brought him waited. The warlock took the seat to the side of Bourne's normal spot at the end of the table, leaving it open for him.

Another change was that the serving women were dressed for once. As Bourne slowly took his seat, Greta put down a glass of tea. When she scurried away, Beth put down a plate with a thick slice of roast beef, fresh bread, and steamy mashed potatoes. Among the smells of the food was a hint of garlic. It made Bourne salivate.

Bourne sighed. There were just too many changes in all of this. He wanted to dig into the food, but he also wanted to keep an eye on his captors. The meal certainly was fitting for a final meal, though.

Knives scraping plates and the chewing from the men filled the air. Over the din, McKinley said, "You missed the prayer."

Bourne hadn't cut into his roast yet, and he didn't know how to respond.

The warlock who brought Bourne said, "Sorry, Bishop. I misjudged the time."

"No excuses," McKinley called around a mouthful of food.

"Not an excuse, my lord. I am simply saying I know what I did wrong, and I will fix it in the future. Please forgive me." The warlock gave a nod at the end.

McKinley swallowed, pointing his knife at the man. "See that this doesn't happen again."

The warlock nodded again.

Bourne was glad he hadn't been called out for this. He did wonder if he shouldn't offer a prayer on his own. Bowing his head, he whispered his prayer. "Please Lord, hear me out. If this is my last meal, please bless it as well as your soldier about to receive it. I hope that when you take me home, you recall all the good that I have done. I thank you for the time you have given me on this Earth and for receiving my sister and nephew in your glorious kingdom. Amen."

He didn't think his whisper could even be heard by his neighbors as quietly as he spoke, but Bourne looked up and found McKinley staring at him, fork and knife hovering over his food. "So, you think this is your last meal?"

Bourne shrugged, feeling his face flush. "You could hear that?"

McKinley grunted. "You know people with magical abilities can hear, see, smell, taste, and feel better than normal folk, right?"

Bourne shrugged. He recalled Marta mentioning something like that.

"So, back to you thinking this is your last meal. I find several things curious here. Do you feel like you've accomplished your goals in life?"

"That was between me and my God." Bourne picked up his steak knife, wondering if he could use it as a weapon, but it seemed as dull as a butter knife.

"I am your God," McKinley said coolly. He still stared.

Bourne raised his eyebrows, glancing at the others at the table. Some nodded and smiled. Instead of questioning the madness of the statement, Bourne shifted his attention to cutting his roast beef.

"What's with us having company today?" Bourne asked.

McKinley shook his head. "I always eat with different soldiers every lunch and dinner, depending on who is free from watch duty. I've made exceptions the last couple of evenings to talk to you alone."

Bourne paused his fork and knife. "So, this is a normal lunch?"

McKinley smiled. "Normal, though it's usually taken in silence. Since you are talking, how about answering something I've wanted to know? Tell me, Jethro Bourne, why are you a sheriff?"

Bourne stopped cutting his beef. This wasn't the type of question he expected from the man, especially after declaring himself a god. "I've got my reasons."

McKinley rolled his eyes. "Come now. Let's not play games. I want to know your reasons."

Bourne huffed. He would rather they all ate in silence like the warlocks seemed to be doing. "I want to help people."

"There are tons of ways to help people. Why are you a sheriff, though?" McKinley inquired.

Bourne shrugged. "I guess I could set out to rule the world."

The warlocks around the table stopped eating, almost seeming to freeze.

McKinley straightened, arching his eyebrows. He broke the silence by saying, "I'm not trying to rule the world. I want to lead it to greatness. Get everyone to live together in peace and harmony. Unite the people to where there is no war."

Everyone returned to eating.

Bourne was dismayed that his dig hadn't enraged the psycho. Instead, he had some good thoughts. "The way you are going about it is causing fighting already. What makes you think that will end when you are done? What makes you think someone won't challenge you?"

"Nobody will be able to challenge me."

"Even the greatest conqueror, Genghis Khan, was killed in a revolt. Are you saying people won't revolt?"

McKinley smiled. "But I have magic where Genghis Khan did not."

"And do you trust everyone who has magic to not come after you?"

A few heads turned toward Bourne, and their eyes stared him down. He ignored the looks, especially with others pretending to not have heard.

McKinley frowned. "Of course I don't trust everyone. I do have safeguards in place, though. I've also got two of the three forces of the orb under my control. Once I have Marta, I'll have the most powerful witch and can get the other. Then I'll truly be unstoppable. I'll be an invincible God."

Bourne nodded. "You'll need to be invincible when your Judas betrays you."

The few who stared at Bourne were joined by others. Bourne didn't care if he wasn't liked at the table. What was the worst they could do? Kill him? He was already marked for death.

McKinley huffed, squinting at Bourne. "You'll see. I will be unstoppable."

McKinley pointed to Bourne. "But you haven't fully answered my question. Why did you become a sheriff?"

Bourne shrugged. He wasn't sure how his being sheriff made any difference compared to a god ascending to ruling the world. "Does it matter?"

The warlocks returned to their food, ignoring Bourne again. They maintained their silence, probably finding this questioning dull.

McKinley wagged his finger. "Yes, it matters. Your connection to Marta is the only thing currently keeping you alive, but I've got other ways to extract the truth from you."

Sighing, Bourne stared at the untouched food on his plate. "After my parents died, I had a hard time with the farm. I had to steal to keep food on the table. I fell in with a gang until they started doing more than just stealing. When I went my separate way, I got caught committing a small crime."

"So, you were at a low point in your life?"

Bourne nodded. "The sheriff who hauled me in took pity on me. He got the judge to go light on my sentence so he could train me to eventually become a deputy. My skills with theft were now being utilized to prevent it. I also knew the area, so I could help head off criminals after their acts."

Bourne stopped, satisfied he'd complied fully with answering the question.

McKinley squinted. "You've explained how you became a lawman, but you haven't explained how you became sheriff."

Bourne sighed. "I was finally appreciated, and I was good at it. People took note, and they wanted me to step up when Davis County needed a new sheriff. Being sheriff kept me fed and allowed me to take care of my sister for a time. When she died and I had to raise my nephew, I knew he needed a good role model. Really, though, I had found my calling. It felt good to help people who were wronged. I felt like I was atoning for the sins of my past."

Done, Bourne took a bite of the roast beef. It melted in his mouth as he chewed, and he appreciated the meat. He also lifted his head high to stare at McKinley. "Does that answer your question?"

McKinley blinked a few times. "Yes," he simply said.

Bourne returned his attention to his food. He had his fork halfway to his mouth when McKinley spoke next. "You know your calling sounds a lot like mine."

Bourne put the food in his mouth, smiling as he chewed. He swallowed before he said, "Except in reverse."

"Oh?" McKinley questioned.

Bourne nodded as he readied another bite. "I went from bad to good in my calling. You've gone to evil with yours."

A few warlocks huffed or made their displeasure of what Bourne was saying clear in other ways. Not that Bourne cared. His only goal was pissing off McKinley. Maybe that would be the edge Marta would need in the coming fight.

"Come now, Sheriff. You can't mean that," McKinley said, calmer than Bourne would have expected.

Bourne shrugged. "In fact, I think your madness will be your downfall. Mark my words… Marta may not be able to stop you, but someone can."

McKinley glared as Bourne took another bite. He tried to look hopeful. He *did* hope Marta could stop this man. Bourne wasn't sure how he could go on if he lost her. Especially losing her to this mad scheme and this evil man. She had to come out on top, right?

CHAPTER 35—REVENGE

After leaving the fire and progressing down the trail, Marta found it hard to keep her eyes open. The warm sun made things worse. She nodded off in her saddle several times only to be awakened immediately.

"You need some rest," Wind Rock said.

Marta slowly blinked as she shook her head. "I'll be fine. We need to make it the rest of the way to McKinley's today."

"We'll make it even if we stop to rest for a while."

Marta stubbornly shook her head. They continued, but not for long.

Suddenly, Marta hovered a foot off the ground as she was carried by Wind Rock's air spell. Had Marta fallen from her horse? She didn't remember Wind Rock even grabbing the power, so Marta must have nodded off.

Wind Rock set Marta down with a nice clump of grass as a pillow. She didn't fight the girl. Instead, she let herself drift off into slumber.

She was roused from her nap by Wind Rock shaking her. "How long was I out?" Marta asked.

"An hour. Some men would like a word with you," Wind Rock said.

Marta looked up to find the gang of outlaws from the river. On their horses, they surrounded Marta, Wind Rock, and Phantom. They had gotten free of their bonds and had caught up to them. Wind Rock gave Marta a hand in standing. Phantom just sat on the ground with his eyes closed, meditating yet again.

"Give us back our money and prepare to die," White-Eye called.

He hadn't drawn a weapon, and neither had anyone else. Marta found this strange. "Don't you know what you are up against?"

White-Eye nodded. "Yep."

Marta sighed. It appeared she would have to teach these men another lesson. "You know I have a bunch of tricks up my sleeves, yet you've still come after me. Why?"

White-Eye held up a cross with a ruby in the middle of it. "I've got a trick up my sleeve as well."

Marta's mouth went dry. She didn't have to try to reach the magical orb to know the artifact being held up was a talisman. She did anyway because the sooner she started breaking the block on her powers, the more likely she would succeed before she was full of bullets. Her stomach lurched at not even getting close to a connection.

White-Eye smirked. "So, where is my money?"

"Our money," another gang member corrected.

Without turning from Marta, White-Eye nodded. "Our money. Where is our money?"

Marta was still working on getting through the block.

"It's around," she finally said, hiding her nervousness from her voice.

White-Eye arched his eyebrows. "Oh?"

Marta glanced at Wind Rock. Her head was cocked, her face scrunched. She seemed oblivious. Phantom, still sitting, now stared at a nearby tree with glazed eyes and a half-smirk. "Psst," Marta quietly sounded.

Phantom either didn't hear her or didn't want to break his concentration with the tree he was so interested in. When Wind Rock turned in her direction, Marta whispered, "I'll push you to the orb."

Wind Rock shook her head.

Marta huffed, but she kept her voice low. "This is life or death. I'll help you get connected!"

"Unless you two are whispering about who will be giving me our money, I'd rather your focus was on me," White-Eye called.

Suddenly, Marta felt Wind Rock pushing on Marta's continued effort to reach for the power. Apparently, she would rather Marta get them out of this than do it herself. The problem was that Marta still wasn't even close to being able to connect with the orb. This talisman was stronger than any Marta had run up against before.

White-Eye drew his pistol. "I don't see anyone moving to get my money."

Other pistols and rifles were drawn by the gang, then menacingly waved about. A few people aimed at Marta, Wind Rock, or Phantom, but they seemed to be taking their cues from their leader. Each gun made Marta's gut tighten more and more.

Marta felt her lip quiver. She needed to act fast if she wanted to live through the rest of the day. The talisman gave her an idea. She pointed to it. "Where did you get that cross?"

White-Eye squinted at her. "What does that matter?"

"Well, I know you didn't have it this morning. I'm curious as to where it came from and how you knew it would prevent me from doing my tricks."

White-Eye shrugged. "Is it working?"

Marta gave a nervous giggle. "Of course not."

White-Eye arched an eyebrow. "You seem doubtful. You wouldn't lie, would you?"

"Ha," she spat. Yes, she was lying, but she wasn't going to tell him that. Wind Rock was still trying to boost Marta to reach the magic.

"I tell you what," Marta began as she stepped forward, trying to exude confidence even though her heart wanted to explode. "We're both interested in something, so let's swap. I'll tell you where the money is if you tell me where you got the cross."

"Just like that, you'll give us back our money if I tell you about this..." White-Eye gestured at the cross. "This gaudy-looking power blocker?"

"Yes, the talisman."

"Talisman," White-Eye repeated. "That's what he called it."

"Who called it that?" Marta asked.

"Don't know," White-Eye said as he shook his head. "Never seen the guy before. Didn't see him today either. He just showed up around an hour after you left, dressed in a robe with a hood that covered his head. He said the talisman would let me shoot you all if we wanted to since you would be powerless to stop it. He also said you were heading for Lincoln, and, if we hurried, we'd easily catch up to you on this particular trail."

Marta took this information in stride. The hooded man must have been McKinley. But why would he send these ruffians to do his dirty work? Plus, why kill her when he had sent Rathbone to capture her in the first place? Something didn't seem right.

"So, where's our money," White-Eye asked.

"What makes you think you can trust that person?"

White-Eye shrugged. "They didn't have a reason to lie."

Marta rolled her eyes. "How do you know that artifact can do what they claimed it can?"

White-Eye glanced around. "I don't see any rope snakes and all my men are still armed."

"You and your men are still armed because there is more than one way to stop a bullet."

White-Eye nodded. "This... I've got to see." He cocked the gun.

"Wait," Marta called, raising a hand. How could she be so careless? She didn't have the means to stop bullets. Not yet.

White-Eye smirked.

Marta put her hand down. "You don't need to test me. Besides, I made you a promise I'd tell you where your money is. I can't over the noise of gunshots."

White-Eye sighed. "I feel like you are playing games with me."

Marta closed her eyes. "I'm sorry you feel that way. I..." She didn't know what else to say. All her attempts to connect with the power were coming up short.

She needed to void her mind of all thoughts and emotions to get the power. Letting out a breath, she made the strongest push she could to grab the orb of power. She missed, but it was closer.

She let another breath out as White-Eye asked something. She then made another grab.

Light filled her from head to toe. She opened her eyes, senses more aware of her surroundings even with the tenuous connection. She could hear the heartbeats of the men and horses who surrounded her. The smell of the wheat field they were next to filled her. A wagon was a mile away and coming down the road at top speed, but she could see the lone person on the seat was perspiring with exertion. Even though it was a trickle compared to normal, the power made her feel more alive. Maybe it was facing near-certain death that made her want to bask in the magic.

"I'm sorry. What did you say?" Marta asked.

White-Eye huffed. He cocked his pistol, aiming it in her direction. "I prompted you to continue what you were saying."

Marta took a breath, using the air spell to pack the air between the outlaws and her, Wind Rock, and Phantom. Wind Rock still helped with Marta's connection to the power, so she couldn't grab it herself. Thus, Marta had to work to protect her. Marta still didn't know whether Phantom could protect himself or not, but she thought she could also protect him until his status became clear. He still stared into the nearby cottonwoods, obvious.

Marta nodded. "It is my turn to fulfill my part of the agreement."

She sent a ball of hardened air at the cross. It hit with a satisfying ping, knocking the talisman from the man's hand. It had taken quite a bit of effort to do this stunt, but it should prove to the gang that she could still do her tricks. And since they had seen her do magic with the ropes, she didn't see the harm in doing more magic now.

"I think you are better off taking that thing to church as it is better suited for such a place. Hell, you may even find your money there since that's where I donated it."

White-Eye eyed the cross that had fallen from his hand. As Marta finished her speech, he jerked upright to stare at her with wild eyes. "You've donated our money to some church?"

Marta nodded.

"What church? Where?" the outlaw asked.

"I can't say," Marta said. "I've honestly forgotten." It was another lie, but so what?

White-Eye raised his gun. "Then there is nothing keeping you alive." Others raised their weapons, too, which made Marta want to laugh since her shield would stop them all.

"Wait!" a man called. It was the driver from the fast-approaching wagon. It left the road, heading for the group. Now that he was closer, Marta could tell this was the man Wind Rock had healed that morning.

The man didn't stop until he was behind Marta. Not sure of his intentions, Marta extended her shield behind her and her companions.

"You should be ashamed of yourselves," the man called. "These people saved my life. Isn't that worth anything?"

Apparently, nobody was moved by this plea since the guns all stayed pointed at Marta. She wondered if the newcomer would get shot by his own gang. Hell, they'd probably shot him to begin with.

Building up the shield to surround them with the talisman nearby had been challenging. She didn't see how she could use her power to fight the gang while keeping the shield up at the same time. Somehow, she would need to get away from the talisman to do more. She thought fast for some way for her, Wind Rock, and Phantom to exit this situation. Marta wished she had a better hold on the magical orb. She would be unstoppable if she did.

CHAPTER 36—TAKING THE LEAD

Some of the outlaws seemed unsure about the healed man suddenly showing up. A few even backed away from White-Eye.

"These three have taken our money, Clint," White-Eye spat.

Marta glanced back at the healed man. He jumped to his feet, glaring at White-Eye.

"We can get more money," Clint started. "What we can't do is come back from the grave. These people have kept me on the right side of the dirt for a while longer."

White-Eye waved him off. "Bah. Barely getting by and living a life are two different things. I'd rather be dead than let people walk all over me!"

There were a few shouts of agreement from the others. These were the ones who weren't shying away from the arguing men.

"Is there some bad blood between you two?" Marta asked.

"Stay out of this," White-Eye called.

Clint nodded. "Yes, there is some bad blood. This isn't the first time this yellow-bellied lowlife has tried to take over the gang."

Marta rolled her eyes. This was outlaw politics, and she was right in the middle of it. Hell, she'd thought that White-Eye was the one in charge, not Clint.

"I'm not the yellow-bellied lowlife," White-Eye shouted. "You're the yellow-bellied lowlife, Clint."

Clint chortled. "My, how original. Does your mama know the idiot of a son she raised?"

White-Eye scowled, raising his gun. "Don't talk ill about my mother, God rest her soul."

Clint cocked his head. "Oh, she passed? What? Couldn't live without you?"

"I shot her the day she tried to steal from me," White-Eye roared. "You know that, Clint."

Clint nodded. "So you keep saying." He pointed at White-Eye. "But you wouldn't shoot me, now would you, son?"

Marta's eyes bugged out. Son? The two men both appeared to be around forty years old. Clint must have aged well, and White-Eye must have had a rough life to look older than he was. Plus, they hadn't acted like father and son this entire time. Surely this was just an expression.

White-Eye cocked his gun. "You wanna bet?"

Clint sighed. "You wouldn't dare."

"Are you really his father?" Marta asked.

He nodded, still staring White-Eye down.

At least it put that question to rest. "You do realize a witch is standing between you two, right?" Marta asked.

Wind Rock coughed.

"Well, two witches and a phantom."

Marta looked back and forth between father and son, but neither seemed impressed.

Marta tsked. "I've also got a shield of air up, so you two can't shoot each other."

"Stay out of this, witch," White-Eye called.

Clint groaned. "Listen to her, son. She is educating you better than your whore of a mama ever did."

"Whose fault was it that she was the only one around to educate me?" White-Eye retorted.

"I'm just saying that she is trying to save you some ammunition. Put down the gun, son. Let's hear what else the wise woman has to say."

Marta felt like she was being put on the spot.

White-Eye gave a few sidelong glances at the gang around him. There were more than a few who were moving their horses away from White-Eye, toward Clint's wagon. A couple seemed to square off against others in the gang.

Marta closed her eyes to consider all this. With her power being limited by the talisman, there was only so much she could do to protect herself. Doing more to protect one half of the gang over the other wouldn't work. Did she even care about the lives of these men?

"She's not wise," White-Eye said. "She's a thief and a liar. Hell, she even claims to have given our money to some church. How stupid would I have to be to believe that?"

Clint pointed to Marta and Wind Rock's horses. "Well, I don't exactly see the saddlebags the money was in, do you?"

White-Eye glanced at the horses. "She must have hidden it somewhere. I know it ain't in no damn church."

"So, how are you going to find it?" Clint asked. "Kill her... and then ask her *corpse* where she hid it? Yep, you're a *genius*."

A few outlaws next to Clint chuckled.

White-Eye's face reddened. "She isn't going to tell us the truth, so she might as well die. We need to send a message that nobody can steal from us."

Marta yawned, genuinely tired. Not just from using the power so much today, but from being awakened from her nap and thrust in the middle of this stupidity. Her current use of having a shield up with the talisman trying to block her also weighed on her.

White-Eye aimed his gun at her. "I'm sorry. Am I boring you?"

Marta smiled. "Nope." She pointed at the man. "Though, you do know that I can't be shot, right?"

A shot rang out, and smoke drifted up from White-Eye's gun. Marta glanced up to see the projectile suspended in her wall of air. It looked like it had been aimed straight at Clint.

Clint seemed to perk up. "Wait a second." He grabbed one edge of his bandage, then peeled it back. "Hell, you weren't kidding when you said you were a witch. There isn't even a scar." He turned to show the guy next to him the lack of a bullet wound.

He began scraping the rest of the poultice off, then discarded his bandages. "See, son?" He turned in the other direction to show the others his scar-free skin.

Marta shook her head. "I wasn't kidding." She just couldn't do much since she strained to keep the shield up and going.

Inspiration took hold. Given that she was too weak to cast spells beyond what she already had, she decided to try a curse. She pointed to the two men. "I curse you to be unable to shoot another living soul unless it is in self-defense. If you do, instant death shall befall you and your bullets will go wide of their intended marks."

She gestured to the rest of the outlaws. "That goes for all of you."

Clint sat on the wagon bench. "Damn," he muttered.

Some outlaws started backing up their horses. Others turned and rode away. Marta was glad to see she still had the magic touch.

White-Eye spat. "You can do that?"

Marta smiled. "Of course I can. I'm a witch. I can curse you to death where you sit, but I prefer to preserve life. Even if it is a life that isn't worth preserving."

White-Eye huffed. "And you won't tell me where my money is?"

Marta rolled her eyes. "I've already told you where it is. Do you want me to also curse you from thieving?"

Hell, what was stopping her? "Fine. I curse you from ever stealing anything from anybody ever again. If you try, instant death shall befall you."

Many in the gang turned and left at that point. They must not have wanted to stick around for more curses. Marta tamped down her satisfaction over the turn of events.

White-Eye spat again, squinting as he surveyed her. He then yanked his reins to the side and yelled, "Ha," as he rode away.

Clint had a hand over his mouth, studying the ground next to his wagon. He removed it when he realized Marta's attention was on him. "You just had to do that, huh?"

Marta nodded.

Clint sighed. "Well, I've lost my gang, and I've probably lost my livelihood."

"There are other things you can do to make money."

Clint shrugged. "Stealing was the only thing I was good at."

He bent to grab the reins, shoulders hunched.

Marta took a step forward. "Before you go, would you mind answering a question?"

Clint sat back instead of flicking the reins at the horses the wagon was hitched to. "What's in it for me?"

Marta sighed. She thought he was a little more upstanding than the son, but maybe not by much. "I could curse you more."

Clint shook his head. "I do the same thing to some of my victims. Nothing stops me from shooting them after they've given me the information I want."

Marta's head started to hurt. He wanted something more from her. What did she have to offer? She could give him a new profession. "I curse you to have good luck more often than not at the poker table." Sometimes the power of suggestion would make something vague like that seem true, even when it wasn't.

Clint arched his brows. "That'll come in handy. I'll do my best to answer."

"Who shot you?"

Clint furrowed his brow.

"I mean, I had my suspicions that one of your gang did it. Did they?" Marta asked.

Clint sighed. "You're asking if my son shot me."

Marta kept a poker face as she waited for the man to answer.

Clint smiled. "No, he didn't. Some bank teller pulled a derringer from his sleeve during a robbery. I shot him six times after he shot me the one. Looks like he'll be the last man I ever kill."

Marta wasn't impressed by this.

Clint went on with, "I think Junior genuinely wanted me healed, despite all our fighting over the years. Maybe he does care for me." He looked over his shoulder toward White-Eye and the others.

Marta had another idea. "I don't suppose you saw the man who gave your son the cross, did you?"

Clint nodded, much to Marta's surprise. But then he shook his head, making Marta's heart sink.

"Not a man," Clint started. "It was a woman with a deep, gravelly voice. Never seen her before, but she knew you. She said all the right things to get Junior to come after you. She wants you dead."

Marta nodded. "She'll need to get in line." She figured it was one of McKinley's cronies, but now she wasn't so sure. Why would a collarless woman willingly ally herself with the man?

"I don't suppose you saw anything else or heard anything else about her?" Marta asked.

Clint shook his head. "I was a bit out of it. Heard her say exactly where you would be, so I knew where to find you. I had to catch this horse. It wasn't saddle-broke, though, so had to hitch it to the wagon, which is why I was so far behind."

"Did you at least see where she came from?"

Again, Clint shook his head. "Seemed to come from nowhere. Like, one minute she wasn't there, then she just appeared in the middle of the river."

This sounded like one of Phantom's tricks. She glanced at him, but his eyes were still glazed over.

"Anything else you want?" Clint asked.

Marta couldn't think of any other questions. She shook her head. "You take care," she offered.

He nodded, waved, then flicked the reins to get his horses going. As he left, Marta finally dropped the shield.

"Who could that woman be?" Wind Rock asked.

Marta shook her head. "I guess we'll find out someday."

"She is of no consequence to the task of taking down McKinley," Phantom said. It was the first time he'd acted like there were people around him.

"Who is she?" Marta asked.

"Like you said… you'll find out someday," Phantom replied.

"Is she a Spirit of the Western Sky or something?"

Phantom just cocked his head.

"What do you know about her?" Marta asked.

He shook his head. "Probably as much as you do. We need to focus on our current mission before chasing rabbits."

Marta sighed. He was probably right. If she became a threat, then Marta would deal with her at that point. "What about you? Were you able to do magic this whole time or was the talisman blocking you?"

Phantom hissed. "I'm not reckless. The talisman only blocks your half of the magical orb. The power of the Western Sky comes from both halves, so, in effect, I was blocked. I was doing my best to get around the block."

Marta sighed, glad to know he hadn't been putting her through another trial. It was time they were off. First, she had a task to complete. With the Earth spell and some air, she moved a section of dirt from six feet down out of the ground. With the compacted dirt suspended, she then marched over to the talisman, picked it up, stormed back to the hole, and threw it in. Afterward, she let go of her spell and filled the hole back in with a satisfying *whomp*.

There was one distraction out of her way, and she could feel the magical orb returning to its full strength instead of being tiny and far away. She reluctantly let it go to focus on her quest to save her friends.

CHAPTER 37—LINCOLN

Marta watched a tumbleweed roll through the empty town intersection. The wind was picking up the farther they moved west, but it was the lack of townsfolk that gave her a bad feeling.

"So, this is Lincoln," she muttered. The town had a few more houses than Kent. Looked like Kent, too. A spray of dust hit her face, and she quickly brought out her bandanna to shield herself from more of it.

"Where's everyone at?" Wind Rock asked. She rode beside Marta as usual while Phantom walked just ahead of the horses.

"People come and people go. Spirits are forever," Phantom said. He seemed unconcerned. Marta and Wind Rock had eyes out for a threat.

"Maybe everyone is staying out of this infernal wind," Marta offered, temporarily lifting her bandanna.

Wind Rock nodded, still surveying the buildings.

Phantom shook his head. "Wind is good for the soul. There is bad energy here."

"Why's that?" Marta asked.

Phantom turned his head up to look at the sun, though he might have closed his eyes. "We are close to McKinley's camp. Close enough that his infection on this world and mine is affecting the people and animals more.

They were getting close. That was news to Marta since she'd thought they weren't going to be there until later today, especially with everything that had held them up. "There is no chance of running into McKinley or his men here, right?" Marta asked.

Phantom nodded. "They are a self-sufficient community, so they have no reason to leave their valley." He was no longer looking into the sun.

"So how much farther to this valley?" Marta asked.

Phantom shrugged. "Not far."

Marta's heart skipped a beat. "Do you know where their camp is or not?"

Phantom pointed west. "It is out there. We will be there before sunset."

Marta studied the sun's position, judging there were about four hours before sunset. But what bothered her was how vague Phantom was being. Granted, he was weird, but this seemed weirder than usual.

Marta decided to press the point. "I don't think you know exactly where we are going."

Phantom grunted. "I know where we are going, but you do not

need to."

"Why?" Marta asked at the same time Wind Rock did.

Marta was surprised to hear Wind Rock echo her.

"The less you know, the better," Phantom said.

"Huh?" Wind Rock asked.

"Why?" Marta asked.

Phantom kept walking, not seeming to want to answer. They were passing the last house of the town, but he stayed mute.

"Why are you keeping us in the dark?" Marta asked, her eyes becoming beady on the spirit's back.

Still, there was nothing from him. At least he wasn't skipping ahead like he usually did.

Marta opened her mouth to ask again in a different way, but Wind Rock forestalled her. "We've followed him this far."

Marta shot her a sidelong look. Wind Rock didn't meet her eye.

Marta sighed. She supposed Wind Rock was right. They should be on the lookout for dangers this close to the enemy camp. She just had a bad feeling about this.

***

Sunset had come and gone. Now, in the twilight, the three weary travelers were still making their way west. Marta had enough of this. "Where is the camp?"

Phantom didn't acknowledge that he had even heard her. He hadn't wavered from the path he was on all day. He didn't even really look at other trails or roads. Instead, he kept them on the trail they were on. Did this mean he did know where he was going?

Suddenly, he stopped. Marta and Wind Rock had to stop their horses before running into him.

"Why have you stopped?" Marta asked.

Phantom didn't say anything. They were in a lull between two hills. Phantom turned, gazing southwest.

Marta peered in that direction, but she didn't see anything that would have drawn his attention. A grassy hillside with pockets of rocks was all there was.

"Can you feel it?" Wind Rock asked.

Marta was about to ask what, but then she looked into the space with the magical orb. There were half a dozen connections to it. This close, she could see them, even though they had to be half a mile away. But new connections were being made and others dropped all the time. The direction of the connections was coming from the same way Phantom was looking.

Marta's mouth went dry. Had they arrived? Her arms tingled as her mind went blank. Now what?

"Phantom pointed south. "I think you should tie your horses up to those trees so we can approach on foot."

Scouting! Yes, they were here to scout. She found it hard to swallow, her chest tight.

"Won't they see us?" Wind Rock asked.

Marta hadn't been able to stop looking in the direction of the power users. She almost didn't want to breathe as she scanned the hill for a threat. Her hands trembled. "Shouldn't we stay quiet?" she whispered.

Phantom walked through the prairie grasses to the trees he indicated. "They can't hear us."

Marta reluctantly followed Phantom, but Wind Rock didn't. "I guess we could crawl through the grass to keep out of sight," Marta offered in response to her question.

Phantom nodded. "Yes, we must stay out of sight. Better to slither on our bellies."

Wind Rock finally turned her horse after them, but her attention was on the hillside. "Surely, there is a better way," she said.

Marta shrugged as she gave the hillside another look. In the twilight, it was hard to see all that much, but her enhanced vision did help. She hoped the camp was illuminated so they could see what they were up against.

Marta pointed to a rock outcropping near the top of the hill to their right. She was amazed her hand didn't waver. "We can use those rocks to mask our approach. Then we can crawl from there."

Wind Rock stared at where Marta pointed. "There is still a hundred yards, and it looks rocky up there. Not the best conditions for crawling."

Marta realized Wind Rock was right. She sighed at the thought of the scrapes and bruises they would have to endure. Healing each other wasn't an option this close to the camp since any witch would be able to feel the connection Wind Rock or Marta made. While she was sure most witches wouldn't purposefully give them away, she didn't want there to be any accidents.

Once they reached the trees, they made quick work of tying up their horses.

Wind Rock didn't seem to be shaky at all compared to Marta. "Why aren't you nervous?" Marta whispered.

She whipped her head toward Marta, then looked her up and down. "I guess I'm good at hiding it."

Marta shook her head, studying Phantom for any clues he was nervous. He ignored the women, only having eyes for the hillside. Not only toward the multitude of connections, but also all along the hill. It was like he was a sentinel searching for an enemy combatant.

"Do they have scouts roaming around?" Marta asked.

Phantom shook his head. "McKinley is too arrogant to do something that smart. He thinks nobody would move against him here, so he doesn't bother to guard himself. Even if someone were to, he thinks he is invincible."

"Is he?" Marta asked with a crack in her voice.

"Invincible?" Phantom questioned.

Marta nodded, then realized Phantom's attention wasn't on her. "Yes."

Phantom sighed. "Nobody is invincible. They can be hard to kill, though. McKinley's knowledge of magic has made him comfortable in believing he can do whatever he wants."

Phantom focused on her. "He doesn't know what you can do, though."

Marta squeaked. "Me?"

He nodded, then he pointed a little south. "There looks to be a gully over there where we can hide while we scout the camp."

Marta stared where he pointed. It took a minute for her to find what he saw in this low light. When she did, she thought it was much too narrow. They would have to scoot through sideways, but it was better than crawling over rocks.

Still, Phantom didn't move from where he stood. "Do you want to wait here while Wind Rock and I scout?" she asked, thinking he was done leading them since they were here.

He shook his head. "Before we go up there, there are three things I wish to say."

Marta shrugged, sparing Wind Rock a glance. She watched him, waiting for him to go on. Phantom wasn't paying them no mind, so Marta prompted, "What?"

"The first is that I have enjoyed traveling with you humans," he started. "I know you are frustrated with me for how I do things, so I thank you for your patience. You'll be rewarded for this."

There was a sense of finality to his words that confused Marta. "Are you not staying with us while we wait for the dream council?"

Phantom cocked his head. "I will be here a while yet." He wagged a finger. "The second thing I want to say is I want you to remember everything you have learned on the journey here. You'll need it in the coming fight."

Marta already knew this, so she didn't know why he was repeating it. Although she wasn't sure what she had learned, there was hopefully time before the fight for him to explain all of that.

"And the third?" Wind Rock asked.

Phantom huffed. "You will not like what you see tonight. Keep your head. Keep cool. We have a plan, and we must stick to it for you to succeed."

Marta felt goosebumps form on the nape of her neck. Phantom was saying the conditions in the camp were shit. She was going to want to fight when she saw it. Hell, just thinking the worst she could imagine made her want to rush into the fight now.

But Phantom was right. They had a plan, and they needed to stick to it if they had any chance of defeating McKinley and rescuing Bourne, Greta, and Beth.

She took a breath. "Well, let's go see the shit, shall we?"

CHAPTER 38—SCOUTING

Phantom lagged as the trio made their way up the hill. He wasn't going to be reporting to the council in the dream realm, so Marta wasn't too concerned. Instead, she focused on her walk. She tried to maintain a nice, steady breath rate to keep calm, but that didn't help much.

Marta turned sideways at several points. She even had to climb over some protruding rocks to get through the narrowest portion of the gully, which Wind Rock managed to get through sideways. Wind Rock's smaller form and undeveloped chest worked to her advantage.

The gully was uphill the whole way. Near the top of the hill, Wind Rock had to crouch. Marta followed suit as she was taller and needed to do so earlier to not be spotted. Soon, they were crawling out of the gully where they could see over the hillside.

Crawling was a chore, especially with shaky limbs. Marta did her best to ignore the scrapes and bruises her body was taking. She crawled to Wind Rock's right side when she stopped. Soon, Phantom was on their left. The entire way, Marta had seen the magic being performed through her mind's eye, but now she could see the magicians in the river valley. Torches and fires lit the camp, and it was about three hundred yards to the closest tent.

At first glance, the camp looked normal enough. The city of tents was arrayed in rigid rows and columns, men and women going about their business. It took Marta a moment to realize all the women wore collars, and they were the only ones doing chores. The men watched the women work or gave orders. Even from this far away, she could hear them, though it was probably her enhanced hearing aiding that.

"What are they building?" Wind Rock asked.

Marta focused to the left where Wind Rock pointed. A large, gaudy house overlooked the valley. Next to it was the beginnings of another building. Marta spotted a huge, gold cross. "It looks to be a church," she said.

She could see women working with magic to cut boards and place them on the frame. It reminded her of Beth and Greta helping Marta build a new room onto her house.

Thinking of her friends, she started to search for them. After surveying the camp, Marta realized none of the women seen were Beth or Greta. None of the men were Bourne, either. Where were they?

Wind Rock shook Marta's shoulder, then pointed toward the middle of the camp. Thinking Wind Rock had spotted Marta's friends, she looked for them there. It took Marta a moment to realize Wind Rock had no idea what Beth, Greta, and Bourne looked like.

Instead, Wind Rock pointed out a confrontation between a man and a woman. The woman babbled apologies, which Marta could hear clearly even from this far away. The man didn't respond. Instead, he held up a large coin, almost lording it over her. Her apologies turned to agonized screams.

Marta's breath caught. The screaming continued until the woman dropped to the ground. Marta wanted to rush down and heal the girl before she died. Was she dead already?

What had the girl done to deserve such a fate? Marta hoped the woman still lived. Why wasn't anyone helping her?

After a minute, the woman's foot moved, making it clear she was alive. Marta exhaled. The man, still standing over her, pointed to another woman. He made her carry the passed-out one away.

"What is that?" she muttered when she had her breath back. She wiped a tear from her eye.

"Magic?" Wind Rock offered.

Phantom shook his head. "Pain can be inflected without magic through the collar."

Marta set her jaw. She wanted to run down the hill to kill the man who had inflicted pain on the poor woman.

"I thought the collars controlled the women," Wind Rock whispered.

"They do," Phantom said. "They can control a woman to use their magic or their bodies to do anything the man wants. This includes making it feel like the woman is walking through fire."

Marta shivered. "Can the women fight back?"

"Sure," Phantom said. "As long as they do not mind the agonizing death accompanying it." He said it so matter of fact that Marta ground her teeth to avoid lashing out at him.

Marta watched the woman being carried to a tent close to where she had fallen. It was one of the larger tents, so it was probably meant for four or five people to sleep there. Letting out a breath, Marta asked, "But would she be able to kill her keeper?"

Phantom shook his head. "The person holding the token would send the same thing he felt to the collar but tenfold. Long before the token bearer died, the woman would from the pain being inflicted."

Marta shuddered. She now knew why these women couldn't and wouldn't fight back. They would rather live in pain than be dead for no damn reason.

Still, Marta couldn't see her friends. "Where are Bourne, Greta, and Beth?"

Wind Rock whipped her head in Marta's direction. "You don't see them?"

Marta shook her head.

"What do they look like?" Wind Rock asked.

Marta closed her eyes, visualizing Bourne. "Bourne has a square jaw, and he's ruggedly handsome. He'll probably have scruff as he only shaves once a week. He has sandy brown hair with gray in his temples. Oh, and chicken feet from riding in the saddle so much."

"Chicken feet?" Wind Rock questioned, eyes still on the camp.

Marta nodded as she opened her eyes. "Skinny ankles and impressive thighs."

Wind Rock gave a nod. "And the others?"

"Greta is a tall blonde. Strikingly beautiful and the envy of any woman who looks upon her. Hell, her bosom rivals mine. Beth is plainer, though still pretty, with wide eyes and dark hair. Also smaller in stature than even me, though a little bigger than you. Luckily, I had a dress still from when I was a teen for her to wear."

"I saw them last year, but don't see them now," Phantom said, somberly. "They might be in the tents or the house. Too bad we can't see through walls."

Marta agreed with that sentiment. Seeing through things would be an awesome ability.

"But then you'd see through clothes," Wind Rock said. "I don't know if I'd like that."

Marta could have laughed if they weren't staring at a bunch of captive women being controlled by men. But she did crack a smile at the thought of being able to see right through Bourne's clothes. Though, it didn't take much to get him out of them.

Phantom grunted. "You are a prude since you grew up in a white community rather than with your own."

Wind Rock scoffed.

Marta swallowed as she tried to focus. What could she report on to the dream council that would sway them to join the cause?

"I count at least thirty women and almost all are medicine women," Wind Rock said. "I only see ten men, though."

Marta thought this was something good for them to share with the dream council. "I think we are only seeing about half the occupants of the camp. Wouldn't you agree?"

Both Wind Rock and Phantom nodded.

"Any idea on which one is McKinley?" Marta asked.

Phantom pointed to the only permanent structure currently standing. "I think he lives in the house, so he's probably in there."

"Makes sense," Marta said. She focused on the house for a bit. There was smoke coming from a chimney pipe, and several windows glowed from the light within. She tried to see if she could spot people inside, but she couldn't. Either no one was there, or they weren't close to the windows facing them.

"Where's Bourne?" she muttered after a while.

Neither of her compatriots answered. Marta continued to survey the house and the camp. It took a while, but she noticed a single tent off by itself.

"What's that?" she asked as she pointed toward the lone dwelling.

"Hmm," Wind Rock said. "Looks to be a single tent with a chair in front of it. Appears normal, other than its position away from everything else."

"Yes, away from the order of the camp," Marta said, getting excited. "It's gotta be Bourne's."

Wind Rock scoffed. "You can't know that."

Marta felt like Wind Rock was letting her down. "Then why is it isolated?"

Wind Rock shrugged. "It could belong to whoever is second in command or some other high honor."

"I'd think it would be bigger in that case."

"Maybe it is a sick tent or a bleeding tent for the medicine... er, the women in general."

Marta's spirits deflated. Men pushing women who were on their cycle or sick to an isolated tent made sense. She studied the tent, trying to figure out if Wind Rock was right.

After a while, she gave up. Nobody was going in or out of that tent. There was no indication anywhere of Bourne, or even Greta or Beth for that matter. Had this trip been a waste?

Marta's eyes blurred. She had to blink the tears from them before she could see straight again. Did this mean Bourne was dead?

Wind Rock put a comforting arm on Marta's shoulder. "I'm sure your friends are alive. You'll see."

Wind Rock indicated the gully behind them. "Come, let's go talk with the dream council to see if we can't get more help to fight McKinley."

Marta sniffled and swallowed, trying to harden her resolve. There was only so much she could do now, and Wind Rock was right about the upcoming meeting. She still needed to come up with a good argument on why they should help. There was still much to do before the battle began, and Marta needed to get ready for it.

CHAPTER 39—LAST SUPPER

Just after dark, Bourne was surprised to be summoned for a second time in a day. After he was ushered inside McKinley's house by his guard, Bourne found the dining room empty. The double doors across from the entrance were open, and a light shone from in there. He peeked inside.

Bourne staggered back when he saw a cannon pointed right at him. He reflexively ducked, even though there was no evidence it was loaded or even manned.

After getting over his jumpiness, Bourne realized that a warlock was even worse than that cannon. They could kill a man with a look. A cannon took time to ready and fire. Bourne took a few steps into the room and stopped.

The room was huge with glass cases hung on the walls. Inside the cases, rifles, pistols, swords, uniforms, and flags were displayed. It didn't take long to see a theme, with the northern half of the room decorated with Union items and the southern half with Confederate. Even though the cannon was a smaller one, it made the room feel tinier than it was.

"Beautiful, isn't it?" McKinley asked.

He was standing to the left of the door while polishing a revolver. Bourne eyed him warily. "What is this? A memorial to the war?"

McKinley cocked his head, but he still eyed the gun in his hand. "I guess you could call it that."

Bourne sighed. "Well, what do you call it?"

McKinley waved a hand around the room. "I call it a tribute to one of the greatest things to happen to the United States."

"Greatest?" Bourne questioned.

McKinley nodded. "Six hundred thousand killed in action. Who knows how many more died from disease or maltreatment in prisons? We're talking about fifteen percent of the country dead in a handful of years. Great."

Bourne shuddered. How was death great? It reminded him that his date with the executioner was coming. "Since Marta is almost here, how long before you kill me?"

McKinley tsked. "What's your rush?"

Bourne eyed the revolver McKinley still wiped down. "I don't want to die. I'm tired of being toyed with."

McKinley eyed Bourne. Bourne met McKinley's suspicious gaze with a defiant glare. He even set his jaw.

Finally, McKinley nodded. He returned his attention to his gun. "If it helps any, tonight is your last supper before you journey to your next life."

The finality of the words hit Bourne like the limestone coming down on Goodman's head last year. Bourne found it hard to breathe. So, this was it, huh?

Bourne looked around the room. His vision clouded, and it took him a moment to realize there were tears in his eyes.

Bourne took a deep breath, refusing to break down. He wouldn't give the madman the satisfaction.

With so many guns and other armaments in the room, surely there was something he could use. He spotted a grenade on a wall. Bourne wondered if the ordinance was live or deactivated for display. He could do some damage with it if it were still usable. Then Bourne noticed its case was locked, realizing all the cases were. He'd have to break the glass to get to it.

The snap of the revolver being closed drew Bourne's attention. McKinley was gently laying the piece on a battle flag for some Northern regiment.

"It's a Colt Model 1860," McKinley said. "It just arrived this afternoon. I had to donate a lot of greenbacks to Bowdoin College in Maine for it."

Bourne saw no connection to the weapon and some college back east. He huffed but didn't respond.

McKinley pointed to the gun. "It belonged to Brigadier General Joshua Chamberlain. Now that he is president of the college, he's willing to part with his war items in the name of improving the college."

Bourne smacked his lips. He was impressed with the credentials behind the gun. Chamberlain was a hero in the eyes of Federalists, so his deeds had even reached Kansas.

And just like that, he thought about his brother-in-law. Surely, he'd never met Chamberlain since he'd served under Grant in the Mississippi valley before he was killed and before Grant took command of the whole Union Army.

It was another person Bourne would soon get to see again. Heaven housed his brother-in-law, his sister, his nephew, Brandon, and Bourne's parents. So much death in Bourne's life. Could he face his death with dignity? A tear made its way down his cheek.

McKinley wasn't paying any attention to Bourne. "Now the revolver is mine. No one can pay me any price to take it from me."

Bourne shook his head. Who gave a damn about a stupid gun? McKinley only saw death, destruction, and war in this room. Bourne saw a tragedy. It was a conflict between brothers and people who once stood for one another, but somehow couldn't reconcile their differences.

But this was years ago. Did it even matter anymore? Maybe it did in the eyes of a madman.

McKinley turned to Bourne. "You've been quiet."

Bourne sighed. "What would you have me say? Are you waiting for me to give my final words or something? Do you want me to beg for my life?"

McKinley shook his head, his smile wry. "Come, now. You aren't dead yet."

With that, McKinley strode to the door. Bourne had to move to allow the man through.

Bourne turned to follow the man to supper, but he stopped. The case McKinley had just put the revolver in was unlocked. His heart leaped. Before he could think, he grabbed the gun. A box of cartridges was also in the case, so he snatched it as well. He lifted his shirt, stuffing the gun in his belt. As he threw his shirt down to hide the gun grip, he jammed the cartridges in a pocket.

"Hey," McKinley called from the dining room.

Bourne jumped. "Yes," he tentatively answered.

"Turn out the light in there before you come to supper."

Bourne breathed a sigh of relief. He hadn't been caught. "No problem," he replied.

He strode to the kerosene lantern hanging from the ceiling above the cannons, then twisted the knob, retracting the wick.

Bourne turned back to the door and the only source of light. Now he just needed to keep the gun hidden, bide his time, and then somehow use the weapon on a magical being. Easy!

Bourne stopped in his tracks—this was a little too easy. Had McKinley set Bourne up? Why else would he walk off and leave a gun and cartridges out for Bourne to grab?

He huffed. Did it even matter? He was given this small chance, and he had to take it. Even if this were a setup, he was doomed anyway.

"Are you coming?" McKinley called.

"Be right there," Bourne said. He sighed. If he couldn't figure out how to kill a warlock, then this would be his last supper. He marched toward the door and his future—however much was left.

CHAPTER 40—DREAM COUNCIL

Marta shot Phantom a look, but he was busy staring out into the darkness. They were in the patch of trees they had tied their horses to earlier. The trees should hide them while Wind Rock and Marta visited the dream realm. Marta tried to relax, but she was uneasy this close to the camp.

Marta closed her eyes, letting the masked dream spell wash over her. She didn't feel any physical sensation, but she was suddenly among the stars. Dreams. Lots of red ones tonight.

Marta twisted around, searching for Wind Rock. They would go before the dream council as a united front to present the facts as they knew them. Together, they could get the help they needed. She just wasn't there yet.

Was something wrong? Marta thought Wind Rock would be right behind her. Surely nothing had gone wrong after Marta had entered the dream realm.

Wind Rock appeared beside Marta, making her yelp. She took a breath. "Took you long enough."

Wind Rock nodded. "I have a bad feeling."

"About our meeting with Runs With Does?"

Wind Rock shrugged. "I can't put my finger on it."

Marta waved a dismissive hand. "I think Phantom's behavior is getting to you." She could act braver than she felt to hopefully lift her friend's spirit.

Wind Rock drew in a deep breath. "He is acting strange. Er, strange for him, I should say."

Marta rolled her eyes. "I think he knows he can't defeat McKinley alone, and he doesn't like that he has to rely on us to take him down."

Wind Rock sighed. "I think you're right, but I'm not sure if that is the cause of my unease."

"Well, I've got a lump in my throat thinking about clashing with Runs With Does," Marta began. "Can you tamp down your feelings while we convince a bunch of women to join our fight?"

Wind Rock straightened. "Yeah. What's the plan?"

"Plan?" Marta asked. She had already explained what she thought would work to fight McKinley.

"Your plan to convince the council to help us."

Marta relaxed. "I figured we could start by giving them our estimate of our foe's strength. Then we need some way to relate where the camp is."

"I can make a map," Wind Rock said.

Marta nodded. "That'll work. Then from there, it is convincing them of the danger McKinley represents if he isn't stopped."

Wind Rock scratched her temple. "I think we should be ready for some people's unwillingness to risk their lives to stop McKinley."

Marta sighed. "I'm also afraid of that. I'll only ask for some women to help. I think we can succeed with ten or so extra medicine women."

Wind Rock drew an unsteady breath. "Ask for more and expect the number to be cut down."

Marta nodded. "Good call."

Wind Rock gave a half-smile. "I'm ready then."

"On three," Marta called.

"Three," Wind Rock said. She winked out from her spot next to Marta.

"Ah," Marta called. She meant to count to three, not just say the word and go. She quickly visualized the meeting spot for the dream council, then exerted her power over this place to move her there. She was there in an instant.

She appeared next to Wind Rock. The council stood around them in a large circle. They had the floor, and the council was ready for them.

"What happened to coming here together?" Wind Rock whispered.

"Later," Marta replied. She didn't want to get into the meaning of counting to three right now.

Instead, she looked for Runs With Does. She stood with a staff and the peace pipe in her hand. She held up the pipe. "During tonight's discussion, we'll dispense with the pipe to allow for free speech to rein. No talking over another person, though." The pipe disappeared. "Marta, start us off."

Marta stiffened. Runs With Does seemed to be trying to be helpful, and Marta was glad for it. "Thank you," Marta called. "I'll get right to it. From what we can see of McKinley's camp, there are twenty or so warlocks and forty or more captive medicine women."

A few women in the circle gasped. Marta took this as a good sign

Marta kept cool. "We witnessed a woman being tortured to within an inch of her life. We didn't see the reason for this, but it appeared the pain came from the collar controlling the woman and not magic."

Marta expected some reactions like she had gotten from the numbers. Instead, there wasn't one. Though the women who kept themselves hidden by hoods were harder to figure out.

"The camp is in the Saline River valley, northwest of Salina and just west of Lincoln Center. Wind Rock and I are currently on the other side of the hill from this valley while we plan our next move."

As Marta finished, Wind Rock drew a map in the air, showing where Marta indicated. Marta recognized the river, the road they had taken, and the approximate location of Lincoln Center on the map.

Wind Rock pointed to a spot in the drawing. "That's where the camp is."

Marta saw several women studying the map. Did that mean they were ready to mobilize? Runs With Does even looked at the map with interest.

"I think if we can get even just twenty of you to come, we can sneak into the camp, free our fellow medicine women from their collars, and fight the warlocks with superior strength. We can succeed since we will be well-coordinated," Marta said.

Wind Rock only nodded. Just because they didn't know how to free a person from the collar yet didn't mean they couldn't figure it out before the medicine women got there.

"So, how about it?" Marta asked. "Can I get twenty of you to join us? We'll make plans for the battle while we wait for you to arrive."

There were some murmurs at this, women putting their heads together. This was a good sign, wasn't it?

Runs With Does raised a hand to silence the room. "I'm still not sure why we should help with this. What do we get out of it?"

Marta thought this had been made clear days ago. She kept a poker face, though. "Besides freeing our fellow medicine women, we can ensure that none of us are next. Defeating McKinley will mean that we aren't made his magical slaves. Plus, whatever he is planning with so many magical beings will be stopped, making our world a better place."

"We've left him alone, and he does the same in return," someone called.

"Is he leaving us alone?" Marta asked. "My friends were abducted just a few days ago. When was the last time he abducted a medicine woman? Hell, when was the last time he killed one of us?"

Marta avoided eye contact with Wind Rock. While McKinley hadn't directly killed Wind Rock's mother, his actions had ultimately done her in.

"McKinley is powerful," Runs With Does started. "With the men and women at his disposal, he'll be hard to stop. You're proposing a suicide mission."

Marta shook her head. "I think we'll overwhelm him and his men."

Runs With Does shrugged. "You might. But what if he gets wise to what you are doing before you free the medicine women in his camp? You'll be outnumbered."

Marta cocked her head. Planning a contingency to her plan was good, right? She shouldn't argue that they would succeed at getting all the women freed before they fought the men. Finally, she said, "Then send more than twenty. We can use anyone you can get here in time."

Marta glanced around the room. There had to be fifty medicine women there tonight. Runs With Does could not wield magic, but most could.

Another thought came to Marta. "I also have a warning for you. A woman has moved against me by giving the outlaws a powerful talisman. Probably a woman under McKinley's control, but it didn't sound like she had a collar, so she must be working with him willingly. It sounds like she can instantaneously transport, too."

"Traitor," someone hissed. Others gasped.

Marta gestured at the person who had spoken out of turn. "Yes, a traitor."

Runs With Does glared. "I assure you that no one here would willingly work with McKinley."

Marta realized her words had took a different direction than she intended. "I didn't say anyone here was."

Runs With Does huffed. "You might as well have."

Marta shook her head vehemently. "My apologies. I was just giving a warning should this woman move against any of you. I didn't mean to accuse anyone of being a traitor."

Runs With Does scowled. It was time Marta returned to her task.

"Anyway, I think we can work together to figure out this new threat once we have taken care of McKinley. Or, if she is in the valley when we make our move, we can get two birds with one stone."

Wind Rock nodded.

Another woman moved forward, almost in between Marta and Runs With Does. This new woman had a hood on her cloak, disguising her. She was one of the few present who couldn't wield magic.

She pulled back her hood. Marta's eyes went wide. "Chassidy?"

Chassidy gave a nod. "I first want to express my gratitude to Runs With Does for allowing me, a pale face, the honor of spying on Marta and Wind Rock. Due to me always appearing before you hooded, Marta and Wind Rock did not know who I was. I tricked them into thinking I was a desperate soul in need of help. Marta was adamant about helping me even though she had her journey to complete."

Marta's mouth had dropped open at this. She recovered quickly, but could feel the heat in her cheeks.

Chassidy was addressing the crowd, but she turned on Marta. "Besides rewarding her help by sending her the fighters she needs, I also think her behavior exemplifies us as a whole. She is caring for more than just herself and her wants. Her desire to get her friends back is one thing, but I think this proves she is out to make the world a better place."

Runs With Does tsked. "Her intentions may be good, and she may deserve help, but the fact remains that some of us will die in an attack on McKinley. Some we hope to rescue may also be lost in the fight as well."

Several people were nodding in agreement.

Marta wanted to refute this, but what could she say? She certainly couldn't guarantee everyone's safety. Maybe she could argue that this was worth the risk. It was worth it to her, but how could she convey that to everyone?

"Wind Rock and I are going to fight no matter what is decided here," Marta said while fixing the crowd with an unwavering gaze. "If you care for us, your fellow medicine women in the camp, and any future who may be captured and killed, then you need to join us."

Marta stopped scanning the room, focusing on Chassidy. "I wouldn't hesitate to help any of you."

Chassidy smiled.

Runs With Does. "Aw, to be young and think you can win when the odds are stacked against you. I am not ready to leave this plane of existence. I want to live to see my next summer."

Marta eyed everyone. Runs With Does certainly had their attention. Did they also think they were preserving their own lives by not mobilizing?

"I, for one, am ready to vote," Runs With Does called. "Is there any more to be discussed?"

Marta had a sinking feeling in her stomach that a vote right now wouldn't go her way. She started another plea, but she was no longer in the dream realm. Something or someone had yanked her out. She thought she had mastered that aspect of the dream realm.

It was then that she felt a cold, metal collar around her neck.

CHAPTER 41—TORTURE

"On your feet," a man demanded. He stood over Marta.

This man was better dressed than the other ruffians surrounding them, and he had a commanding presence. Marta recognized the man from Bourne's dream and from when she had fallen into his. "McKinley," she whispered.

She tried to grab the magical orb, but failed. It was there, but dimmer. Not the faraway sun like when she was blocked by a talisman. No, this was more like her arms were pinned down from reaching for it instead.

Wind Rock stood stiffly, a gold collar also around her neck. Phantom squatted on his haunches, a bronze collar around his neck. Marta had only seen gold collars up to this point. Did it prevent him from instantaneously transporting away? He wasn't disappearing, though he hadn't done that for days now.

"I said to get on your feet," McKinley called.

Pain, like being struck by lightning, emanated throughout Marta' Her body spasmed as the electricity coursed through her. She couldn't move while it attacked her. All she could do was cry out.

It felt like minutes, but it couldn't have been more than a few seconds, before the attack was over. She had felt the magical orb pushing power to the collar, which had been the source of the pain. She struggled to catch her breath.

McKinley took a step forward, raising a golden token in his hand. "Stand up… or I'll do worse."

Marta's hand went to the collar. The feeling of fire, without there being one, met her fingers. She screamed in agony, but she didn't let go.

"Don't touch it," Wind Rock said.

Realizing Wind Rock's advice was sound, Marta let go of the collar. The pain stopped instantly. She sniffled.

"Stand," McKinley commanded.

Marta nodded as she fought for breath. A tear leaked from her eye. She didn't want to draw notice to it by wiping it away. Slowly, she rolled to where she could kneel before pushing herself up. She turned to face McKinley.

He smirked, taking Marta in. "You're stronger in your abilities than I thought." He closed his eyes, breathing deeply. He rubbed the silver-dollar-sized token like a blind man reading Braille. "Yes, very strong."

He opened his eyes, waving the token like a knife slicing her in half. Marta gasped as power flowed from the orb through the collar, then sliced her clothes in half. The garments flew away with a little help from the air spell. The men cheered. Marta moved a hand in front of her groin, putting her other arm across her breasts.

McKinley arched an eyebrow. "And beautiful to boot. Though, you hiding that beauty is upsetting." He raised the token.

Marta set her jaw. She could feel her heart hammering away, but she suppressed a shudder.

Lightning struck, or at least it felt like it. Marta yelped, her skin on fire. Hell, her muscles were on fire. Every drop of blood was on fire. She could feel the power keeping her from falling, but she wanted to let it engulf her.

It was over in a blink. The echoes of Marta's screams died. Her arms were at her sides, fists balled to help keep her steady. She cried, snot flowing into her mouth. Marta didn't bother to look for wounds. She doubted there were any. She just stood there, shaking, and did her best to ignore the world around her.

"Strong in more ways than just the power," McKinley called. "I can see why Bourne likes you."

Marta's heart skipped a beat at the mention of his name. "Is he alive?"

McKinley cocked his head. "In his current form? For a little while longer, yes."

He eyed her again, making Marta's skin crawl. "But you have other things to worry about."

Marta thought fast about how to forestall the next round of punishment. She closed her eyes as she prepared for it, trying to think faster.

"I don't think you captured us just to torture Marta," Wind Rock said with a steady voice. How was she so calm?

Marta opened her eyes. The teen hadn't been stripped of her clothes or given the same shocks Marta had. Was Wind Rock now bringing McKinley's wrath on her to save Marta for a time?

McKinley turned to the girl. She met his eyes, her chin high. She had her jaw set, too.

"You've got some nerve, daughter," McKinley said.

"Daughter?" Marta questioned.

"Don't call me 'daughter'," Wind Rock spat. "You may have fathered me, but you are no father to me."

McKinley shot her the same smirk he'd had since Marta had first seen him. "You are just like your mother."

He raised another token. Somehow, Marta knew it wasn't the one he lorded over her. Wind Rock eyed the token, standing even taller than she had before.

"If you pledge your devotion to me, I'll free you from that collar," McKinley said.

Marta's heart jumped. Freedom was at hand!

Wind Rock shook her head. "I assume I'll have to swear some oath with the power that will kill me if I don't obey."

Marta's heart sank, knowing what was to come.

"Of course," McKinley said after a pause. "Trust must be earned, not given just because of your bloodline."

Wind Rock spat in his face.

Marta felt a moment of joy as McKinley slowly wiped the spit from his eye. "What is she to you, anyway? Why not accept your birthright?"

Wind Rock glanced at Marta. "She has nothing to do with my decision to not help you. You can torture me and do whatever to my body, but you'll never have my soul." In a louder voice, she addressed the sky. "I am Wind Rock, daughter of Quail Heart." She faced him again. "And I have brought your destroyer."

McKinley laughed. "Marta?" He pointed at her. "She is my destroyer?"

Wind Rock continued her icy stare. Marta gulped.

McKinley turned to the men around him. "You hear that, my flock? Marta is here to destroy me." He laughed again, and the others joined in.

McKinley stepped in front of Marta. She felt her knees threaten to buckle, but she eyed him the best she could. The tears were only coming at a trickle now.

"Some destroyer you are," McKinley said with a snarl. "What do you have to say for yourself, destroyer?"

Marta closed her eyes in a long blink. She should say something that warranted Wind Rock's faith in her. Hell, Phantom still hadn't said anything or moved since his capture. Did that mean his faith in her had waned?

"She's speechless," McKinley called after a few seconds of silence.

His men laughed.

"Pathetic," McKinley spat.

He rushed forward, almost butting his head into Marta's. She took a step back, even leaning away from the assault. McKinley just chuckled. The other men also laughed.

"Kneel, Marta Farragut, and offer your fealty to me," McKinley said, pointing at the ground.

Somehow, Marta shook her head.

"If you swear to me, then do a vow with magic so that I can have you, mind, body, and soul, I'll let your friends go," McKinley offered.

Marta's heart leaped. She could save Bourne, Greta, Beth, and now Wind Rock and Phantom. All she had to do was give up her own life in trade. What was one person compared to five?

McKinley's smirk grew. "I can see it in your eyes. You know that you have to do this."

Marta pictured Bourne's smile instead of this madman's. There was something special about that man. Something more than just her love for him. He was destined for great things.

Not to mention Wind Rock and her powers. At only sixteen, she was doing magic at a far greater ability than Marta had even just a year ago. Her fate wasn't to be here with McKinley.

Then Marta thought of Quail Heart and all Wind Rock had said about her—the abuse she had taken at McKinley's hands, being burnt out from doing magic, and then her eventual insanity. The same insanity that led Rathbone to take his own life.

Was that Marta's destiny? Her friends would live, though. But surely there was some other way. A way she could save everyone, even herself. She just needed time to figure out how to do it.

"No," someone said. It came out a barely audible squeak.

Marta lifted her head. Louder, she said, "No." It was more forced the second time. More controlled. It felt right.

McKinley's smile faded. "Join me or Bourne dies."

Marta blinked, but she refused to let more tears fall. "Then he dies. You have no hold over me, not even with him. You think I'm here to save him when I am really here to stop you."

McKinley's smile returned. "Then you need to learn that there is no stopping me!"

The collar issued more pain. Lightning, fire, and ice hit every nerve in her body. And hit hard. Marta convulsed as she fell to the ground. Some part of her registered the pain of that fall, but it paled in comparison to the agony from the collar.

Marta barely endured the pain, crying out, whimpering, and even losing control of her bladder. She didn't care. She knew that it had to end at some point. She would welcome death rather than feel this pain, but she rode it, living for the sake of living.

She blacked out within moments.

CHAPTER 42—FAMILIAR VOICES

Pain. Swirling images of women in collars. More pain. Marta screaming. The nightmare restarted with the cold feel of the collar snapping around her throat.

Then a whisper on the wind, "We are coming."

Marta struggled through the fog, fighting off the loop of nightmares. Was hope lost? The magical orb was still just a dim reflection of its normal self—there, but inaccessible.

"Who's coming?" Marta asked in a barely audible whisper.

"She's coming to," Greta said. Surely it wasn't Greta who whispered, though.

That stalled Marta's thought. She opened her eyes to find Greta hovering over her. Beth then slid in beside her. Several medicine women were also in the tent. Everyone wore simple gray dresses. Marta was surprised to find she had on the same thing. She grabbed her head to stop the pounding.

"I'm glad to see you, but I wish you weren't here," Beth offered.

Marta smiled, weak though it was. "Glad to see you, too," she croaked. She raised a bit to pull both Greta and Beth into a hug. They were alive. Marta wasn't too late.

"Where's Wind Rock?" she asked.

"I'm here," Wind Rock said from behind the others.

Marta's concern shifted. "So, being the daughter of McKinley doesn't afford you the special privilege of a private tent or something?"

Wind Rock didn't say anything for a minute, and it made Marta wish she could see her face. Finally, she answered, "He offered me a room in the mansion, but I refused. I figured I was needed here."

"Needed?" Marta questioned.

"I thought you would need me," Wind Rock huffed.

"Go easy on her," Beth said. "Being under the control of the collar is a lot, and McKinley tortured her until she passed out because of her refusal of a better bed."

Marta sagged. "Oh, I'm sorry, Wind Rock."

"It's okay," Wind Rock murmured. "You didn't know."

Marta turned to find she was on a cot. "How long have I been out?"

"Long enough," Greta said. "It's getting close to ten AM. Most of us are usually put to work before the sun comes up, but, for some reason, we've been left alone today."

Marta tried to make sense of the change of routine. Then again, how a madman's mind worked was hard to figure out.

"Where's Bourne?" she asked. Surely he wouldn't be in a tent with a bunch of women, but stranger things had happened.

"We're not sure," Beth said. "He has a tent of his own. He's usually chained to a stake through the night and into the day, but…"

Marta waited for her to go on. When she didn't, Marta prompted, "But what?"

Greta and Beth exchanged a look. Still, neither said anything. Greta shook her head.

"But we did see him at supper last night," Greta rushed out.

Marta closed her eyes, taking a deep breath. She slowly exhaled.

"Tell her the rest," Wind Rock insisted. "It is obvious to everyone here that there is more to the but… And Marta knows you two better than the rest of us. Hell, I just met you an hour ago when I woke up, and I already know you well enough to know you are hiding something."

Marta loved her new friend. She was older and wiser beyond her years. Marta wished she hadn't gotten Wind Rock involved in her quest though. However, with the relationship to McKinley, the girl was already involved.

Beth and Greta avoided each other's gazes, only glancing at Marta occasionally.

"But," Marta interjected, "Bourne is going to be put to death if he hasn't been already."

Beth trembled, and Greta's eyes widened.

"Who told you?" Beth asked as she was the first to recover.

"McKinley," Marta said. "So you might as well tell me what you know."

Greta nodded. "Well, we're McKinley's serving girls."

"Naked serving girls," Beth added.

Greta nodded. "We were there last night when McKinley told Bourne it was his last supper."

"It was like McKinley knew you would be here today or something," Beth said. She swallowed. "Previously, he'd said he could feel Phantom coming closer."

Greta shook her head. "No, he said you had something that belonged to him. He then started to talk about Phantom, but I have my doubts that Phantom belongs to McKinley."

Marta closed her eyes as she remembered something. "Phantom said McKinley had breached the power in the Western Sky—that he could sense it. It was why he wanted to see McKinley defeated."

"It wasn't Phantom who belonged to him," Wind Rock offered. "He was referring to me. You know, his daughter."

Marta slid that piece of the puzzle into her mind. "And you've been connected to him, too. That's why you want him dead."

Wind Rock pushed in next to Beth. She had tear tracks on her cheeks, but otherwise looked fine—if the collar around her neck was discounted, anyway.

"I didn't realize he could also feel me," Wind Rock started. "Phantom only knew the way to Lincoln. I've been leading us ever since I started to feel him. Being this close, I could feel exactly where he was." Another tear streamed down her face.

Marta smiled weakly, raising her arm. "We'll get out of this. You'll see." Maybe if she said it and thought it enough times, she would believe it.

Wind Rock breathed a bit easier as she took Marta's hand. "Thank you for not blaming me," she whispered.

"No time for blame. We've got to figure out how to escape," Marta said as she sat up and swung her legs to the side of the cot. Her head swam at the movement. She wanted to lay back down, but she fought through her headache.

Someone handed her a tin cup. She drained the contents in three gulps. "Where's Phantom?"

"I haven't seen him since last night," Wind Rock said. "Maybe he was taken somewhere else to be better watched over."

Marta nodded. It was another piece on the chessboard that may or may not be a factor in the end game. It was time to get answers. She eyed everyone's plain clothing. "What's up with the dresses?"

"McKinley likes order," Beth said. "But when any warlock wants to take a woman to bed, they must marry them. There is no premarital sex here."

"Except for McKinley's concubines," Greta said.

Marta eyed her, but Greta didn't meet her look. When Beth also averted her gaze, the plural to 'concubines' took on its full meaning. Marta shuddered at the thought of rape.

It was time to move on. "What about the collars? What do we know?"

"Not much," Greta said.

"The warlock who holds the token controls the wearer's magic, and each collar is controlled by a unique token," a medicine woman put in. Marta could tell her magical abilities were fairly weak compared to Marta's. She was young, though, so maybe her abilities would grow.

"I've seen a warlock have as many as five tokens, but usually they have fewer," the medicine woman continued.

"Unless the warlock wants the same thing done by each collar, they only hold one at a time, though," another medicine woman said. She had stronger abilities than the first and looked older.

"Do warlocks do their own magic?" Marta asked.

The women in the tent seemed to give it some thought, but most shook their heads.

"I've never seen a warlock do magic," the older one said, "and I've been here the longest, I think."

Marta soaked that in. Slavery had never been allowed in Kansas, but here it was, alive and well. Though there was nothing an officer of the law could do to prohibit this form of slavery, it did tell her the type of men she was up against, even if they were Christians. "How is this okay?" Marta asked.

"McKinley fancies himself some sort of Messiah or even a god," Beth said. "The warlocks go along with this, or they are given a sermon."

"If the sermon doesn't work, torture is threatened until they are brought into line," the older medicine woman said. "It never gets that far, though. Warlocks tend to be loyal to him no matter his faults. He manipulates them, and they fear him."

"Why?" Marta asked.

The older one shook her head, while the others didn't seem to want to answer.

"Maybe it's the same reason why we follow you," Wind Rock said. "He is the strongest warlock here."

Marta gulped. Feeling out the other's abilities, she realized she was the strongest magic user here, though she was barely stronger than Wind Rock. Were they following her?

"The question is, though, if Marta is stronger than McKinley?" Greta asked.

"We'll find out once we remove the collars," Beth said.

"How?" several women put in.

Marta wondered this herself. "Has anyone seen a collar removed?"

Again, more shaking heads. "The only time a collar is removed is if the wearer is dead or they've burnt themselves out," the younger woman said.

"And they do that out of sight of the rest of us," the older one said. "It also doesn't happen all that often. I think five have died and another five have been burnt out since I've been here."

"How long have you been here?" Marta asked.

She shook her head. "At least ten winters, I think. It's hard to keep track as time seems to a blur here."

"And people don't fight back?" Marta asked.

"How can they?" the elder answered. "If they touch their collar, the collar sends them a shock. If they try to touch the token controlling the collar, they get a double dose of pain. Strike a man, and the pain triples. Escape is impossible because you can't go more than a few hundred paces from your token without a debilitating shock."

More and more, this situation screamed it was unwinnable. She hadn't counted on not being able to remove the collars.

They were stuck. Without being able to get out of the collar, how could she save Bourne? How could she save Greta, Beth, and Wind Rock? How could she save herself?

CHAPTER 43—MCKINLEY

"Someone's coming," the medicine woman who stood as the lookout whispered.

Marta was about to ask a new question, but she refrained. Instead, she tried to relax as the warlock entered the tent. He just stood there a moment, blinking.

"How may we be of service to you?" a woman called.

The warlock shook his head. "Your service is to Bishop McKinley. He has summoned all of you for the execution of Sheriff Jethro Bourne."

Marta heard a gasp, and she felt the blood drain from her face. It took a moment for her to realize she'd made the sound. Before, Bourne's health was questionable, but to find out he was about to be executed made his death a reality. Her bravado from before slipped away like a speck of dirt caught in a river.

"Come along now," the warlock demanded. He opened the flap of the tent, holding it for the others to exit.

Marta met Greta's and Beth's gaze through tear-filled eyes. Her hands shook, and her body refused to move in any other manner. Greta frowned, and Beth's lip quivered.

"We can't just sit here," Wind Rock said, offering a hand to help Marta stand. "Maybe we can stop this."

Other women exited the tent, but Marta's body still refused to move. She eyed the hand in front of her like it was a snake.

"I don't have all of your tokens, but I can have those of you under my control light a fire under the rest of you," the warlock shouted. "Now move!"

Marta thought about letting the man set her on fire. She had no reason to follow where he led as it only led to death. The death of her best friend in the entire world.

Beth and Greta both stood, making their way to either side of Marta. "Grab her hand," Greta murmured.

Marta's mind had trouble grasping her surroundings, but she somehow grabbed Wind Rock's hand. Beth and Greta aided her until Marta was able to stand. Wind Rock led them out of the tent.

Other tents were emptying, everyone heading for the big house on the hillside. The sun was at its peak. Marta, still held up by Greta and Beth, reluctantly marched on. She searched for Bourne the entire way.

It took a matter of minutes for them to walk to the house. There was still no sign of Bourne. Warlocks took up positions around the throng of women, but McKinley was nowhere to be found.

"It looks like everyone had the morning off, not just those of us in our tent," Greta whispered.

Beth nodded. "Something is different about today."

Beth, still holding Marta, moved next to the elder medicine woman as the entire encampment stopped in front of McKinley's house. "Has there ever been a meeting like this?" Marta asked.

The woman shook her head. "We've also never had an execution before. Women have been put to death, but not like this."

Marta didn't look toward the speaker. Instead, she continued to search for Bourne. Where was he? She bit her lower lip, her breath coming in quick, short gasps.

She surveyed the warlocks. There had to be about twenty, and they all looked like jailers watching prisoners. They gazed at the collared women with beady eyes and furrowed brows, appearing ready for a fight.

There were around sixty women in the camp. Marta didn't count them, but that was the number discussed in the tent earlier.

"Where's Phantom?" Wind Rock asked.

Marta shook her head. She hadn't seen the spirit today. Maybe he was already dead.

Marta pushed aside the bleak thought. Phantom was annoying, but she would miss him. She hoped his absence meant he had managed to escape. Besides, he was already dead. How could he be killed again? Maybe he'd been banished back to the Western Sky.

Marta became fixated on the collar of the woman in front of her. There wasn't a seam anywhere. Nor a clasp to open it. She wondered if she could free herself if she got her hands on the token controlling the collar. Would that open it? How was she going to get her token?

Suddenly, the energy of the crowd shifted. All eyes were on the front door as McKinley walked out, holding a thick chain that trailed behind him. Marta was surprised to find Bourne on the other end of the chain. A shackle was on his right foot, and he moved forward willingly so the chain wouldn't trip him up.

His eyes went wide when he saw her. Bowing his head, he muttered, "Fuck." Her enhanced hearing clearly heard it.

"No cursing," McKinley ordered.

The ball of chain then fell to the porch boards. It made Marta realize McKinley hadn't actually carried the chain, but instead had manipulated it with magic.

Louder, he proclaimed, "It is about time for the vengeance of God to strike this man down." He held up a token. "The instrument of his death is to be Marta Farragut." He smiled.

Marta's heart sank. She couldn't kill Bourne, but she knew

McKinley could make her. The token McKinley held must be hers. Her hands shook as she tried to find any way out of this.

McKinley raised his other hand, palm toward him with only his index finger up. He then slowly curled and flexed his finger a few times.

Marta recognized she was the target of the gesture, but her mind didn't want her feet to comply with the order. In fact, Greta and Beth were still holding her up.

McKinley wolfishly grinned. "I guess I should have a little fun first."

Marta felt the magical orb push magic into her collar before it radiated out. Instead of shocks, the power worked as an exoskeleton and moved her limbs. First, she was forced to let go of Greta and Beth before she was walked forward, then made to stop before climbing the steps to the porch. Then the magic quit controlling her.

The entire time, Marta couldn't look at Bourne. What must he be thinking—knowing he was about to die and Marta was the one who was going to do it? Did he resent her? Hate her? Or was he resigned to his fate? Her cheeks were hot, and the rain of tears on them didn't help.

McKinley pointed to Bourne. "Are you ready to kill him so he may be reborn to enact God's plan for him?"

Somehow, Marta managed to shake her head. Her vision blurred, and there was a lump in her throat. Her hands trembled as she waited for what was to come.

"Come now," McKinley urged. "Sure you are."

Again, Marta shook her head. Surely, the madman would just demand she do it at any second, and then the real pain in her heart would begin.

"How should he die?" McKinley asked. "Fire?"

Her arm was controlled and moved until her hand was straight up. Fire then shot into her palm. It didn't hurt her, but she could feel the heat. It would hurt someone else if it were shot from her hand.

"Nah... I'll not get rid of the stench for weeks," McKinley said. "Drowning sounds interesting, though."

The fire winked out, a ball of water forming in its place. It was drawing in more and more moisture from the air as it grew until it was the size of a watermelon.

"Too easy," McKinley said dismissively.

The water released, splashing her before hitting the ground.

"What we need is something painful," McKinley mused.

Thorns, splinters of wood, bits of gravel, and other small objects were all plucked from the ground and nearby bushes. This debris, gathered by the air spell, made its way to above Marta's arm before aiming at Bourne. It was like a wad being fired from a shotgun. Marta watched it with a quivering lip.

McKinley tsked. "But that'll make a mess."

The debris dropped to the ground. Some bounced off Marta, but a few of the thorns and splinters found purchase. Marta sucked in her breath to steel herself against the pain.

"How about some lightning?" McKinley asked.

The collar then shot power into the sky. Thunder boomed, but no lightning struck the ground.

"Ah, again, there would be a smell," McKinley said. "But..." He shrugged.

Time slowed. Marta heard her heart—*tha-thunk, tha-thunk.*

From on top of the hill, magic of a kind Marta had never seen before was performed in an amount so huge it was blinding, Blinding in her mind's eye, anyway.

Tha-thunk.

McKinley sighed. It came out as a slow hiss.

Marta shifted toward the magic, but it was hard to move in this time dilation.

Tha-thunk.

Marta took in the magic. It was beautiful in its complexity—more complex than the healing spell and the death curse combined. It took Marta's breath away.

Tha-thunk.

A black hole opened in the sky. It spread to be about six feet tall and three feet wide, hovering just a few inches above the ground. There was no witch or medicine woman there making it. It was just a black-edged hole lined with more sky, but a different sky than the one here.

Tha-thunk.

An Indian woman appeared on the other side of the hole. She jumped out, running straight down the hillside.

Tha-thunk.

Marta's breath caught. The medicine woman dropped her spell to begin aiming death curse after death curse at the warlocks.

Tha-thunk.

Marta blinked, and time returned to normal. She recognized the woman from the dream realm. Marta's heart skipped a beat. The woman was here to help!

"Stop her," McKinley yelled as he pointed up the hillside.

Warlocks shook themselves out of their stunned inaction. But it was Marta, or rather her collar, that struck back first. The death curse shot up the hillside at the approaching woman. She had been so focused on killing warlocks that she hadn't seen the curse coming.

It was like she tripped and fell. She hit the ground, face first, and tumbled through the grass. She was dead before she fell, though the fall also broke her neck. Marta squeaked, horrified.

She struggled to take a breath. She hadn't expected this woman, but she hadn't wanted her to die, either. And it was Marta's hand that had killed the woman. Sure, she hadn't been in control, but it still made her feel like a murderer.

The death curse was still being issued from Marta's collar in many directions. She couldn't stop it. Couldn't even fight for control. McKinley owned her power. She blinked tears from her eyes to see what was going on. Who was he targeting with these curses?

Women appeared in holes all over the hillside. First ten, then twenty. At least forty women, most Indian, fought their way down the hillside. They blocked Marta's death curses and the other spells, so they were aware of the need to defend themselves. Some were familiar while others had been there in the dream realm like the first gal. The 'we are coming' in Marta's sleep took on a new meaning.

Marta's elation was swiftly replaced with fear. The magic from her collar was going to fight the women on the hillside. Fireballs, lightning, death curses, and other nasty spells flew through the air. Marta wasn't the only collared one doing magic, so other warlocks were also putting up a fight. Shields went up on both sides to block most spells, but some made it through.

"Get the tokens," a warlock yelled. He scrambled to the nearest dead warlock to grab more. The dead warlocks were rushed by women and men alike. They snatched up tokens off the ground, out of hands, and out of pockets. As women claimed tokens, collars fell away. They must have found out how to release them.

Excitement filled Marta at seeing a few women being freed from their collars. But then they became targets to Marta and the other captured women. Some died. Others fought and blocked spells as they retreated up the hillside with the newcomers.

Marta stared up at the porch where the person she needed to take her token from was. McKinley watched the battle with fire in his eyes. Marta couldn't tell if he was doing magic, but he was making her do plenty.

Bourne was now next to her, taking shelter behind the steps. He breathed deeply, brows furrowed. He had no idea what was going on, and Marta couldn't fill him in. How was he still alive? Had McKinley forgotten about him in the attack, or was he saving his execution for when he could savor it? Marta shuddered at the thought.

She indicated for him to leave the area with a jerk of her head. He shook his in response, shielding himself from a barrage of fireballs nearby.

The attack came from Wind Rock. She sent fireballs, lightning, and bombs up the hillside, tears on her face. Greta, Beth, and a couple of others in collars were doing the same. In fact, groups of three or four women all over the yard were as well. That had to mean they were controlled by the same warlock.

Some of the warlocks picked up discarded collars, doing their best to get them on any woman without one. Mostly, this was done with air spells, but some were doing it by hand. They worked fast and furiously.

Marta wished there were something she could do to stop the men. Instead, her magic was going up against women attacking from the hillside. Those who were freed made their way to join them, but some stayed and fought in close quarters with the men.

It was then Marta saw what was wrong with the picture before her. The women who appeared from the holes and those who had been freed were only attacking warlocks. They were defending themselves from attacks from the captured, but it wasn't enough. They were being overwhelmed.

Marta gritted her teeth as a bomb spell was issued by her collar. It aimed at some of the women who had just been freed and were moving up the hillside. They hadn't counted on this, so their shields hadn't been enough. Body parts went flying. The death curse followed to put the screaming survivors out of their misery.

More bombs detonated. It wasn't just Marta sending them now, but the women were ready for it. Their shields held, and they continued to fight. None of the warlocks were going down. They held their ground.

Marta counted ten dead warlocks. Close to twenty women were dead, about half free. The odds weren't looking good.

Someone on the hillside must have come to the same conclusion. The women slowly started backing away from the house. It was a slow retreat with spells still flying. They weren't turning and running, so Marta was grateful for that. They just didn't seem to be fighting as fast and furious as they had before.

It was easy to figure out why. The women were fatigued. The spell to create the hole for them to travel here had taken a lot out of them. They weren't fresh for the fight.

Now what?

"We've got them on the run now," McKinley hollered with glee. "Try to capture a few if you can."

Marta resented McKinley's mirth. If she could, she'd strangle the man. Instead, she found that she couldn't move. Not only were spells being sent up the hillside to attack, but her magic held her in place.

A hole appeared on the porch, and Marta caught her breath. She watched in absolute disbelief as Reverend Hubbard stepped from the portal. He *was* a warlock.

Marta had given the outlaws' money to a damn warlock. What was more, with him here to join McKinley and the other warlocks, the women would lose. More death and carnage were coming.

And there was nothing Marta could do to stop it.

CHAPTER 44—CURSE

If Marta could control her magic, she would kill Reverend Hubbard. Hell, if she could move, she would beat and choke him with her bare hands. Then again, she could say the same of any warlock around her.

"Reverend, so nice of you to join me," McKinley called with a bright smile. "That's a nifty trick, appearing from nowhere. You'll have to teach it to me."

Hubbard smiled back, but it looked forced. "It's called hopping, but I can't teach a dead man how to do something."

Three men in front of the porch fell, dead before they hit the ground. Fireballs flew from Hubbard's hands toward the other warlocks, including McKinley. Marta's jaw dropped.

The shield issued by Marta's collar that protected McKinley and herself deflected the fireballs. She could feel the heat as close as she was. Marta assumed the death curse had been cast from both sides, but neither landed. McKinley had Marta issue fireballs, which Hubbard blocked.

"You dare to move against me, Hubbard?" McKinley bellowed. "You'll pay for this!"

Other collared women began throwing their life-threatening magical spells toward Hubbard. He stepped back on the porch to evade them, but the spells were coming up short. It was evidence of a shield protecting Hubbard.

Elsewhere, the battle still raged. Fireballs *popped*, bombs *exploded*, and thunder *boomed* in the valley while death curses killed with silence. There were two pockets of women—one on the hillside and one at the corner of the house. The warlocks kept their collared women in front of the house, doing their best to fight.

Marta's mind struggled when it came to Hubbard. Wouldn't all warlocks work together? Surely a man of the cloth, any cloth, wouldn't fight another. What's more, did that mean he was helping witches when there was this rumored war between witches and warlocks? Didn't the abduction of witches and medicine women by McKinley and his ilk prove there was such a war?

Marta shook her head. She needed to concentrate on the opportunity to free herself. So far, it looked like the only way was to get her token.

The three dead warlocks weren't far from her, but her midsection was pinned down like there was a weight on her back. Other collared women were free to move, though. "Get the tokens from the dead," Marta shouted, pointing.

The collar issued a slap across her face. She was then gagged, air used to keep her from speaking out again. McKinley must have heard her.

A few women realized what Marta wanted. They moved toward the men, but other men ran in to grab tokens, too. The women were too late, and Marta's eyes widened at this.

The women stopped. They stared at the men who were now their new handlers, but the men were examining the tokens as if they were foreign.

The first collar sprang open. Then, a man said, "You just have to think it." He held up four tokens, and three more collars unlatched.

Marta couldn't count them from there. All the other women who had rushed in to grab their tokens had their collars drop away. Marta studied the three men. They seemed different somehow.

There were now warlocks fighting other warlocks. Well, more like warlocks were fighting the women controlled by other warlocks. The difference between sides was that McKinley's men were dressed like cowboys. A little more upscale than a typical man working the land, but underdressed compared to Hubbard and the others who fought with him. Hubbard was in a black shirt and black pants with a clerical collar. Other men had black robes, but they had clerical collars, too. The men who freed the women were robed.

Marta's collar issued spells at the men and the women they had freed. One of Hubbard's men was taken out by a death curse. A medicine woman failed to protect herself from a bomb. She erupted in flames, screaming. Marta's hackles rose. The smell of burnt flesh saturated the air along with the acrid scent of smoke.

So much pain, suffering, and death. Not to mention the women on the hillside who still fought. They looked to be getting in a lick or two, but it seemed like warlocks who went down had their tokens picked up by others. So, not many women were getting free. Marta grunted as she tried to fight the air spell holding her down so she could join the fight against McKinley and his men. She tried to do a push-up, but it was futile against the magic holding her down.

Hubbard had climbed over the porch railing. He was now down in front with a couple of others who were still alive. The free women who survived had also joined with them, and they were protecting each other while getting their licks in where they could. The pocket of women at the corner of the house merged with that group.

"Stop!" McKinley commanded, enhancing his voice with Marta's air spell. Where she was, Marta had to cover her ears.

"Warlocks need to stick together," McKinley called. "Witches are evil, and they need to be controlled or eradicated. Hubbard, join me in my glorious quest."

"Only evil people do evil," Hubbard replied. He didn't enhance his voice. "Marta doesn't do evil. She has proven that."

Marta felt heat in her cheeks for being called out.

"Yet, you and your men have proven you are evil time and time again," Hubbard finished.

A resurgence in fireballs and other magical weapons went up, but it looked like everyone was firmly entrenched in their shields and other protections like pendants. Nobody seemed to be going down at this point. It was as if the two sides were in a stalemate, but were still trying their best to win.

Marta coughed as a wave of smoke rolled over her. She still couldn't see an opening for herself. How was she going to get free and fight *against* McKinley instead of for him? Something had to change.

"Men, use your own abilities in this fight, not just your bondwomen's," McKinley ordered.

Marta could feel a shift in the power being called upon by her collar. It seemed less focused, and she didn't think as much magic was getting thrown against the enemy. She wondered why McKinley called them to use their own powers. Marta's ability wasn't being stretched to the limits, and she didn't think the others were either. None of the women had passed out.

What was now lacking from her collar was more than being made up by McKinley himself. Although she could only see the fireballs coming from him, there were more bombs, lightning strikes, and other spells thrown at the different pockets of McKinley's enemies. Marta couldn't see this magic, so it had to be coming from McKinley and other warlocks.

A few things did make it through the shields as they weakened and collapsed in the new onslaught of attacks. For the most part, the people against McKinley were able to rebuff these new attacks while a couple of Hubbard's men lost their lives.

Marta shivered, goosebumps forming on her arms as she realized there was another shift in the fighting. The people against McKinley were throwing fewer fireballs, death curses, and other spells. Instead, more and more shields were going up. Marta couldn't see the men's magic, but this was the pattern she saw in the women's. It was the benefit of McKinley's men also fighting.

McKinley's forces were winning the fight. It was only a matter of time before it was over. Marta huffed, and a tear leaked down her cheek. Why couldn't she think of a way out of this?

She stared at McKinley, zeroing in on the token he held in his left hand. She wanted that token—*her* token. She wanted it so she could free herself—to rain her fury down on the madman who was the source of this fight.

He took something from his pocket. It was a medallion on a leather cord. It could have been a talisman, but before she could get a better look, he swung it over his head like a lasso.

McKinley let the medallion fly right toward the group in front of the porch. At first, Marta thought the shield would stop it, but it somehow sliced through. The leather cord burned up as it passed through, though.

The medallion then transformed into a gold collar, open and ready for a neck. The group was so taken by surprise that they didn't have time to react. The collar closed around Hubbard's neck.

A medicine woman and one of Hubbard's warlocks went down in the next instant with what had to be death curses. The rest of the group shifted the shielding until it excluded Hubbard.

"You're mine," McKinley whooped. A token was held in his right hand. Hubbard was now fighting against his own people. His bug eyes made Marta feel for the man. He was now in the same boat as she was.

She glanced around to find a few other men collared. They had somehow been surprised like Hubbard.

Marta grunted. Even men could be collared? Then inspiration took hold. *Even men could be collared.* How could she collar McKinley? She had to figure it out.

Marta glanced toward where Bourne still hid behind the porch steps a few feet away. She wanted him away from here, but she didn't see how he could scramble free. Besides, he was protected by her shield where he was anyway.

He locked eyes with her. She expected to see pain or softness. Instead, they were piercing. Pure determination exuded from him. He still had faith that she could turn this around.

She closed her eyes to think, Phantom's words playing in her mind. "I want you to remember all that you have learned on the journey here. You'll need it in the coming fight."

What had she learned on her journey that she could use while she was collared, pinned to the ground, and helpless? Phantom knew something. Why couldn't he ever say anything outright?

"Phantom said you have to learn." It was Wind Rock's voice from a memory that was only yesterday but seemed like long ago.

Marta sighed, recalling the journey here. Somewhere in her memories was a clue to get her out of this. She just had to recognize and act on it.

In Marta's mind, the sounds of the battle diminished to nothing. Everything from her going to Council Grove, finding Wind Rock, and then them hitting the trails played in her mind. Losing the track near Abilene,

Phantom showing up, and the ensuing battle with Rathbone came next. Then there was following Phantom, meeting Chassidy at the Solomon River, and the run-in with the outlaws, which went by in a blink. Next was her conversation with Hubbard, the donation to his church, and fighting the prairie fire. Nothing seemed all that spectacular. Nothing seemed like it would help her here. She found it hard to swallow

For some reason, Wind Rock's voice echoed in her mind, "You have to fight fire with fire."

Marta took stock of her current situation, trying to calm her trembling hands. She attempted to reach for the orb, but it just slipped through her fingers. She wasn't blocked from it, but it was dimmer than usual. The collar around her neck was accessing the orb. Could she reach for the magic in the collar?

Marta opened her eyes, seeking out McKinley. He surveyed the battlefield, focused on sending his and Marta's power against his foes. She focused on her token in his hand. That was what controlled her collar.

She could see her power flowing out of the collar. When she had control of her power, it would go where she directed. So, it was somehow the replacement for the orb or some sort of intermediary. She knew physically touching the collar was out of the question, so she grabbed fistfuls of grass to steady herself.

In her mind's eye, she didn't see a collar. All she saw was the orb and the different magic flows of herself and the other women. She studied a thread that came down to her collar. It was like the magic was in her mind's eye and then went into the physical world at the juncture with her collar, but she couldn't see the collar itself. Maybe if she took her eyes out of her sockets and turned them to look at her neck, she could see, but she shuddered at that thought.

Wind Rock was near, so Marta looked at the current through her collar. The magic flowed toward Wind Rock, aimed at her neck. Then it changed direction and streamed out into the battlefield. The collar was at that change of direction, but she still didn't see it other than as a physical piece on Wind Rock's neck.

She was on the verge of something, and she licked her lips. It was like it didn't exist in the space with the magical orb. How could something that didn't exist have so much control over magic? Was it something like how she couldn't see the men's magic? It was there—she could see the effects in the real world. But if it was like the men's magic, then how did it also work on men?

Another piece fell into place, and she began to breathe easier. Phantom had been collared with a brass collar, not gold. Everyone else was getting gold ones, so there had to be a distinction aside from the metal.

Phantom even admitted McKinley had some influence on his control of the magical orb.

"It's the magic of the spirit world," she muttered with awe. "Phantom's magic is what's working the collars."

This meant the brass collar was made by a warlock since she hadn't seen it as something made from witch magic.

Another sickening thought was that this wasn't helping. Men and women were still being hurt and even dying around her. She wasn't helping them.

So, why did the memory of fighting the fire with fire hold so strongly in her mind? There was something to it.

"Phantom!" she called as it hit her. He'd said McKinley had somehow gotten hold of the power from the Western sky. If he could do it, couldn't she? Couldn't she fight the magic of the collar with that same magic?

Phantom said the orb had different sides. One half was for women and the other was for men. Somehow, Phantom's powers came from both halves. Being blocked by one half blocked Phantom's magic as well.

She closed her eyes, studying the magical orb again. Supposedly, she was only seeing her half, like the sun in the sky. She wanted to turn the sun in her mind to see the other half. She tried to imagine it rotating or something, but it didn't budge. It was made more difficult by not having direct access to it due to her collar. Instead, she flailed around like a blind, frustrated bat.

Then she thought about looking through the orb. Somehow, the orb turned in on itself at this thought, then lengthened. A tunnel formed in the middle, making it appear more like a thick, oval ring. The right half issued spells for women or through collars. The left half issued spells for the men. In the middle were the collars. She could see them now as entities of magic. She reached for her own.

"Fight fire with fire," she muttered as magic from both halves of the ring flowed to her. Calm took over. The world around her didn't exist. Only the magic did.

The air spell held her down, but she struck through the thread of magic in an instant. She felt her physical body stand. Still holding the new magic, she took in the world through new eyes. Everything was so different. Small and insignificant. Nothing mattered.

She turned toward McKinley. He no longer mattered. He was just a bug to be squashed.

He gaped at her. "How?"

She issued the death curse, but he expertly turned it aside even though he couldn't see it. He must have somehow known it was coming. She issued another, yet it was again struck down.

She studied the magic flowing to him from the left half of the ring. He had built a weird shield that was striking out constantly. It was like a rolling mess of snakes surrounding him, turning aside curses and spells.

Marta issued the same shield around herself, but with both halves of the magic. She then cut the shield spell around them that came from the collar. She replaced it around herself with the new power to prevent physical objects and spells.

Lightning flew from her fingertips as she issued another death curse. She tried multiple things to throw him off balance.

"You've transcended," McKinley muttered with wide eyes. He smirked. "You're still not as powerful as me."

Death curses, persistent lightning, fire, and bombs struck out at her. They all bounced off her new shielding. She was surprised to find she wasn't afraid of his magic. Instead, she was fascinated by seeing this other half of things. It was all new to her.

"You'll die if I overwhelm you," McKinley said as he held up the token. "I still control your witch magic, and I will burn that from you. Without that, you'll lose access to both halves."

He continued to rain curses down on her, but some now came from her collar. Her new shield was blocking him, but the collar was another matter. She was having to kill the spells as soon as they were made. It was hard for her to keep up. She clenched her fists as she worked.

Part of her wanted to reinforce her shielding while another wanted to strike back. She thought that was the wrong thing to do. Something about what he said rang true, and it was already using a lot of her energy to keep up the lightning and shielding while stopping the collar spells.

She gasped at how overwhelming it all was. This was it. Her overconfidence in her newfound ability would be the death of her. She gritted her teeth, perspiration forming on her brow as she fought for her life.

McKinley kept issuing more magic. A fireball formed from the collar. Marta couldn't stop it before her dress caught fire. She turned to a skeleton to protect herself, snuffing out the fire and fireball with her new magic.

Lightning came down and struck her. It was a McKinley spell. Her rolling mess of snakes hadn't been enough protection from above. Since she was a skeleton, she bucked and gasped at the effects, but it wasn't fatal. She adjusted her shield to block the lightning.

Still, she couldn't strike out. McKinley had the upper hand and would destroy her sooner rather than later. Marta couldn't give up. She had to live. If she failed, Bourne would die. Wind Rock and everyone else who had come to their aid would also be enslaved. There was no telling what

McKinley would do to the other witches and warlocks who wouldn't come to his side. What would he do with so much power and no one to stop him?

A shot rang out from next to Marta, startling her. The token in McKinley's hand now sported a bullet hole through its middle. The collar around Marta's neck sprang open, falling to the ground. McKinley gaped at the token.

Both Marta and McKinley turned toward Bourne, who stood next to the porch steps, pistol smoking in his hand. "Did you forget to shield yourself from bullets?" he asked

Marta had been the one to kill that shield. McKinley had forgotten to replace it with his own magic. Before Bourne fired the pistol again, McKinley added a new layer of shielding to protect against bullets.

Marta knew she needed to act now that he was distracted. She readied a flow from the right side of the ring now that she had access to it again, another from the left, and yet another from both. Three different severing curses flew at McKinley. These were similar to what she had severed Rathbone's connection to the magic with.

The curse from the men's side sliced through McKinley's bullet shield. The one from both halves cut through his rolling snake shield. Then Marta's hit McKinley.

Bourne hadn't stopped firing. He emptied his revolver, the last two striking McKinley in the head since he was without a shield by that point. Without his magic altogether, really. To make sure he was well and truly dead, Marta issued the death curse.

Marta closed her eyes, breathing deeply. They had defeated McKinley.

In her mind's eye, she saw the collars in the middle of the magical ring. She pushed those collars into the ring, making it collapse in on itself. A bright shiny orb took its place. It was only her half of the magic.

"Hello, friend," she said as she connected with it and only it.

"Whoa," Wind Rock said from behind Marta. It made her realize there was more to the world than just the magical orb now that McKinley was dead.

She opened her eyes, ready to fight, but nobody was fighting anymore. Instead, everyone stared at Marta. Shields were still up to protect people, but nobody had a collar on. In fact, the collars weren't even discarded on the ground. They had disappeared.

"What did you do?" Wind Rock asked.

Laughter came from the porch, drawing Marta's attention there. Phantom chuckled. "You've done well." He didn't have a collar on, either, but she didn't think her actions had freed him. He must have been freed when McKinley died. He laughed even as he slowly dissolved to nothing.

Marta felt heat in her cheeks as a sheepish grin formed on her face.

She enhanced her voice. "If you have been duped by McKinley, you should back slowly away and only issue magic for defense. You're outnumbered, so leaving with your life is a good deal."

A few warlocks eyed each other, but some were already on the move. The others soon followed. There were only six of McKinley's men still alive, so they had no chance against the sixty or so men and women previously under their control or coming to Marta's aid.

A hand touched her shoulder. "Man, I'm glad to see you without a collar on."

Marta beamed at Bourne. "I couldn't let my best guy get hauled off without at least trying to save him."

Bourne nodded. "Much obliged, ma'am."

He pulled her in close for a kiss. It seemed like it had been ages since they'd last done this. Bourne needed a shave, too. She pulled back, lifted a hand to his cheek, and rubbed the stubble of whiskers there. "I could take care of that if you want."

"What?" he questioned. "You don't like kissing sandpaper?"

Marta laughed, staring into his shimmering blue eyes. She cut her laugh off to kiss sandpaper some more, ignoring its roughness and giving in to her heart.

She had her Jethro back!

CHAPTER 45—HOME

Marta felt dizzy. She made it a couple of steps to the porch before plopping down there. Bourne sat beside her, studying her with a furrowed brow.

"I'm all right," Marta said.

"How did you do that?" Wind Rock asked.

Greta and Beth turned toward her. The other medicine women and warlocks moved in closer. Most had dropped jaws.

"I accessed Phantom's magic," Marta said. "With it, I could stop the magic coming from my collar. Eventually, I figured out how to destroy the collars."

She tried boring through the orb again to access the oval ring, but it appeared she could no longer do it. "It would seem destroying the collars repaired the rift that allowed me to access Phantom's magic."

Wind Rock's eyes went wide. Everyone else moved, and it didn't take Marta long to figure out why. She hung onto Bourne as holes were dug with Earth spells to bury those who hadn't survived. Wind Rock, Greta, and Beth were the last to move to help, leaving Marta and Bourne alone.

Bourne nodded toward the others. "Why aren't you helping them?"

Marta scoffed. She leaned on his shoulder, in part to shield her tears. "I need a moment." She wasn't going to complain to him about being tired and dizzy from her use of magic. Plus, she had her guy back and she wanted to be with him.

Bourne breathed deeply. "I'm not going anywhere. I promise."

"Damn right you're not," Marta whispered, feeling an ache in her chest. "Even if the devil were to take you, I'd go to hell to retrieve you."

Marta heard Bourne gulp. Maybe that had been a little over the top.

Hubbard broke off from the others, heading toward them. Marta still held the magical orb, so she readied a defensive spell.

"Speak of the devil," she said.

"Give him a chance," Bourne whispered. "He did come to our aid."

Hubbard stopped before them. If he'd heard any of their exchange, he didn't show it. He put his hand out to Bourne. "Sheriff, I'm Reverend Hubbard of Salina's First Methodist Church. I've heard a lot about you."

Bourne shook his hand. "Unfortunately, I haven't had the pleasure of meeting your acquaintance. How did you get roped into this mess?"

Hubbard smiled. "I wouldn't say I was roped into it. Marta gave a compelling case on the need to save you, though I was more interested in destroying McKinley."

Hubbard looked directly at Marta. "Though, you probably don't recognize me."

Marta nodded. "I take it you were one of the hooded figures at the meetings?"

Hubbard shook his head. "I have a better disguise than Chassidy's hood." He shrugged. "People usually refer to me as Runs With Does in the dream realm."

Marta gasped. She couldn't picture that strong old woman as this man before her. She knew people could alter their appearances there, but he went to the extreme with his disguise.

Hubbard glanced over his shoulder. "Don't tell anyone, though. I'd lose a ton of credibility with the others if they found out I was white. Or, well, a male. Plus, people respect me as an older person. They must consider me wise."

Marta drew in a breath. "I can see that. Before today, I thought all warlocks were evil."

Hubbard whistled and shook his head. "I've seen evil witches and warlocks in my time, but some of us just want to live quiet lives."

Marta giggled. "I hear you there."

Hubbard cocked his head. "Do you? You seem hell-bent on sticking your nose into fires."

"Well, I feel the need to put them out." She offered her hand. "Thank you, Reverend. You've saved my life."

Hubbard gestured around. "I think it was you who saved us. I thought for sure we were all goners."

Marta took in the scene. Bodies were now being moved into graves. Was this counted as a win?

"Was there a death count?" Bourne asked.

Hubbard closed his eyes. "About fifteen hostiles and forty-two friendlies. Some of those were lost while collared."

Marta deflated, gripping Bourne tighter. Another tear rolled down her cheek. So many had died. And for what? Why did evil have to exist in the world?

"May they rest in peace," Bourne added.

Hubbard nodded. "And may they reap the benefits of their heavenly bodies."

"Amen," both men said together.

Hubbard smiled at Bourne. "You're a good man, Sheriff."

"Thank you," Bourne replied. "You as well."

Hubbard addressed Marta. "I'll be seeing you from time to time in the dream realm, right?"

Marta smiled. "Of course."

"Good," Hubbard said. "You'll make a good addition to our council."

"Why were you so adamant about not helping us even after I donated to your church?"

A smile flickered on Hubbard's face. "Besides wanting to lead a peaceful existence, I couldn't trust Wind Rock not to expose us to McKinley. I'm probably the only one who knows her connection to him, and I hid that from the rest. I had to pretend like we weren't going to help. Meanwhile, I sent Chassidy to find out your true nature, but then you came to me with a bunch of money, so I saw you for what you are."

"Which is?" Marta asked.

"A helping soul," Hubbard answered. "You, by being only yourself, convinced an entire council to move against McKinley when they hadn't done so in the decades since finding out he was a threat."

Marta felt her cheeks flush.

He frowned. "I better head back to Salina before I'm missed. The new church isn't going to build itself."

One of those weird holes opened next to him. Marta could see brick on the other side. "What is the difference between hopping and instantaneous transportation?"

Hubbard was about to step through his hole, but he stopped. "Instantaneous transportation is a lost art, I believe. I've only heard of Phantom being able to do it. That's what he did on the porch a little bit ago. I think it allows you to move between our realm and the Western Sky. Hopping brings two points on this realm together."

"Ah," Marta said. Instantaneous transportation wasn't as useful as she'd thought.

"I'll be off now, but I'll see you soon," Hubbard said as he stepped through his hopping hole.

Marta waved.

Bourne pointed at the closing hole. "Can you do that?"

Marta thought about the other medicine women who had made the hopping holes. She remembered the different flows of magical elements, how they combined, and what proportions to use. She produced the spell in front of them. It was a little tricky since she was already exhausted. A small hole opened to show a shallow river. It was the Solomon River where she'd met Chassidy.

"A simple 'yes' would have sufficed," Bourne said.

Marta smiled as she watched the serene river. Smells of clean air wafted in through her hole, and it made her want to bathe in that water. It wouldn't get the smell of blood and burnt flesh out of her pores, but a few baths might do it. Either that or hours of letting the water flow over her.

Marta reluctantly closed the portal. Greta and Beth were walking up the hillside. Some of the women were already leaving as the graves were all filled in now. "Where's Wind Rock?" Marta asked.

Greta pointed toward the camp. "She said she wanted to find your horse."

Marta straightened, noting the pen set up on the far side of the camp. There were a few medicine women down there, taking a few horses.

Marta turned to Bourne, but her question died on her lips. He pushed dirt around with the toe of his boot, not meeting Greta's or Beth's gazes. "What's wrong?"

Bourne gulped, his wide eyes meeting hers. "Who said anything was wrong?"

Greta laughed, but Beth nudged her in the ribs. "Let's just say he's seen us in our birthday suits."

Bourne's mouth opened and closed like a fish out of water. Marta suppressed her laughter, trying to look as serious as possible. She had already heard that Greta and Beth had been forced to do labor while naked. It made sense McKinley wasn't the only one to see it.

"I was forced to," Bourne finally rushed out with. "McKinley…"

Marta couldn't help it. She chuckled. "Well, now I know how you'll act if you ever go to a whorehouse or something."

"I'd never!" Bourne exclaimed, face flaming

Marta chuckled, pulling his arm until he was close enough for a kiss. "You're forgiven," she said after the quick peck.

"But I didn't do anything wrong," Bourne protested with his hands out imploringly. "I even did my best to close my eyes when I knew they were in the room!"

Marta giggled, pointing between the two. "So, which one is better looking?"

Bourne rolled his eyes. "They don't hold a candle to you, Marta."

"Hey," both gals complained.

Marta ignored them, beaming at Bourne. He kissed her then, long and desperately. It was a kiss she could get lost in. A kiss to say he'd missed her, and she'd missed him. A kiss that said, "I want to do more than kiss, but now isn't a good time."

A horse snickering returned her to reality, and she reluctantly pulled away. Shadow approached, led by Wind Rock. She rode Greta's mare bareback, but Marta only had eyes for her horse. She gingerly rose to walk to him. "Come here, you," she said as she threw her arms around Shadow's neck.

Shadow whinnied in delight.

"We couldn't find the tack," Wind Rock called. "I'm afraid we couldn't stop a medicine woman from exacting her revenge, so we had to shorten our search." She dismounted.

Marta looked down the hillside at the fire raging through the camp. It was a small display of revenge, and she didn't blame whoever started it.

"Oh, can I do the same to the mansion here? Please?" Bourne asked. He grabbed a tuft of tallgrass. "Can someone give me a light?"

Greta jumped at the chance, lighting the end of the grass. Bourne ran inside the house with it, then exited quickly. He waved everyone back.

An explosion shook the ground, and the roof seemed to jump a foot up. Smoke and flames soon coursed throughout the house.

Marta eyed Bourne. Had he just done some sort of magic?

Bourne beamed. When he saw her expression, he said, "Gunpowder."

Marta scrunched her nose. "What would McKinley need gunpowder for?"

Bourne shook his head. "He didn't need it. He wanted it. He collected Civil War mementos."

"Is that what was in the room we weren't allowed in?" Beth asked.

Bourne nodded, still watching the fire with a weird smile. He brandished the pistol. "It's where I got this."

Marta eyed the gun that had ended up being crucial in the day's events. There was a story there, but it could be told later. "Come on," Marta said. "Let's go home."

"Your house?" Beth asked.

Marta shook her head. "They torched it after kidnapping you two. We'll go to Bourne's house."

"If it's all the same to you, I should probably get back to my grandfather," Wind Rock said.

Marta's heart skipped a beat. She took in the young woman who had been her companion—even her teacher at times—over the last few days. Marta gulped. "I'll miss you." Tears welled in her eyes.

Wind Rock shook her head. "I'll see you every other night, won't I?"

Marta nodded vigorously. "Of course, but I still feel like I'm being robbed of time together."

"Then this isn't a final goodbye, just a bye for now," Wind Rock said with a smile. "Whose horse is this, anyway?"

"She's my nag," Greta said.

"She was good to me," Wind Rock said. "Thank you, horse, for a smooth ride."

"Thank you for coming for us," Greta said.

Marta smiled at the exchange. "Thank you isn't good enough." She hugged the girl, surprised she was being hugged back.

"You were right, by the way," Wind Rock whispered.

"Oh?"

Wind Rock nodded. "I don't feel any better for getting revenge for my mother."

Marta drew in a breath, afraid of what was to come next.

"But I sure am glad that infernal man is gone from this Earth," Wind Rock said.

Marta sighed, glad Wind Rock had some peace. "Me too," she finally replied.

"See you tomorrow night," Wind Rock said, appearing a little more bubbly than Marta had ever seen her. She waved before making a portal to hop out of there.

Only after she was gone did Marta remember Wind Rock's donkey was still at her neighbor's. Marta also wondered how long the girl had known how to hop. That would have saved them so much time. Though, then Marta wouldn't have learned what she needed to on the journey.

"What does she mean by she'll see you tomorrow night?" Beth asked.

"Yeah, and Hubbard seemed to suggest you would be seeing him every other night, too," Bourne added.

Marta turned to her friends. It was great seeing them all. Hell, it was great seeing them safe. "All in good time. Let's get home."

Marta opened another hopping hole, this time to Kent next to Bourne's house. She had to make it bigger for the horses to fit through, so it took more magic. It was more difficult as tired as she was, but she managed. Marta glanced around one final time.

A gust of wind rustled the prairie grass. There was a new sense of peace through the land. Marta hoped this continued instead of only being a temporary reprieve.

THE END

Also by Matthew J. Olson:

Shorts: A Collection of Stories (2014)
Dark Matter: A Collection of Stories (2015)
Alien Fear (2016)
Gun Smuggler's Tale (2016)
Tech Fear (2017)
Twisted: A Collection of Stories (2019)
Flaming Curse (2019)
Whispers Within (2021)
Infinite Horizons (2022)

See my website (olson777.com) to sign up for my newsletter and be one of the first to know about my new releases! Look for Marta, Bourne, Greta, Beth, Wind Rock, and Hubbard to return in *Thunderbolt Curse*, coming soon!

Made in the USA
Monee, IL
15 March 2022